A DUBIOUS TOAST

"To my beautiful fiancée. A diamond of the first water."

A roar of approval went up throughout the breakfast room. Tears of humiliation filled Elizabeth's eyes, though everyone seemed to think they were tears of joy. But she gave a sweet smile and raised her glass of champagne, drinking it down in one long gulp. Ha, see how Lord Clearbrook likes a wife who drinks, she thought, feeling a buzz in her head. How dared he call her beautiful and make fun of her? She wondered if he ever looked ugly. Maybe she could prolong the engagement for at least a year. That would surely give her time to think. She would not marry this brute.

"I think you have had enough champagne, Elizabeth."

"We are not married yet, my lord," she said through clenched teeth, "so do not try your heavy hand with me."

Stephen stared in amazement at the woman before him. The girl was half drunk. With those dancing eyes, rosy cheeks, and her disarrayed hair, she looked beguiling. The thought unnerved him, especially when he peered over his shoulder to the sound of clapping heels coming their way. Lord Githers and Mr. Blundly had stopped and were now staring at Miss Shelby as if she were a prize for the hunt. In fact, they seemed to notice the same thing Stephen had. Miss Elizabeth Shelby was enchanting, and she didn't even know it.

ALSO BY TERESA McCARTHY

The Rejected Suitor
To Marry a Marquess

The Wagered Bride

Teresa McCarthy

A SIGNET BOOK

SIGNET
Published by New American Library, a division of
Penguin Group (USA) Inc., 375 Hudson Street,
New York, New York 10014, USA
Penguin Group (Canada), 10 Alcorn Avenue, Toronto,
Ontario M4V 3B2, Canada (a division of Pearson Penguin Canada Inc.)
Penguin Books Ltd., 80 Strand, London WC2R 0RL, England
Penguin Ireland, 25 St. Stephen's Green, Dublin 2,
Ireland (a division of Penguin Books Ltd.)
Penguin Group (Australia), 250 Camberwell Road, Camberwell, Victoria 3124,
Australia (a division of Pearson Australia Group Pty. Ltd.)
Penguin Books India Pvt. Ltd., 11 Community Centre, Panchsheel Park,
New Delhi - 110 017, India
Penguin Group (NZ), Cnr Airborne and Rosedale Roads, Albany,
Auckland 1310, New Zealand (a division of Pearson New Zealand Ltd.)
Penguin Books (South Africa) (Pty.) Ltd., 24 Sturdee Avenue,
Rosebank, Johannesburg 2196, South Africa

Penguin Books Ltd., Registered Offices:
80 Strand, London WC2R 0RL, England

First published by Signet, an imprint of New American Library,
a division of Penguin Group (USA) Inc.

First Printing, December 2004
10 9 8 7 6 5 4 3 2 1

PUBLISHER'S NOTE
This is a work of fiction. Names, characters, places, and incidents either are the prod-
uct of the author's imagination or are used fictitiously, and any resemblance to actual
persons, living or dead, business establishments, events, or locales is entirely coinci-
dental.

To Tina Brown,
Editor Extraordinaire

Chapter One

*L*ord Stephen Clearbrook was leaning back in his chair, studying the cards on the leather-topped table before him, when suddenly the hint of rich tobacco teased his nostrils. Irritation spurted through his veins at the pungent odor.

It had never bothered him before, but the Spanish cigar habit had gained momentum in London Society ever since the war with Napoleon, and blast it all, the wartime vice resurrected memories Stephen would rather forget.

With the grace of a gentleman about to win a good deal of money, Stephen casually gathered his hand and raised his wineglass to his lips. He tipped the drink back, letting the sweet red liquid trickle down his throat as if he had not a care in the world. *And if that were the cursed truth, Napoleon was the sainted king of England.*

As Stephen dared another glance at his cards, his hand tightened on his empty glass.

"More wine, my lord?" the cheerful voice uttered from across the table tucked in a darkened corner at Baxley's Gaming Hell.

Lifting a cool brown gaze, Stephen eyed William Shelby's fat white hands tapping against the table while a neatly rolled cigar hung carelessly between the man's stubby fingers.

"I am immune to wine, Shelby. Two bottles or three, I am as sane as when I walked in here."

Two shaggy white brows drew together in thought. "Certainly, my lord. Certainly. Ain't wanting you to lose on account of a few drinks, now, would we?"

Ignoring the comment, Stephen followed through with his discards, playing out his hand.

The ticking of the mantel clock was barely heard over the murmur of the gaming tables spread throughout the room. Faro, piquet, whist, vingt-et-un, and a variety of other amusements hovered in the distance, but every bit of Stephen's concentration was on the two-man game being played at his table.

When the last of the cards were laid to rest, Stephen showed no outward sign of disgust.

Across from him, Shelby shook his head regretfully and sighed. "Ain't one to take things from a lord, don't you know, but the game was as fair as any gentleman could want."

Stephen calmly slipped the deed from his coat pocket and handed it to the man without a word. Earlier this week, Stephen's solicitor had thought to take a look at the deed to make certain all was in order, and now it seemed Stephen would no longer be depositing the papers in the family vault as planned.

It surprised Stephen the way Shelby seemed to relish the win, as if the man had secured his entire fortune in one sweep of his hand. But the cit was as rich as Croesus. He didn't need a pound of Stephen's money or his land.

"Hear tell Creighton Hall is a prime estate." Shelby's eyes gleamed with appreciation as he pressed the papers to his protruding stomach. "Good hunting, they say."

The man's fleshy lips suddenly took a downward turn. "See here, the duke ain't going to come after me, now, will he?"

Stephen's eyes narrowed dangerously. "My brother is not the owner of my life or Creighton Hall, Shelby. The property is not entailed—it belonged to me through my maternal grandmother—if that is what you fear."

Shelby clapped his hands together and patted his prominent belly. "Then I daresay it will make a nice addition to my holdings, now, won't it?"

It was all Stephen could do to hold his tongue. How the man knew Stephen was carrying the papers to the family property he would never know. Had he made mention of it at the club, or perhaps Newmarket? He had no idea, but somehow Shelby already had been informed of the fact when they sat down to play. But it was Stephen who had made the stupid wager and lost, not Shelby.

"Your lordship ain't going to call me out or something like that, are you?"

Stephen cracked his knuckles and leaned back in his chair, stretching his long legs languidly beneath the table. It was amusing that Shelby harbored thoughts of a duel between the two of them. It was absurd, really.

At four and twenty, Stephen was known to be the most carefree of all the Clearbrook males. It could almost be said that his easygoing nature was epitomized by the casual manner in which he wore his cravat. Nothing mathematical about it. Even his wavy chestnut hair fell over one eye, suggesting his approach to life. Simple and relaxed.

But his handsome profile boasted of an inner strength and power not to be ignored by the most confident of men. Moreover, a willful stubbornness lay in the square cut of his chin and the firm set of his lips. His nose was what most Englishmen would call perfect—a Roman nose, many called it. His eyes were dark with touches of humor lines fanning about the surrounding skin, making him appear fetching, his sister would say.

He knew most women found his charm appealing, but some men perceived that beneath his easygoing exterior lay a cunning intelligence that was not to be dismissed. Even Wellington himself had found the youngest of the Clearbrook brothers prodigiously useful during Napoleon's fall at Waterloo.

Though nothing seemed amiss with Stephen's appearance, upon closer scrutiny, one could detect a cold logic in his brown gaze, a sign to the more discriminating that said Lord Stephen Clearbrook stood acutely aware of his surroundings.

In fact, Stephen had always been good at hiding his innermost turmoil, and it seemed that precise trait was work-

ing for him now. He would have to buy the place back as
soon as his business venture with Lord Brule came through.

"Exactly what kind of man do you think I am, Shelby?"

The older man drummed his fingers against the table, the
dying cigar all but forgotten. "Ain't one to meddle with the
fourth son of a duke. You know, I ain't looking for trouble."

Stephen quirked a brow and waved his hand for a servant
to pour him a glass of brandy. "My birth has nothing to do
with this. The cards were what talked tonight, not my peerage."

After letting the fiery liquid slide down his throat,
Stephen peered over the rim of his drink, giving Shelby his
most brilliant smile. "Men lose at cards all the time, my
good man."

Surprise, along with a hint of confusion, seemed to
flicker in the older man's eyes at Stephen's response. Shelby
bared his yellow teeth and pushed away from the table to
stand. "You ain't one to shrivel from a loss, are you, my
lord?"

Stephen said nothing, his discerning gaze intently studying the man. After serving with Wellington during the war,
Stephen recognized the gleam in Shelby's eyes for what it
was, pure, unadulterated greed. Yet there seemed to be
something more . . . . .

"'Course, if you're hoping to retrieve this"—Shelby patted the papers tucked beside his tight-fitting waistcoat—"I
will be attending Lord Harmstead's ball next week. Always
a game to be had there." A flash of hunger appeared in the
man's gray eyes that sent a twist of warning to Stephen's
gut. "Perhaps you might want to wager, hmmm, something
else, my lord?"

Stephen knew he should cut his losses and buy the place
back later, but the more he thought about it, the more he realized that his mother would never forgive him for losing
Creighton Hall in such a manner, and he would never forgive himself. After his father's death, his mother had remar-
ried and was much happier now. He wouldn't puncture that
bubble of happiness for the world. Although he might not be

able to wait for his money to come in before his mother found out about the matter.

"Another high-stakes game?" he asked Shelby, considering it as a possibility.

The fat man's gaze glittered expectantly. "Indeed. But cash on the barrel, mind you. No notes accepted."

Stephen's brow rose in surprise. "No debts taken at the table? How very unconventional. An easy mark for a thief, I would venture."

"The footmen will be armed. Of course I don't take you for a coward, my lord. I do have contacts at Whitehall. Heard you saved Wellington's life at Waterloo."

Stephen stiffened. "You have eyes everywhere, Shelby."

No one in Stephen's family had a notion of the extent to which he knew Wellington. His eldest brother might have known, but as to the other two, they probably had no idea. Once, at a ball, his own mother had introduced him to Wellington as if the two had never met. Stephen had never batted an eye.

"Indeed, but that don't change the fact that you are a brave man, your lordship. Not many men would put themselves between Wellington and a Frenchman's rifle, no matter what the cost."

"A ball knicking one's thigh was small payment for the freedom of our country, Shelby, and I would consider it a favor if you kept the incident to yourself."

Shelby heaved an appreciative sigh. "A war hero you are, and humble, too. Heard the ball went clean through you. But never fear, my lips are shut, always have been. There are those at Whitehall who would have my head. But you'll do."

Do for what? Stephen was stunned to know the man knew about secrets he would rather keep quiet. Playing the war hero was something Stephen had never felt comfortable with. And a hero he was not, even if he had saved Wellington's life and sent the attacker to prison.

He spun his brandy glass between his fingers. "As for Harmstead's ball, I fear next week I go to Brighton. Regent's party and all that, you know."

"Suit yourself, my lord."

Stephen saw the flash of disappointment that crossed the elder man's face and wondered what else was hidden behind the dangerous glint in those intelligent eyes.

He regarded Shelby as the man lit another cigar from one of the flickering candles resting on the table. It had been a bad night for cards, that was all. At the Harmstead ball, he would repossess Creighton Hall within an hour of playing with this rich cit. Just a little more baiting, and the pot would be his.

"Of course, Lord Harmstead is a longtime friend of the family," Stephen added, as if an afterthought. "I have not replied to the invitation yet."

Shelby placed his hands on the table, leaning forward, the smoke of his cigar swirling toward the high ceilings like the remnants of a dragon's breath. "I would give you a chance to regain Creighton Hall. That I can promise you. Heard your mother is quite fond of the place."

Stephen's jaw hardened. What else did this man know? Waterloo was one thing, his family quite another. It seemed money bought many things in this world. "I should make a point of it, then, shouldn't I?" His lips fell into a twisted smile.

Shelby's eyes twinkled with satisfaction. "Good. Good. See you then, my lord."

Stephen saluted the man with his glass and watched him depart. Now what the deuce was the old man up to? Creighton Hall was no great estate, and the man had enough money to line Prinny's pockets. It wasn't as if Stephen had anything more to lose to the man. Or had he?

Stephen unfolded his body from his chair and stared at the door, pausing. Shelby was known to be a shrewd businessman, having made his money by using his brain and his wit, marching over anyone and anything in his path. A bit like old Boney, Stephen thought with a bitter tightening in his chest.

He grabbed the brandy decanter and poured himself another drink. *Waterloo.* He would never forget. The blood. The screams. The death. The killing. He had been on his way to warn Wellington of a spy in the trenches when it happened. The Frenchie had come out of nowhere.

Stephen tried to shake the disturbing thoughts from his mind, but they would not let go. Taking a man's life was something he would never forget. Saving Wellington's life minutes after the killing had not even lifted his spirits. Snuffing out a man's life was not something he was proud of.

He downed his drink in one long swallow and slapped the snifter back onto the table. No. It wasn't just one man's life snuffed out, it was two—the Frenchie at Waterloo and his very own father, the duke, at Elbourne Hall.

"Papa, you cannot mean this."

Elizabeth Shelby paced the floor of the family's London hotel apartment, not able to believe her father's words. Wisps of wheat-colored hair, highlighted with strands of honey blonde, fell about her face as she stopped and looked at her father's frowning gaze in the gilded mirror across the room.

Tears of frustration pooled in her intelligent blue eyes, but she refused to let them fall. Her father had hurt her deeply, and whether he thought he was doing this in her best interest or not, she could not agree to his plan.

"Papa, please don't do this to me."

"Now, Lizzie, be a good girl and don't argue with me. It ain't seemly."

Elizabeth's gaze began to blur, and she turned toward the window, glaring past the carriages clattering along the street. She could not let this happen. She would not marry some lord for the sake of his name and title. She could not.

She gripped the crimson curtain beside her and drew in a shaky sigh. It would do her no good to argue with her father. She would have to take action instead.

Oh, she knew her father had always wanted the best for her. Even their present lodgings were the finest the hotel had to offer.

Crystal chandeliers hung in every room. Rich red velvets decorated most of the seating. Rosewood tables and sideboards with intricate inlays of contrasting wood sat beside stately marbled fireplaces. Sparkling silver covered the breakfast table from the teapots to the utensils. Even the bedchambers boasted luscious blue- and cream-colored coverlets with mounds of matching pillows and plump feathered beds.

Elizabeth dragged a hand over the curtain's gold brocade trim and bit the inside of her cheek. Kings and queens were said to reside in these very chambers when visiting England. And why not the best for William Shelby, too?

After going from rags to riches in ten years, he was going to make sure he lived like a king, and if that included marrying his eldest daughter to a lord, so be it.

"Don't you go moping on me, girl. You've had the best money has to offer. Why, I sent you to Miss Horatio's Seminary in Bath, did I not?"

"Yes, Papa."

"And you can speak French, Italian, and Spanish. How many girls your age can do that?"

"Not many, Papa."

"See there," he said, as if making his point clear. "All I ask of you is this one simple thing, and you have given me nothing but grief on the subject. And what about Millicent? Your sister should have a chance to live in the splendor that high society has to offer, should she not? See here, now, if you marry a lord, she can have that too, my girl."

He puffed out his chest and grinned as if everything was settled, then sank into a chair near the hearth. "That and more. Don't you agree?"

"No . . . I mean, yes . . . I—oh, you don't understand, Papa."

Elizabeth felt her world slipping out of control. Her father's sudden announcement of her upcoming marriage to some lord she had never met made her ill. She didn't want a peer of the realm; she wanted a man who loved her.

And who was to say her father would not buy a lord for Milli too? He had made no promises.

At nineteen years old, Elizabeth had her own plans. She loved her father, yet she knew he had a head as hard as Henry VIII when it came to decisions. Once the man's mind was made up, there was no turning back. He wasn't one of the richest men in England because of an indecisive streak. No, indeed. But this blatant command was insufferable!

She kept her gaze on the parade of carriages below, her chin taking on a stubborn line. "Whether I speak one language or fifty, Papa, it does not signify. I will not marry a man I do not love and that is final."

She turned suddenly when her father rose from his chair, blurting out a sharp curse, stabbing the air between them. His pudgy cheeks turned bright red.

"Listen here, Lizzie. You will marry him. This ain't your decision. I have always done right by you, haven't I? He's a right one, he is. He hasn't asked for you yet, but he will soon, I tell you. Handsome as Apollo. Comes from good stock, too."

"Good stock? People are not cattle, Papa!" Clenching her hands, she shifted her gaze back toward the street. "Besides, if you must know"—she spun around—"I love Mr. Fennington."

Dead silence blanketed the room. Elizabeth regretted her outburst immediately. She should have used a bit more tact in explaining her position.

"*Who* in the blue blazes is Mr. Fennington?" Her father all but growled out the words through his clenched jaw.

"Oh, he's the man Lizzie *thinks* she loves." The sweet voice came from Millicent Shelby, Elizabeth's younger sister, who had been lounging on the settee in the corner of the room, reading her newest romance novel from the Minerva Press.

"Milli," Elizabeth scolded, walking toward her sister, instantly inhaling the strong scent of lavender that the girl seemed to always wear. "Thank you, but I am in no need of comments from a girl still in the schoolroom."

The fourteen-year-old rolled her gray eyes, as though she were an expert on the subject of love. She had a slim, modest body for a girl her age, making her seem younger than she was. Dark chestnut hair framed a heart-shaped face, giving her the appearance of a bewitching elf, and Elizabeth adored her.

"Fudge, Lizzie. I am not two, you know." Milli slapped the book closed, slipping her body sideways, feigning a swoon. "Oh, woe is me. My heart is but a palpitation of my innermost core."

Elizabeth stifled a laugh at her sister's antics. "Milli . . . you are incorrigible."

Large gray eyes twinkled above a pert little nose, giving the false impression of a very innocent and manageable female, an impression Elizabeth had told her sister would find the girl in more trouble than Milli could handle some fate-filled day if she did not curb her theatrics.

William Shelby waved his hand in agitation at his youngest. "What in heaven's name are you talking about, Milli? There ain't nothing wrong with your heart!"

Milli shut her eyes and heaved a groaning sigh. "My love, my love, why have you failed me? Come to me and save me from these woeful ingrates."

"Ingrates?" William took a menacing step forward. "Listen here, my girl. Enough of this foolishness. You may want to be an actress in Drury Lane, but I will have none of that entertainment here."

Milli peeked out from one eye. "Papa, how could you disrupt my performance? I am only—"

"You are disrupting my conversation with your sister, and if you think for one second that I have forgotten your mischief with your last governess, you are sorely mistaken, girl."

Sitting up, Milli gave her father a mulish expression, then looked at Elizabeth with a shrug. "Well, I tried, Lizzie."

Elizabeth managed a smile, realizing Milli had only wanted to obtain her father's attention in order to divert the man from his goal. "Yes, you did, dearest. But I think this is something Papa and I need to discuss alone."

"Oh, very well." Milli stood solemnly and with the air of a queen, threw a righteous hand to her breast. "But never fear. Your knight in shining armor will come to you on his white horse and swoop you into his arms"—her arm swung wide, pointing deliberately at her father—"saving you from this conniving and despicable villain!"

William Shelby, his gray eyes widening in shock, shook a fat finger at his youngest daughter. "Now see here, Millicent, you have exactly five seconds—"

Milli frowned. "Well, I can see that you have no taste for theater, Papa. Did you know that Elizabeth thinks I'm wonderful? She thinks—"

"Millicent!"

"Oh, very well."

Putting a hand on her small hips, Milli lifted her chin toward her sister, gave a mischievous wink, and sashayed from room as if she were a flamboyant opera dancer luring the London bucks to her side like hapless, tongue-wagging puppies.

William Shelby blinked hard.

Elizabeth chuckled. "You must admit she is quite the little actress, Papa."

Shelby shook his head and turned a confused face upon Elizabeth. "She is that, my dear. The thing is, I have no idea where she gets it from. I fear she will never be as biddable as you."

Elizabeth raised a delicate brow in protest. "Biddable? I am most certainly not biddable. I will not marry a lord, Papa. I want to marry for love, like you and Mama."

Something flickered in the back of the older man's eyes, and Elizabeth's breath hitched. "You did love Mama, did you not?"

William Shelby fiddled with the fob on his waistcoat. "Certainly. Certainly. But that ain't the point, Lizzie. I want you to marry into a good family. Have a name for yourself. Blue blood, my dear, that's what counts."

He swallowed visibly and looked up. "Now that's the ticket for the good life. Once you are married into the *ton*, little Millicent will have her choice of husbands. It ain't much to ask, poppet. That's all I want for my girls. A place in Society. A place where they belong."

Elizabeth frowned. *A place where they belong.*

And there lay the crux of the problem. Her father was accepted in Society because of his money, yet there was always the hushed snicker, the snide remark, the malicious smile of a haughty dowager or another snob of the *ton*. To them, blood was everything, and William Shelby's blood was as contaminated as the Thames.

Elizabeth crossed the room and held her father's hand in a gentle grip. "But I don't want to belong to those people, Papa," she said, her voice softening. "Being part of that group means nothing to me. My life would be over if I married one of those stuffy lords. He would only be marrying me for my money, do you not see? I want love, Papa. Is that so much to ask?"

Her father gave her hands a squeeze. "See here, Lizzie. You are a beautiful girl. There are many men who would want you for a bride. Why not have a handsome lord if you have the choice?"

"But I don't seem to have a choice, Papa." Elizabeth jerked her hand away. "And besides, I am not beautiful. I am plain. My hair takes hours to curl, and at the end of the day it is as straight as a pole. As for the color, it is a drab mousy brown, nothing to fetch a man's eye."

"That ain't so, Lizzie."

"Oh, Papa. You are blind to my faults. And as long as we're speaking of eyes, see these?" She raised a finger to her brow. "My eyes, Papa—well, they are a dull blue, and I cannot read unless I have those stupid spectacles." She pinched her cheeks. "And look at these. I still have baby fat. I am not at all the thing. So the person who marries me will either love me for my heart or love me for my money. I choose my heart, Papa."

"You are not ugly, Lizzie. You are . . . well, rather tall and pleasantly plump. And as for your eyes, they are, er, a very nice blue. But as to your marriage, I am only acting in your best interest. Believe me, I know about Society, my dear."

The door sprang open, and Milli appeared, dancing into the room with a tray of lemon cakes swaying in her hands. "No, Papa, they are the color of a mountain spring."

William's lips curled in exasperation at the outburst. "Millicent, by heaven, I have had just about enough out of you."

Milli batted her eyes. "But I have a tray of lemon cakes, Papa. Your favorite."

William's face softened. "Very well. Come in. We can always take a break for food. Ain't going anywhere, are you, Lizzie?" He chuckled as he swiped a cake off the tray. "Not as if some knight is going to break through the barriers here, eh?"

"No, Papa," Elizabeth said somberly. "No knight here."

William stuffed the cake into his mouth, wiping his lips with a napkin. "No one is going to tell me you're ugly, Lizzie. You are a very healthy female, and that's all a gentleman wants in a wife. Prime stock, you are."

"Papa, please."

William lifted his brows. "Well, you are a capital girl, Lizzie, and don't you forget it."

Milli glanced admiringly at her sister. "And your face, Lizzie, is like a whisper of heaven, with angelic cheeks of celestial rose. Your skin is as flawless as a diamond of the first water. Your hands are as soft as a lamb." She sighed dreamily. "Your knight will want to sweep you away forever."

William stuffed another bite into his mouth. "Life ain't a flight of fancy, Milli. Depend upon it. You've had too much of that Shakespeare and what not. My Lizzie has a head on her shoulders, she does. She's a practical girl, and doesn't fill her head with knights and white horses."

Milli's gray eyes flashed. "Oh, yes, she does! Why the other day she told me—"

Elizabeth interrupted her sister, placing a meaningful grip on the girl's arm. "Milli, please, not now."

"Oh, very well, but she does not want some pompous lord."

William patted his youngest daughter's head. "Yes, yes, now go on, Millicent. Your sister and I have more to discuss."

Elizabeth curled her hands by her sides. "But we have nothing to discuss, Papa. I will marry for love. I will not marry some money-hungry lord. I don't care who you have in mind. I won't have it. I may have been biddable in the past, but this time I will put my foot down."

William squished the cake in his hands. "By Jove, you are going to marry a lord, Elizabeth!"

"I won't!"

"You will, even if I have to drag you to the altar myself."

"Papa!" The color drained from Elizabeth's face. Her father had never spoken to her with such anger. But she knew he meant what he said. There was no doubt about that. Without another word, she bit her lip and hurried from the room.

Milli gasped. "Oh, Papa," she said in a disgusted whisper.

William flushed to the roots of his white hair. "I ain't one to drag you, Lizzie," he shouted. "You know I ain't. Something in those lemon cakes, you know. Always bothered me."

Milli turned on him when she heard her sister sob. "She will have her knight, and I will see to it."

With a hand to her forehead, Milli fled the room, her voice dwindling to a theatrical whisper. "Oh, treason of thy very blood, murder not my heart for I have only one."

Muttering a curse, William Shelby sank into the plush velvet beneath him and pulled out the papers in his jacket pocket. Lizzie would thank him later. She thought he was misguiding her, but he was doing this for her own good. Creighton Hall would be a nice summer home; now all he had to do was nab the lord along with the property. He would make a nice husband for his Lizzie. A nice husband, indeed.

Chapter Two

"*L*izzie, what are you doing?"

Taking her spectacles off the bridge of her nose, Elizabeth looked up from her dressing table, turned toward her sister, and feigned a smile. No use letting Milli know how miserable she was about her father's demand. "I'm writing a letter, you silly goose. What does it look like I'm doing?"

Milli frowned, plopping on her bed and drowning herself in a heap of silk and damask pillows. A shaft of sunlight illuminated her impish face, and Elizabeth wondered for the thousandth time how they could ever be sisters. Milli was such a fetching little thing.

"Papa loves you, Lizzie. The thing is, he wants a lord in the family so badly, he will do anything to have one."

"I know, dearest. But it is my life, not his." With a tired sigh, Elizabeth switched her gaze back to her letter and raised her spectacles to her eyes once again. She only needed them for writing and reading, but they were so very ugly, she tried to avoid using them in public.

After signing her name, Elizabeth placed her pen into its holder and stood, hoping Mr. Fennington would respond quickly. She was doing this for Milli, too, she reminded herself. If she married of her own free will, Milli would know she could do the same, whether her suitor was a gentleman of the *ton* or not. Papa would not be able to lock her sister into a marriage of convenience for the sake of a name or a title, even though he had said otherwise.

"Woe is me. Oh, woe is me," Milli exclaimed, putting a

hand to her head, striving for her sister's attention. "I will be forever a spinster—" She stopped and sat up. "Do you know, Lizzie, I believe these pillows smell of vanilla?"

Laughing, Elizabeth walked toward the bed and took Milli's hands in hers, drawing the girl out of the pillows. "Yes, they do smell of vanilla, and now they smell of your lavender bouquet. And you are the silliest girl to tease Papa. He almost had an apoplectic seizure when you sashayed from the room like that."

Milli giggled, twirling about the room. "Oh, Papa reminds me of one of those stuffed antler heads in Lord Pommly's study. You know, all stiff and inflexible."

"And when have you been in Lord Pommly's study?"

"I met his daughter in Bath. We are good friends." Milli's eyes twinkled mischievously. "But do you think Papa knows about my visit to the back stairs of the opera house?"

"Good heavens! *I* never knew of it until this instant, Millicent. You little minx!"

Milli's face took on the soul of innocence. "I took his mind off you for a bit, did I not?"

Elizabeth caught the wicked gleam in her sister's gaze and chuckled. "I can fight my own battles, dearest. You must not compromise your own situation with Papa."

Milli whacked her hand against a pillow. "But, Lizzie, I do so want you to be happy. Papa likes to have a hold on everything we do, as if we lived in medieval times. It is not quite the thing today, you know. A woman can do many more things than she could have done hundreds of years ago."

"Like what?" Elizabeth asked skeptically.

"Well . . . like acting!" Milli put on a militant face when Elizabeth's brows rose.

"Yes, I know what you think of that," Milli went on. "And I daresay Papa does care about what we do; however, sometimes he treats me as if I am a four-year-old."

Elizabeth's blue eyes twinkled. Milli did act like a four-year-old sometimes. "And?"

"Well, never mind me, but he means for you to marry a nobleman or at the very least some odious lord, Lizzie. That is the point I am trying to make. You are going to have to do it, you know."

Elizabeth frowned, thinking of her letter. "I am going to marry Mr. Fennington. He loves me."

"You mean that blond-haired gentleman you met at the lending library? The one with that monstrous quizzing glass?"

Elizabeth smiled. "The very one. I have even danced with him at Almack's. Papa is a friend of the patroness, Lady Sefton. Anyway, my gentleman says he loves me. He will do anything to have me."

Milli closed her eyes, a simpering smile upon her lips. "How utterly romantic," she drawled.

No sooner had she uttered those words than her eyes snapped open in horror. "But Papa will not let you marry him. You heard him. Even I could not sway him. He has a plan and that always means trouble, Lizzie. You might be locked away until your wedding like a princess in hiding. What will you do?"

Elizabeth strode back to her writing desk. "I have a plan."

"Goodness, I must know it then. For depend upon it, I have no wish for this to end like *Romeo and Juliet*. I always believed the lovers should have told someone, at least someone who could have done something other than get them killed."

Elizabeth grinned. "I am not Juliet. And you are not going to do anything. However, I believe it best that you know I am going to elope with Mr. Fennington the night of the Harmstead ball. It will be an easy feat to accomplish since we will be staying as guests of Lord Harmstead. But if you dare tell Papa, I will never speak to you again."

Milli's eyes widened. "Elope! Well, I certainly will not tell him. He will find out soon enough, I daresay."

Milli swayed slowly toward the bed. "But woe to the man who separates thy daughter from her father's breast. He is like the thief who plucks the rose from the king's garden, stealing into the night, never to be seen again."

Elizabeth smiled and looked thoughtfully out the window where the sun pierced through the clouds, teasing the cool spring day. "I am marrying for you, too, Milli. If Papa marries me to some lord, he might do the same to you. But you must see that you have a choice. Papa means well, but sometimes he becomes misguided. He does things 'for our own good,' as he says."

"Oh, I won't mind if he tries that on me."

Elizabeth spun about. "You won't?"

"No. I am going to run off to the theater. But don't worry. I will write every day. Papa will eventually see that I will not cave into his plans. No more governesses either, and I am certainly not going back to that stupid Seminary for Young Ladies. Many of the girls are all nasty, like Lady Odette."

Elizabeth frowned. Lady Odette, a noted schoolmate from Elizabeth's time at Miss Horatio's Seminary in Bath, would be staying as one of the guests of Lord Harmstead, too. Her father had mentioned that fact in passing.

Odette may have been the most beautiful female at school, and at the balls for that matter, but she was also a spiteful, selfish girl who had contrived to make Elizabeth's life, and that of many of the other girls at the school, terrible.

Elizabeth quickly switched her thoughts away from the memories of Odette's cruelty and back to Milli. "If you run away, dearest, what will you do for money?"

Her sister chewed her lip. "Well, I will have to lie, cheat, and steal to make my way." The girl's eyes glowed with adventure. "Would it not be famous, Lizzie? Me, an actress? Just imagine. Princes from other countries would come to see me."

Something in Milli's words worried Elizabeth. "One day your stories will go too far."

Milli slipped off the bed and marched toward the door. "I daresay you think I have forgotten *your* stories?"

"What stories?"

"Oh, the ones you told me when I was young. The stories about the knight coming to save you, vowing his love, and sweeping you into his arms." Milli glanced over her shoulder, her cool gray gaze daring her sister to deny it. "Those stories."

Elizabeth remembered all too well the stories she told Milli when her sister had awakened in the middle of the night from a bad dream. Years of warm memories tugged at Elizabeth's heart.

She had been like a mother to Milli. When Milli had been ill with the measles, Elizabeth had come home from the seminary to nurse her. When Milli had fallen off her horse and broken her leg, it was Elizabeth who had sat by her side and kept her company. Elizabeth loved the girl and wanted only the best for her, not foolish dreams that would never come true.

"Being an actress is well and good for some people, but not for you, dearest. My stories were only dreams, Milli." Dead and gone.

Milli's face paled. "Dreams? Ah, yes, I understand now. You can live with the stories in your head, but when I want to act them out, I am scolded for it. I daresay I would rather have dreams than wait for fate to bite me in the—"

"Millicent Harriet!"

Milli's eyes flashed with defiance. "Well, I am still going to dream, Lizzie, and no one is going to stop me, not even you!"

The door slammed closed, the sound of its echo hammering in Elizabeth's ears as she sank into her dressing chair and frowned. Dreams of knights and white horses were fairy tales for little girls, not grown women.

She spread her fingers over her letter and heaved a tired sigh, wishing she could ask her mother what to do. At this point, she was not about to ask her godmother, for Aunt Polly might very well tell her to marry the lord if the man were from a good family. One never knew with Aunt Polly.

For a moment Elizabeth wavered before she folded the letter and sealed it. Mr. Fennington was not a knight in shining armor, but he loved her, and that was all that she needed, was it not?

Stephen's head ached like the very devil. He had been rash and foolish, but a mere loan of twenty thousand pounds should be nothing to his brother, the Duke of Elbourne. Nothing at all.

As he strolled past the library doors of Elbourne Hall, the duke's country estate, Stephen took in the mingled scent of leather and books that reminded him of his youth . . . and his father. His stomach went taut at the thought.

It was here where Stephen had seen the last of the man that sired him, here where they had the argument that killed him.

Forcing away his frown, he managed a smile as he walked across the Aubusson carpet and greeted his eldest brother. "Roderick, my dear duke, where is that lovely wife of yours?"

The duke lifted his dark head from the papers on his desk, his mouth splitting into a full-fledged grin. "Where the devil have you been? It's been ages since we've seen you!" Roderick instantly stood and shook Stephen's hand. "Come. Have a drink. Didn't hear you come in."

Stephen raised a discerning brow. Roderick had always been a bit pompous, even at a score and eight, but it seemed marriage had changed him. His heart lifted considerably as Roderick stepped to the sideboard to pour the brandy. Perhaps this meeting would be fruitful after all.

"Married life becomes you," Stephen said, taking the drink offered him.

"Never thought I would say it. But, yes, it does indeed."

The duke moved back to the desk with a decided spring in his step. Stephen's eyes widened. Jane's doing, no doubt.

"You are staying, then?" the duke asked, taking his seat. "Jane would love to cater to you, for a few days at least. And Mother is visiting as well. Depend upon it, little brother. It will be hard for you not to stay here."

"I would love to stay, but I have a slight problem." Stephen shoved a hand through his brown locks and fell into a chair near the hearth where an orange glow rose from the coals.

For a moment the air sizzled with unanswered questions.

Roderick dropped his tall form into his chair and steepled his fingers near his chin. All the Clearbrook brothers were athletically built, with broad shoulders and long, muscled legs, but Roderick had always been the largest of them all.

"A problem?" the duke asked, concern lacing his tone.

Stephen had never liked asking Roderick for money, and blast it, he didn't like it now. "It's like this, Roderick. Had a bit of bad luck in Town. Nothing to worry about though."

Roderick's face darkened. Now this was the old Roderick. "Bad luck? The only bad luck you have is your stupid head."

The clock in the hall chimed three, and Stephen's head began to throb again.

"What was it this time—piquet?" Roderick's tone hardened.

Stephen groaned. "Yes, but dash it all, I have the funds, only they are tied up in a business venture with Lord Brule."

"Business venture?" Roderick snorted as he sipped his brandy, his piercing gaze never leaving Stephen. "Lord Brule is out of the country. Never mind. How much do you need?"

"About twenty thousand."

The hard lines around the duke's mouth froze as his snifter clanked hard against the table. "Only twenty? My, why not make it an even thirty? What did you do, lose Creighton Hall, too?"

Stephen's eyes flashed, giving away his secret. Not many men could read him like Roderick could, but it had taken the duke years of practice to do it so well, a lifetime, in fact.

Roderick shot from his seat, cursing a blue streak, tearing apart Stephen's character as if he were shredding a paper doll.

As the yelling began to subside, Roderick paced behind his desk. "Confound it! I mentioned Creighton Hall in jest."

He paused, his gaze drilling into Stephen like a fiery cannon ball shot at close range. "You have been quite the idiot upon several occasions, little brother, but hell and thunderation, Mother's childhood home? How could you?"

Stephen glared at his brother. "Forgive me for taking up your time," he said sharply as he rose.

He turned to leave when the door opened, and Jane entered, looking like an angel with her fair hair and baby blue eyes.

"Good day to you, Duchess," he said, his lips curving upward for he was not able to frown at the loveliness before him.

A warm smile broke out on Jane's face as she ran to Stephen, throwing her arms about him. "You heartbreaker! How long have you been here? How long can you stay?" The scent of rosewater lingered about the beauty.

"Roderick, you should have told me your brother was here."

Roderick fisted his hands at his sides, glaring at Stephen. "He won't be staying, sweetheart. He has a prior engagement."

She turned back to Stephen. "Is that true?"

Trying to avoid a confrontation, Stephen took Jane's hands in his and stepped back, smiling. "But how wonderful you look. You must have taken Paris by storm."

Jane's blue eyes danced. "You are ever the flatterer, Stephen. Now, please, say you are staying."

Stephen saw the curl of his brother's lip and released Jane's hands. "Forgive me, Duchess. But I have already made plans. I will be taking my leave within the hour."

Jane frowned. "But you will visit us in Town? Soon?"

"Of course. Must greet Mother before I depart, so if you will excuse me." He brought her hands to his lips, kissed them, bowed, and started for the door.

"Stephen," the duke ground out.

Stephen glanced up. He had asked Roderick for a favor, but by heaven, he would not beg. "What is it, your mighty dukeness?"

As the youngest of the four brothers, Stephen seemed to annoy Roderick the most, especially with his dry humor.

Roderick regarded his wife. "We have unfinished business, sweetheart. If you would please close the door on your way out."

Blue eyes snapped. "Are you dismissing me, *Your Grace*?"

Roderick raised his right brow at his wife's defiance, a

gesture Stephen was all too familiar with. He had always wondered how the new duchess would take Roderick's overbearing, self-righteous attitude after she had lived with him for a while.

Stephen turned around, taking Jane's hand back in his, using his utmost charm. "You'd best leave, Duchess. It seems Roderick has a few choice words he would like to say to me."

Jane's bosom swelled as she glared at her husband. "Well, I believe I heard a few of those words, and I am ashamed of you."

Roderick's eyes rounded. "This is between Stephen and me. It is not for a lady's ears."

"How dare you speak to me as if I were a . . . a peabrain."

"I am your husband, a fact perchance you have forgotten."

"And I thought I was your wife, a fact *you* seemed to have forgotten entirely."

"Not entirely," he drawled, his gaze moving lazily over her person, "but as my wife you will do as I say."

"Whatever gave you that silly notion?" Jane uttered.

Stephen thought the entire scenario hilarious until Jane took a menacing step toward Roderick, blocking Stephen from the duke's glare. Stephen frowned. Shame heated his blood as he realized that he had sunk very low indeed if he needed to have a lady defend his honor, and his brother's wife at that.

"Jane," Stephen said hoarsely, "please leave, dearest. I know you mean well, but this is truly between Roderick and me."

The lady gave Stephen a tremulous smile. "If you wish. But please promise me you will not be a stranger. You must stay with us in London when you come to Town. Those apartments you have are not quite the thing. The food is no good at all."

Stephen kissed her hand. "Your servant, madam."

Roderick let out a low growl as soon as his wife departed. "How dare you use Jane for your own interests."

Stephen's jaw hardened as he turned toward his brother.

"I would never use a woman to defend me, and you know it."

Roderick's eyes challenged him. "Do I?"

"There is nothing more to be said. Good day, *Your Grace*."

"I will never give you another guinea to be thrown away on gaming. Do you understand me? Your gambling and drinking have gone far enough. You are a disgrace to the El-bourne name."

A muscle ticked in Stephen's jaw. "Devil take it, if you were not my brother, I would call you out."

"Do not let that stop you. But pray, have you considered Lady Odette's reaction to your loss of Creighton Hall? If you think she will marry you now, you are very much mis-taken. That prime piece of land backs up to her father's. Whom did you lose it to? Tell me, so I may buy it back. Mother need never know."

Stephen's expression grew dark as the memory of the card game drummed in his brain. "I am only telling you be-cause I know you will find out by other means. Shelby holds the papers."

Roderick let out a low whistle. "William Shelby? That rich cit who made his money in spices?"

Stephen grimaced. "The very one, but if you dare take one step in that direction, I will tell Jane of your dalliance with that opera singer. Arabella, was it not?"

"That . . . that was years ago," the duke stammered.

"But you know women. I mean what I say. Stay out of this."

With Roderick sputtering about the injustice of younger siblings, Stephen glanced over his shoulder for the last word. "And forget I ever asked you for a thing. Because if you think I will ever come begging for a loan again, I will die first."

Slamming the library door, Stephen strode down the hall. He would gain back Creighton Hall if it killed him. He would never hurt his mother. And then there was Lady Odette . . . .

"Stephen."

He spun on his heels. "Mother?"

The lady stood before him dressed in a gown of blue sapphire, her arms holding her fluffy white feline Egypt against her shoulder. "Were you going to leave without saying hello?"

Stephen came forward and kissed his mother's cheek. "I confess it was not well done of me, was it? Where is Bringston?"

Stephen's mother had recently married Lord Bringston, a man who had loved the duchess from afar for years. Though Stephen's father, the duke, had been dead for almost four years, Stephen could still recall the pain his mother had endured at the notion of the duke loving another in the course of their marriage.

His father's death had plagued Stephen every day of the past four years. Stephen had argued with the duke minutes before the man had taken that fatal fall from his horse. The quarrel had dwelled on the manner in which the duke had treated his wife.

Stephen had asked the duke why he had even married his mother. The man's anger had escalated to monumental proportions as he told his youngest son that his heart had always belonged to another, and Stephen had no right to interfere in his life or his mother's. In that moment, Stephen vowed to marry for love.

His mother let out a sigh of delight at the mention of her new husband. "Alas, my love is visiting his estates the next few weeks and I decided to help Jane acclimate to Elbourne Hall. However, duty will soon return me to Town to be with Emily."

Emily was Stephen's younger sister, and in a month or so she would be having his mother's first grandchild. Emily had finally married Lord Stonebridge, a suitor once rejected by the duke.

His mother's smile soon turned to a frown as she shifted her cat in her arms. "You know, Egypt is getting ever so heavy lately. Don't know what's come over her."

Stephen gave the mewing feline a knowing look but prevented himself from saying anything more. Letting out the secret that the cat was going to have kittens in the near future would put the house in an uproar—something Jane did not need at the moment.

"I wanted to tell you," his mother went on, "I will be visiting Creighton Hall when my dear husband returns." Her eyes softened with emotion. "I intend to show him the tree I played on when I was small. The swing is still there, is it not?"

Stephen pulled at his cravat. "Creighton Hall?"

"Rope must be frayed to pieces by now," his mother sighed.

"Indeed," he muttered. "Frayed to everlasting hell."

"What was that?"

"It will be swinging like a bell, Mother. I will spend my last farthing on that swing. See if I don't."

She kissed his cheek. "Don't go to too much trouble now."

"It's no trouble, Mother." The light in his mother's eyes sank his spirits to a new low. "No trouble at all."

Chapter Three

W hile most of the guests were settling into their chambers at Harmstead Hall, Elizabeth was on a mission to acquire a rope long enough to lower her trunk from her chamber window to the ground below.

It was early afternoon and a crisp cool wind blew across the courtyard as she hurried to the stables. She lifted her face to the cloudless blue sky and hoped the weather would stay fair, for tonight she would elope.

A niggling doubt pinched her heart at the thought of hurting her father and making a bigger mistake than he would with her life, but she had to do this. She would not marry some lord who only wanted her for her money. She would not.

"My lord, someone will see us."

Elizabeth stopped outside the stable, recognizing the sensual female voice immediately. Lady Odette—of all people!

Smells of horses and hay filled Elizabeth's nostrils as she peeked through the crack beneath the hinge in the stable door. Her eyes widened in shock at the sight of a tall gentleman with his arms wrapped tightly around Lady Odette's curvaceous figure.

"One little kiss, Dettie," he pleaded with a hint of amusement lacing his voice.

Dettie? The odd silkiness of the man's tone sent Elizabeth's face flaming with embarrassment. Yet she stood frozen, watching as the man leaned toward Odette and pressed his lips to hers.

Odette giggled, pushing the hair from the man's face

where dark coffee-colored locks curled boyishly at the nape
of his neck. "Stephen, you odious man."

The man's hearty laugh echoed in Elizabeth's ear and
shot straight to her stomach. Even from this view, she could
see that he was extremely handsome.

And for some insane reason, whether it was the musical
sound of his voice or the sudden stab of jealousy in her own
heart, Elizabeth fervently wished that the man would know
Lady Odette for what she was before it was too late.

She hadn't seen Odette since leaving the seminary two
years ago and hoped never to see the loathsome creature
again. But Stephen looked as besotted as a little boy receiving his first pony.

Elizabeth couldn't take her eyes off him. Long muscular
legs filled a pair of buckskin breeches as he stood back and
studied Odette in amused silence. He crossed his arms over
his wide chest, pulling his deep brown jacket tight against
his shoulders. But it was when he grinned, baring a set of
beautiful white teeth, that Elizabeth's heart stopped.

This was no mere boy. This male specimen was a man of
power and determination.

Putting a hand to her mouth, Elizabeth stumbled back not
wanting to see this supreme male make such a fool of himself. Odette could lure a man into a lion's den if she wanted
to.

Elizabeth knew she should leave, but this would be her
only chance to snatch the rope the groom had told her would
be hanging beyond the door.

She hurried around the back of the stables, her mind trying to block out the mumbled conversation inside.

When the voices finally ceased and she heard footsteps
heading away from the stables, thinking all was clear, she
peeked in the back door and made her way inside, stepping
lightly about the hay. Still hovering in the shadows, she eyed
the rope hanging in the shaft of the sun's rays directly beyond the door—exactly where the groom had said it would
be. Her heart lifted. She paused. Then, without warning, a
strong arm grabbed her and whirled her around, hauling her
up against a hard chest.

"Back so soon?"

Shocked, Elizabeth found herself speechless as she was pulled further into the shadows. It was Odette's suitor! Her heart hammered wildly as she fought to maintain a calmness she didn't feel. Did he know about her elopement?

"Nothing to say, little one? Coming back for another kiss?"

Before she knew it, warm lips pressed against hers. She pushed her hands frantically against the muscled chest that held her. The scent of bayberry assaulted her nose, making her all too aware of the man holding her. And "little one"? Was he making fun of her height and girth? She may take an extra roll at breakfast, but this man had no right to speak to her that way.

"Unhand me, sir!"

With a jerk, he drew her into the dappled sunlight and immediately dropped his hands. "I thought you were . . . never mind."

The truth of the situation finally hit her like a fireball to her face. He thought her Odette! Heat flooded her.

"I beg your pardon, Miss—"

Elizabeth's lips thinned as dark brown eyes laughed back at her. Why, the man was not sorry in the least. He was enjoying her humiliation! The cad!

Ignoring him, she skirted his tall frame and grabbed the rope that hung on the wall.

"Do you need help carrying that?" the voice said dryly. "Ah, you are going to string me up for a little kiss, then?"

Elizabeth spun around, her eyes flashing. Something in the carefree way this man stood there sent her hackles rising. He was a peer of the realm—the enemy—one of many her father would love her to marry.

"That was a kiss?" she said, lifting her chin. "I've enjoyed a lick from a horse better than that *kiss*."

A horse neighed in one of the nearby stalls. The man's eyes suddenly darkened to a foreboding black. Elizabeth felt as if she had waved a red flag in front of a bull. She managed a feeble smile, backing up toward the open door.

"You have, have you?" He took a step toward her, his powerful form sending a distinct warning to her brain.

She pressed the rope to her gown and backed up slowly. "Yes, well . . . if you had not—"

Before she could finish, she tripped over her feet and went sprawling to the ground with a thud.

The man stood over her, his eyes alight with laughter. "Best take care where you walk with a rope, little one. Never know where it might lead you."

"Little one" again! Elizabeth pulled the rope back to her side and glared up at him in stony silence.

"Ah, the silent treatment, eh? I have a sister and know all about that. Won't work on me, I assure you."

In one swift move, his hand whipped out and he gently pulled her to a standing position. She came within an inch of him and her heart stumbled. She could only attribute her sudden reaction to the bayberry soap he had used this morning. Yet perhaps it was the independent streak in this man that captivated her. It was unquestionably something.

Holding her breath, she stepped away. He let her.

"Thank you," she said, finding her tongue growing thick.

He bowed over her hand and kissed it. "Your obedient servant, madam." With one last look of amusement, he strode from the stables, leaving her with the rope lying at her feet.

"Help me pull my trunk beneath the window, Milli."

Elizabeth finished tying the rope around her jam-packed trunk and heaved it toward Milli. They were in Lord Harmstead's guest bedchamber, readying for Elizabeth's escape with the romantic Mr. Fennington.

But to Elizabeth's displeasure, instead of her thoughts dwelling on her intended as they rightly should, they veered toward a tall gentleman with buckskin breeches and dark, laughing eyes.

"I think this is a big mistake, Lizzie," Milli grunted, helping her sister move the trunk. "Papa is not going to be happy. Besides, I don't think Mr. Fennington is planning to take all this to Gretna Green. It might slow him down."

"Don't worry about Mr. Fennington. Your job is to stand below the window at midnight. No one will suspect you. I will come down the tree after my trunk. Understand? You are only there to coordinate."

Milli grunted again. "I know you are supposed to have the headache, but can you not come down the stairs like me?"

"No, I cannot. I will be stopped for sure. I am supposed to be ill and will not attend the ball. You are not out, and therefore, not expected to be at the ball. But if you are walking about for some fresh air, who is to stop you?"

After they had pushed the trunk to its desired destination, Milli sat on the ornate luggage, breathing hard and shaking her head. "I don't like it. I don't like Fennington being such a coward that he cannot face Papa. He's acting like one of those dastardly villains in the play I just read."

"He is not a coward. Now are you with me or not?"

"Okay, okay. I'm with you."

Elizabeth heaved a relieved sigh and sank onto the trunk beside Milli. "Let's go over the plan one more time."

Stephen felt a cool numbness taking over his brain. Whether it was from the wine or the cards, it didn't matter. Nothing mattered anymore.

He looked around the salon and realized that he and Shelby were the only two men still in the room. The rest of the gentlemen had left to attend to their required dances or other less costly adventures. Another salon in Harmstead Hall hosted lower stake games of faro and whist. But in this room, high stakes had been the order of the night, and those without the ready did not apply their skills.

Beyond the oak doors, the sound of violins lifted in the air like a melodic summer breeze, like the setting of a beautiful dream. But it was no dream at all. It was one devil of a nightmare—one that Stephen had stepped into with his eyes wide open.

And meeting an old friend of his father's earlier today had not helped his disposition. The elderly gentleman had been abroad for years, seeing to his plantation in the

Caribbean, and though it was a bit late, he had expressed his sympathy concerning the duke's untimely death to Stephen personally.

Pushing back the unbidden memory, Stephen peered at the bottles of wine beside him and felt his head buzz. Across from him, Shelby leaned back on his chair, puffing on a cigar.

"Have you the blunt or not, my lord?" the man asked, his gray eyes narrowing.

"I can have it for you tomorrow, Shelby. Won't be a problem." Now he had only to contact Brule and tell him he wanted out of that little business deal.

Stephen would have enough money to pay off his debt, but he would not have Creighton Hall back. He would have to buy it back at a later date. His mind raced. But then again, if he waited a bit on the business venture, he could have more money than the Duke of Elbourne. Blast it to hell, he was in a fix!

". . . Cash on the barrel, my lord. Those were the rules. As I said, my offer of marriage is the best you will get tonight."

Marriage? The man had used the word a few times in the last minute, but Stephen hadn't been registering much of what Shelby was saying. All he knew was that he did not have the funds at hand to pay the man. But the way Shelby was uttering the word *daughter* finally pierced through the numbness of Stephen's brain.

"You want me to what?" Stephen choked out.

Shelby rested his cigar on a silver tray beside him and heaved a perceptive sigh. "You heard me correctly. If you have no funds to pay your debt, then this is my final offer.

"You may marry my Elizabeth," the man went on as if he were entering into a business venture with a sheik, "and I will clear you of your debts. Of course, I will give you Creighton Hall back as a wedding present"—Shelby's lips parted with a grin—"or an engagement present, perhaps?"

Stephen stared back, dumbfounded, as an uneven row of yellow teeth reflected back at him. "You're mad."

"Now, your lordship, I know what I'm about. I ain't mad

at all. But I believe a special license may be the way of it. It isn't something I take lightly now. Elizabeth is a special girl, my eldest, and not without her merits. Schooled down in Bath with the best of the *ton*. Knows a few languages. Can watercolor decent enough. Plays the pianoforte with the fingers of an angel and has a heart of gold. Not many girls like her in all of England."

Stephen could bet a hundred pounds on that fact. By heaven, the chit was probably twenty stone and looked exactly like her father. Yet Stephen's honor was at stake here.

"Be doing you a favor, my lord. Why, think of it this way—you won't have to be part of the marriage mart anymore, eh? Stuffy mamas and all that."

Stephen's lips tightened. *And he would no longer have Odette.* For now it seemed there was no recourse but to agree to the man's insane demand. Shelby might be shrewd but he was not a cheat. The game had been played fair enough.

Stephen dropped a hardened gaze to the empty bottles of wine at the edge of the table and his stomach twisted with guilt. What had he become since his father died? A drunk? A wastrel? A man who thought he could have anything he wanted, including a beautiful woman, and now he had come to this? Would his marriage be like his parents'? No respect, no love? No life at all?

"She may not be a diamond of the first water," Shelby began to idly shuffle the cards, "but as I said before, Elizabeth is not without her merits."

Stephen shifted a wary gaze toward the man who seemed to be choking the life out his dreams. Hell and thunderation! Shelby was serious about this.

"You are demanding that I marry your daughter over a debt of cards? Seems a bit coldhearted, don't you think? Just for a few guineas?"

Shelby's eyes narrowed with a cold and calculating emotion Stephen could not quite put his finger on. "A debt of more than a few guineas, my lord, lest we forget. As I see it, you have no choice in the matter; that is, unless you want me to go to the head of the family. That would be your brother, the Duke of Elbourne, would it not?"

Stalling for time, Stephen began to twirl the stem of his wineglass. This man had unequivocally made his way to the top of the list of England's richest men by the use of his brains. Not only had Shelby increased his monetary worth, he had also gained Prinny's full attention. The cit was heard to even be on the Regent's Christmas list. He had managed an invitation to the most noted of the *ton*'s balls, soirees, and foxhunts. It was amazing Shelby was not in Brighton right now.

His flamboyant use of money, dropped into the right hands, had earned him everything he wanted—everything but a title. He was accepted in Society, but accepted was different from being born into the *ton*, or at least that was what Shelby seemed to think. And Zeus if Stephen had not just handed him a titled son-in-law on a silver platter.

"I need time to collect my sum," Stephen said, stuffing his hands in his pockets. "I can have the money for you by tomorrow." Devil take it. He would sell everything he had to buy back Creighton Hall, too.

Shelby took out his snuffbox and pinched a bit into his nose. "Time? You think I have no knowledge of your past gambling . . . and drinking?"

He glanced purposely at the empty wine bottles. "Knew you would come here tonight. You ain't the kind of fellow who would lose his mother's childhood home and leave it to a man like me.

"Beggin' your pardon, but you do have a conscience, your lordship. Knew that from the start. I ain't wanting my Elizabeth to have a man without morals, you know. Said I knew all about your fight in the war—Wellington and all that. A good man, you are, if you ain't drinking or gaming. Wellington would vouch for you, I'm certain."

"I am certain he would," Stephen said in a clipped tone.

So the man had planned this, knowing Stephen would fold under the sins of the bottle. Shelby had known all about Creighton Hall, too. It was amazing how sane and sober Stephen felt at the moment.

Heaven help him, he'd like to shoot Shelby between the eyes. He could see Creighton Hall, Lady Odette, and his life drifting away like a ship on the distant horizon.

"You may have my hunting lodge as collateral until I make good upon the debt," Stephen offered, trying to compromise with anything but marriage to the man's ugly daughter.

"No. Won't do. My daughter needs a husband."

"A husband?" Stephen said, a steel edge to his voice. "I do believe that what you really want is a lord for a son-in-law."

Shelby flinched, and the ace of spades flew out of the deck and onto the table.

"A warning, my lord?" the man uttered, retrieving the card.

"A threat, Shelby, or are you merely coaxing me with sweet words to wed your *beautiful* daughter?"

Shelby's face reddened. "Now see here. You have lost a considerable amount to me. You have told me that as of this precise moment you are without funds to meet your debt. Therefore, I believe I am being quite generous. Your notes at this time will not do. The stakes were very clear when you entered this room. If you go back on your word, all of London will know you for what you are. Disgrace will follow you like the plague."

Stephen leaned forward, his lips twisting into a cynical grin. "You had this all planned out very well, old man. I have to hand it to you. Very well indeed. Did you ever think that disgrace would follow *you* if people discovered your wager?"

The fat man smiled, sagged against the back of his chair, and patted his waistcoat. "I pride myself on my accomplishments, my lord. Just as you saved Wellington's life and kept quiet, honor will demand that you still your tongue on tonight's game. However, I have one more stipulation."

Stephen laughed. "Only one?"

"One more," Shelby said seriously, his gaze suddenly turning as cold and hard as the emerald sitting on his fleshy white finger. "You will take my daughter as your bride, but you will never tell her of this day. She will believe this is all of your making. Have I made myself clear?"

Stephen stiffened. "Perfectly."

"Oh, almost forgot. As my future son-in-law, I will pay all your debts. Clear the papers, so to speak." The man's eyes sparkled with self-satisfaction. "What say you to that?"

"I have no other debts, sir, but the debt I owe you." Stephen stood, stuck one hand in his waistcoat and bowed to the man. "Your obedient servant," he said with a cool expression. But he would never be this man's servant, obedient or otherwise.

With that, Stephen strode stiffly from the room, his head spinning with reckless thoughts of duels and endless tours of the continent and America. But he was a gentleman and would do what needed to be done.

As he stepped from the room, he thought he heard a muffled laugh from the man behind him, but the sound was lost in the mingle of voices down the hall. Uttering an oath, he hastened toward the gardens behind the mansion. His steps were hard and purposeful as a cool breeze lifted the lock of hair at his temple, and he tried to lose himself in the shadow of the trees.

"Pssst, you there."

Stephen stopped abruptly, glancing past the winding wisteria to his left. Footsteps padded lightly on the graveled path alongside the mansion. The wind lifted and he was slapped by the overwhelming scent of lavender.

He saw nothing until he took another step toward the giant elm brushing against the bricks of Harmstead Hall. To his amazement, a pair of elflike eyes stared back at him.

Stephen fought back a smile and raised a questioning brow. Why, it was not an elf at all, but a tiny chit dressed in some fluffy green concoction, and from all appearances, she seemed about ten, maybe twelve. Probably one of Lord Harmstead's children, he thought, recalling the games of hide-and-seek he had played as a child with his brothers when his parents had held extravagant parties at Elbourne Hall.

His eyes sought hers and he grimaced. The girl should

not be out here alone. Although there was a full moon, and the lamps outside the mansion illuminated the garden quite prettily, dappled shadows concealed places for lovers and predators—places where a little thing like this should never be.

Having a sister himself, Stephen felt his anger rise. Anger at his stupid use of spirits. Anger at his stupid loss. Anger that he had let Lady Odette slip through his fingers. And anger that he had to marry some ugly chit that was probably the spitting image of William Shelby.

"What are you doing out here?" Stephen replied, more sharply than he had intended, giving the girl a hard stare.

He took a step toward her, hovering over her. "You wish a dance, sweetheart?" he said silkily, watching her eyes go wide.

Good! That should scare the tiny thing back to her room.

The girl flushed. "Oh, no. I am not out, you know. Papa says I cannot come out until next year. It's a silly rule, I know, because I am almost fifteen. However, I am not out here for worldly pleasures. I am helping my sister. Of course, I would like to be an actress when I grow up, and this will only help me play the part of, well, a secret agent, I believe."

Stephen began to feel his head swim as he tried to put the girl's ramblings into some kind of sense. "A secret agent for a secret rendezvous?"

She nodded with a hesitant smile, then whispered, "I need a rescuer. A knight of old."

Stephen's lips twitched. This little imp reminded him of Emily when she was young. The girl was up to her elfin eyes in mischief and she was not fifteen.

After the hideous events that had occurred in the card room only minutes ago, Stephen felt a little diversion was in order. This girl's sister was probably sent to her room and needed a few desserts from the kitchen. Stephen knew all about that. There were many times Stephen and his brothers had foraged the kitchen before a big soiree at the Duke of Elbourne's home and eaten half the desserts before they were ever laid out.

"Very well, my lady, let me be your knight in shining armor. What is your sister about? Stealing cakes from the kitchen?"

"We are not stealing." The girl's chin stuck out. "We are eloping."

Now that grabbed Stephen's attention. He felt the corners of his mouth twitch. "Ah, eloping. And the age of your sister?"

"Nineteen." The girl pointed to the elm that brushed up against the mansion. "And in a minute or two she is to be coming down that tree."

Stephen raised his head, his eyes narrowing on the flimsy branches near the mansion. The thicker branches stuck far away from the wall.

"And I do not like the man at all, you see—"

The scene was becoming all too clear. "By Jove, nineteen, you say? Which window is it?"

"The one with the rope."

Stephen eyes widened as he took another step beneath the tree, his head still tilted upward. "The rope?" Something about the rope spiked his senses. "And when is this wondrous sister of yours going to climb down that tree?"

He heard a slight whimper and dropped his gaze. The girl looked ready to cry. Fat tears edged the corner of her eyes, and she gave a pitiful sniff.

"A-at the stroke of twelve she is to meet . . . Mr. Fennington right here . . . and then they are off to Gretna Green. I told her that Papa would not like it but she would not listen to me."

Stephen froze. "Did you say Mr. Fennington?"

When Mr. Fennington had tried to woo Stephen's sister, Lady Emily, all four of her brothers had trussed the man up like a pig ready for slaughter. It was fortunate for him that their mother had come to his aid.

The girl looked up, her gray eyes flashing, her dark hair bouncing about her face. "Yes, the one with that odd quizzing glass. Goodness, you know him, then?" She stepped back, wary. "Are you friend or foe?"

"Foe. And know him? By heaven, I almost killed the man on many occasions."

The girl's eyes rounded with excitement—a fact that made Stephen look at her twice. "He is a fiend, is he not? Like a villain in a Minerva plot?"

Stephen's lips thinned as he watched the girl dance beneath the tree, fisting her hands in the air. "Yes, a veritable fiend." And since when did they let chits her age read the Minerva Press?

"Milli, are you down there?" The husky feminine voice snapped Stephen's gaze back toward the window.

"Your sister, I presume?" he said softly.

Milli gasped. "Yes, and she wants to marry that despicable fellow." She grasped Stephen's sleeve, jerking him back and forth like a church bell. "You must help me. We cannot let her do this."

Just then, Stephen wanted to leave. He had his own problems. Stealing cakes was one thing, stopping an elopement was quite another. But the devil take it, Fennington was involved!

This bit of evening entertainment had only added to the tumultuous emotions flaring up inside him. But honor reared its ugly head again and he knew he would stay. The thought of his sister almost running off with the bastard made him intervene.

If he could not save himself from a horrid marriage at least he could save one wretched soul from a life of doom, even if she was a stupid female who had fallen for Fennington and that idiotic quizzing glass. Obviously the girl's family was from money because that was Fennington's only motive in marriage.

Stephen placed his hands against the tree, the rough bark riding against his hands. At least he knew the imp's name. "Very well, *Milli*. I will stop her . . . for now, at least."

Milli wrapped her arms around him and sobbed. "I knew it the minute I saw you turning the corner. You are a most noble knight, sir. My prayers were surely answered."

Stephen swallowed hard at the girl's innocence. Noble? He was a cad and a drunkard.

He lightly put his hands on her shoulders and lifted her away. "Yes. Well, let us solve this little problem."

Milli backed up, her mouth tilted into a full grin. "How exciting. This is like a play at Drury Lane, is it not?"

Startled, Stephen stared back at the girl. Drury Lane, indeed. There was no trace of tears on her smiling cheeks. And innocent, he thought, his senses coming to full alert. Her acting could put Drury Lane to shame! And where in the blazes was that dashed lavender bouquet coming from? It seemed as if she had poured an entire bottle of the scent on herself.

"Milli," the husky voice whispered again. "Are you down there?"

Milli looked up and squeezed Stephen's arm. "Yes."

"Well, step away from the tree, dearest."

At the sound of the voice once again, Stephen felt a pleasurable familiar tug at his brain. The lady's voice reminded him of the whisper of silk on a winter day. It was inviting, yet oddly innocent and pure. Where had he heard it before?

Milli stared at Stephen as if she wanted him to say something back to her sister. But he held back the urge to shout and decided to follow through with the scenario. It might be the only reckless thing he ever did again.

"Oh," Milli said, her voice trembling with emotion as she raised her gaze, "I think she might kill herself."

After gauging the distance to the ground, Stephen thought the very same thing. "Dash it all," he said to Milli. "Move aside, imp, I'll catch your sister if she falls."

Milli nodded and moved away. "Thank you, *dear knight.*"

Stephen bit back a groan at the girl's lavish adoration. This was all he needed tonight. But he had no intention of catching the descending female. He intended to give her a piece of his mind instead.

"What is your sister's name, Milli?"

She opened her mouth to answer when the branches rattled above them and there was a shout from above.

"Watch out! Here it comes."

Before Stephen knew it, something hard came crashing

onto his chest. Uttering an oath, he fell to the ground with a thud. A blinding pain shot through his shoulders and he lay flat on his back with a sharp rock pushing into his spine.

Muttering another curse, he shook his head and looked to his left. Beside him sat an ornate gold-leafed trunk, worthy of the king himself. Must have weighed a ton, too!

"Hell's teeth! What kind of trunk is that?" Clothing of some kind came flying out of the window and landed on his head.

"Catch my cloak, Milli," the husky voice added in a low hush. "It might prove a bit cumbersome when I climb down."

"Cumbersome is too tame, madam," Stephen mumbled as he threw the cloak off his head, pain shooting down his arm.

By heaven, this was the end!

But as Stephen was just about to rise, he glanced up, his eyes widening at the sight of one creamy white calf shining in the moonlight. He blinked.

"That was the new trunk she got from Papa on her last birthday," Milli whispered in his ears. "Are you all right? Did you break something?"

Stephen gritted his teeth, wondering what star he had been born under to deserve all this tonight. "Break something? Ruined my future is more like it."

"I see her leg," Milli said.

"So do I," Stephen answered, his head throbbing, but not enough for him to stop staring.

"Do something, you ninny."

Stephen blinked again. Was this schoolgirl calling him names?

"Goodness gracious! She's climbing down. Oh fudge. She has never been a good climber."

Brushing a hand over his bruised shoulder, Stephen immediately realized the danger. "Move aside, Milli. Plague take it! Looks as if I may have to catch your sister after all."

"Oh, oh, I cannot hold on—"

Stephen planted his feet apart, enough to brace himself for the fall. The impact of the trunk had been nothing compared to the bang of the woman against his chest. He was slammed to the ground as if he had been knocked down by three of his brothers.

"Mr. Fennington . . . you saved me."

The breathless words were said with such insanity and love that Stephen wanted to box the girl's ears.

"I am not Mr. Fennington, madam. And if you would kindly roll off my chest, I could begin to breathe again."

Elizabeth jumped up and stood with her back against the tree, watching in shock as two glittering eyes glared back at her. She gathered her traveling dress, ripped at the shoulder, and stared back in dismay.

She could not quite see the man's face because he was still sitting in the shadows, but the sheen of the moon illuminated that angry gaze as if it belonged to a sleek black panther. A sudden shiver swept through her as he uttered an oath and stood.

She pressed a hand to her mouth when he stepped into the moonlight. "It's you!" It was the man from the stables, but he didn't seem to hear her.

"That was the most dangerous, stupid, idiotic act I have ever seen in my life!"

Elizabeth lifted her chin, but inwardly her heart was beating like that of a mouse cornered by a cat.

She remembered all too well the athletic-looking man in the stables with his wavy chestnut hair and warm brown gaze. But it wasn't warm now. It was as cold as the icicles outside her window in the winter. He brushed a hand through his dark locks, and memories of his kiss lingered in her mind.

She swallowed as his large form shadowed over her, blocking her view. "I will, er, reimburse you for your clothing, sir."

Dark eyes flashed as he pulled the torn jacket from his shoulders. "You think your intended would allow you to pay for a gentleman's clothing? How half-witted do you think I am?"

His words were said with such contempt she felt the insult all the way down to her toes. Why, he had no idea they had met before. Her mouth opened and closed as she pushed her back into the tree, feeling its bark scratching up against her spine.

Yet, to be quite honest, it was this man's casual elegance that unnerved her. He was a lord. She knew that from Odette's previous rendezvous with him. But there were no brass buttons, no waterfall cravats, no ornate jewelry. His clothes seemed simple and clean—before she had knocked him down, that is. Moreover, there was something about the way he wore them that set him apart from the other gentlemen. He emitted a certain masculine charm that turned her knees to jelly.

Regarding him, she could see that he was much more muscular than Mr. Fennington. Humiliation welled up inside her. How could she have mistaken him for her fiancé?

His eyes gleamed with humor and a sparkle of recognition as he continued to stare at her. "The girl from the stables, I see."

He remembered her, did he? She might not be as pretty as Odette, but at least Mr. Fennington wanted her. She lifted a haughty brow. "My fiancé will not mind clothing a man in need, sir."

The man's face became taut, and for the first time Elizabeth noticed Milli standing in front of her trunk, watching the exchange with wide innocent eyes.

Elizabeth bit her lip, regretting her outburst instantly. Why, she had never treated anyone so outrageously. This man had saved her life, and he had every right to be riled after her idiotic descent from the window.

"Sorry to disappoint you, my dear, but I will not need your assistance in my choice of wardrobe. I regret I am to marry soon."

Her cheeks burned. "That is not what I meant, and you know it." He laughed then, a deep resounding rumble from his chest, making him look even more handsome than he had in the stables.

"You think this funny?" she asked, shaking her free fist at him while the other fist held her gown together.

"Hilarious, madam."

Milli let out a snort of amusement and Elizabeth's icy gaze shot to her. "Sorry," Milli said, lowering her eyes as she sat upon the trunk.

Elizabeth's temper soared. This man was laughing at her as if she were some silly chit. Mr. Fennington was a true gentleman—not at all like this man. Her fiancé would never laugh at her like some uncaring beast. And where was Mr. Fennington, anyway?

Anxiety at the break in her plans soon replaced her rising anger. She needed to rid herself of this detestable lord if she still wanted to make her escape tonight. She took a deep breath, trying to calm the emotions surging through her.

"I thank you for breaking my fall," she said, her tone softening. "However, I am no longer in need of your chivalry. If you would be so kind as to leave, I will be on my way."

The smile in the man's eyes died. Before she could open her mouth, her sister did.

"Lizzie, the man did save your life, and, well, he seems to know Mr. Fennington, too."

A sinking sensation filled Elizabeth as she took in the lord's taut expression when Milli mentioned Mr. Fennington. "You may leave, sir. As you can see, I am not injured. I have no more need of you."

"Too devilish bad," the lord drawled, his gaze locking on an approaching form. Then her dratted rescuer moved into the shadows, appearing even larger than he had only seconds ago.

Elizabeth glanced over her shoulder as a familiar blond head came into view. Relief swept through her.

"Oh Mr. Fennington," she whispered. "Over here."

"I fail to see what whispering will do," the man beside her interjected with a sarcastic snort. "If we have not awakened the entire ballroom by now, you may rest assured you are safe to speak." He shifted back a step and glared at her bare shoulder.

With a quick hand, Elizabeth scooted the material higher, scowling back at him.

"Ah, dearest, I knew you would not fail me. I have the

carriage waiting." Fennington walked up to Elizabeth, his huge quizzing glass in hand as he surveyed her appearance. "But my dear, whatever happened?"

"She fell," came the deep baritone voice from the shadows.

Fennington's quizzing glass dropped to his side. "You!"

"Me." The lord's face took on a threatening twist.

Elizabeth's heart pounded wildly as the tension in the air thickened to the consistency of Cook's holiday pudding. She was surprised when Fennington took a step back. Her fiancé's reaction bruised her pride. Was he afraid of the man?

"Mr. Fennington," she said with a little laugh, "the most peculiar thing happened. I was coming down that tree and thought you were there to catch me. But in fact this—uh—gentleman broke my fall. But as you see, I do have my things ready for—"

"Fennington, how well you move around these days." The sharp words cut through the night like a well-honed ax.

Fennington raised his quizzing glass. "Ah, Lord Stephen Clearbrook, I thought I saw you in a card game earlier."

Elizabeth frowned at the flash of irritation on the intruder's face. He seemed to stiffen at Mr. Fennington's words. It was obvious the lord was readying for a fight. Goodness knows this was the last thing she needed tonight.

"I see you two have met before," she said, her thoughts racing. "Well, Mr. Fennington, as I said before, this man saved me from a terrible fall but I have already thanked him. I believe I am ready to depart on our journey."

Hoping she would not lose her nerve, she turned to her sister and gave her a hug. "Good-bye, Milli. I will write—"

"You, madam, are not leaving."

The commanding words burst forth from the intruder with such imposing clarity, Elizabeth froze. Seething with indignation, she turned around slowly, intending to set this man straight, but she hesitated when she noted the dark scowl that masked his face.

"I do appreciate your help, Lord, um, Stephen Clearbrook, is it not? But Mr. Fennington and I are deeply in love—"

Elizabeth watched his expression change from irritated to amused. The man was mad. He was laughing at her again. "I beg your pardon."

"My dear." Fennington inched toward her, and she breathed a sigh of relief. Thank goodness he would take care of this hateful man. At least she could depend on someone.

"Love is not part of this little escapade, *Lizzie*," the intruder stated in a commanding tone.

A cold knot settled in Elizabeth's stomach. What was wrong with him? "I am Miss Elizabeth Shelby to you, sir. So if you would please excuse us, we will be taking our leave."

For a moment the man stared back at her as if she had grown a beard. A second later his hand shot out and grabbed her elbow. "No doubt someone will be taking his leave, Miss Shelby, but it certainly will not be you."

Chapter Four

*W*ith a decisive jerk, Stephen separated Miss Elizabeth Shelby from Fennington's side.

He wanted to beat his head against the disfigured elm. *Lizzie*, her sister had called her. He should have known.

Dash it all, this was a hideous nightmare. But by heaven, as a gentleman of honor he could not let this little bird fly the coop into Fennington's greedy hands.

Besides, Stephen thought bitterly, as his fiancée, the female belonged to him whether he liked it or not.

He set his teeth. How utterly convenient.

Watching the shocked expression playing across Miss Shelby's face, Stephen felt his maddening emotions gradually fade, only to be replaced by a stir of deranged amusement.

Miss Shelby was, without a doubt, a feisty little creature, and she definitely did not come by her looks from her father's side of the family. She was not what one would call exquisite, but her haughty manner made up for what she lacked in a conventional beauty.

Nevertheless, the chit was rounded in all the right places. He knew that the minute she had dropped from the sky and literally fallen onto his chest. Gracefully curvaceous, he thought, and quite pretty when riled. Her cheeks reminded him of a cherub—plump and rosy. But her big blue eyes reflected an innocence and naïveté that brought his protective instincts to the surface.

He felt her stiffen under his regard. It was obvious this girl had no idea of the depths of Fennington's deceit.

He stared at her lips, recalling the kiss in the stables, realizing he had enjoyed their earlier confrontation immensely. Yet she was so gullible it amazed him.

And here she was with Fennington.

For the love of the king, he had not forgotten the prim little miss at all. But heaven help him, if the lady had wanted to box his ears in the stables, wait until she heard the news that they were to be married.

Dappled moonlight played against her creamy white skin and he caught Fennington eyeing her bare shoulder with the look of a wolf licking his chops.

In one smooth move, Stephen lunged toward the cloak lying on the trunk, grabbed it, and threw it to her. "Here, put this on. Don't want you to catch a fever of the lungs, now, do we?"

Those blue eyes snapped back at him as if he were the devil himself. "What would you care?"

"I think, Miss Shelby, that you may find my answer rather enlightening."

So this was the lady he was to marry. He would have laughed if the situation were not so horrid. And the joke of it was, she thought herself in love with Fennington.

Well he could let her follow through with this little fiasco and relieve himself of the burden of marrying her, but there was no honor in that. And though he was an absolute idiot to drink and gamble his life away, no matter what his excuse, it was no reason to let this girl marry the weasel before him.

"See here," Fennington said, "we have had our differences, but I say, be a good chap and let us be on our way."

Stuffing a hand into his pocket, Stephen turned toward the six-foot worm across from him and gave the maggot a twisted smile. "As a gentleman, I cannot do that. You do understand, do you not, old chap?"

The peabrain had the gall to pull out that stupid quizzing glass and look him up and down. "And pray tell why not? Because your sister could not have me."

Miss Shelby gasped. Milli scowled, slipping beside Stephen.

Stephen's anger at Fennington was past the breaking

point. However, it was Stephen's sense of impassioned duty to safeguard this Shelby woman that surprised him the most. Elizabeth Shelby was too trusting by far. Moreover, though the little sister was a veritable termagant, he discovered, much to his surprise, that in the past few minutes he had become quite fond of the little imp. Having Fennington in their lives would be a living hell.

Stephen leaned against the elm and lazily crossed his arms over his chest. "Fennington, my dear sir, I will give you to the count of three. And if you do not leave these premises, grounds and all, I will call you out."

Fennington's face turned white. "B-but you cannot do this. You have no say in Miss Shelby's life. We have plans . . . Y-you cannot interfere." The monstrous quizzing glass shook in the man's white hands as he shoved it back into his pocket. "Upon my word, this is barbaric. I simply will not allow it."

Stephen raised an irritated brow, pushing away from the tree. "Well to tell you the truth, Fennington, I have been waiting for this time together ever since my sister's wedding. I promised my mother I would not follow you, but since you came across my path, what can a man say to that?"

Fennington gulped.

Miss Shelby threw herself between the two men, fixing an icy stare upon Stephen. "Do not come one step further, you beast!"

Stephen blinked at the lady. She was not a dazzler like Odette, yet those eyes of hers could put a spell on any man if he looked long enough. He stared thoughtfully, then shook his mind free of his fanciful notions. Her wheat-colored hair was escaping its pins and combs, and fell about her face as if she were some ragamuffin with no manners at all, making him wonder about the long years ahead of him.

"Ah, so you love this greedy rake, do you?" he asked her.

The lady wrung her hands on her skirt. "That is none of your affair."

So she was not as fearless as she seemed. He noticed that Milli had left. Good. The poor child did not need to see the blood spurting from Fennington's nose.

Fennington added an agreeable grunt. "Not your affair at all. Not at all."

"Oh, depend upon it. This is my affair," Stephen said calmly, glancing between Fennington and Miss Shelby.

"You're mad," Miss Shelby hissed.

Stephen's lips twisted. "Never said I wasn't, Miss Shelby."

She bit her lips, her face seeming to drain of color as though she believed he was going to pull out a pair of pistols and kill them both. So she had an imagination. Intriguing.

Stephen felt an instant stab of regret. The poor woman had no idea what was happening, but she would know soon enough. Fennington had been a thorn in his family's side for years now. It was time to do something about it.

Without a second thought, Stephen put his hands on Miss Shelby's waist and lifted her from her spot, placing her behind him. She sputtered something incoherent as she stumbled against the tree. He left her flailing in the dark, grateful she could not see him cuff Fennington in the jaw.

The man flipped over the gold embellished trunk and landed on his nose with a resounding thud.

Stephen hovered over him, lowering his voice to a deathly calm. "If you dare ever to come near this lady or her family again, I shan't be giving you a warning. Is that understood?"

Holding his nose, trying to stop the blood from rushing down his face, Fennington nodded.

Behind him, Stephen heard a horrified gasp.

"B-but Mr. Fennington, you are not going?" Miss Shelby's lip trembled and Stephen's stomach knotted at the longing in her voice. "My trunk, the carriage, our plans . . ."

"I fear . . ." Fennington pulled out a handkerchief and held it against his nose which muffled his voice as he backed up toward the wisteria, "dear Ewizabeth, our pwans have changed."

Elizabeth stepped forward and smacked Stephen on the shoulder. "Because of this brute?"

Stephen hardly moved at all, but inwardly his respect for

this female was growing by the minute. By Jove, the little thing would probably call him out if she were a man.

Hand still pressed against his nose, Fennington managed a contorted smile as he took a quick glance at Stephen, then returned his attention to Miss Shelby.

"A wady of your dewicate constitution should never . . . have had to witness . . . such depwaved conduct." He rubbed his jaw, his eyes gleaming with reproach as he glanced at Stephen. "A scandaw may suwound you . . . if I . . . do not take my weave."

"But you cannot leave!" Elizabeth took a hasty step in Fennington's direction but Stephen halted her movement by slipping a strong arm about her waist, hauling her back.

To Stephen's surprise, Fennington took that moment to slip in and raise Elizabeth's hand for a farewell kiss. "Good-bye . . . my sweet . . . good-bye."

"Oh Mr. Fennington," Elizabeth sobbed, "you are too good."

Stephen's hold on Miss Shelby tightened as he watched Fennington depart toward the back of the garden.

Elizabeth heard the towering lord growl something she could not understand and she swallowed another sob as she wrenched free from his hold. "You beast!"

Her heart turned over at the thought of Mr. Fennington's courage. He had left her alone so there would not be a scandal, and hence, this intruder could not smudge her name on the dueling field.

But the man standing next to her looked so smug in his simply tied neckcloth and torn dark jacket, which he had thrown back on, that she wanted to slap him.

He seemed to read her thoughts. "I would not do it if I were you, Miss Shelby." Brown eyes looked into hers with something akin to pity and her cheeks bloomed with color.

Only moments ago, when his hands had rested upon her waist to move her away from Fennington, she had been surprised. He had been gentle but determined. However, so was she.

"You . . . you ruined my life, you fiend!"

His hollow laugh rumbled in her ears. "Ruined your life? This is too rich. Depend upon it. I saved you from a man who only wanted you for your papa's money."

Elizabeth drew in a sharp breath. "How dare you! Mr. Fennington loves me. We will marry; you will see. He has left with his dignity intact." She gave him a swift perusal and snorted. "Which is more than I can say for you."

"Me? By Jupiter, madam. That man is nothing but a thief. He has gone after many an heiress seeking her fortune. Are you daft as well as stupid?"

She tripped back against the tree and held a hand to her bosom. "Why, you insufferable lout. How dare you speak to me as if I were some . . . some tavern wench!"

Stephen knew the moment the words were out he could not take them back. Tears pooled in those innocent blue eyes and he felt a thousand times worse than he had an hour ago. He loved women. Never said an unkind word to one as long as he could remember.

Even when his sister Emily had been in high spirit, he had all but encouraged her manner, vexing Roderick and his brothers Clayton and Marcus to no end. Still, it seemed that this woman irritated him more than she would ever know.

"I beg your pardon, madam." He stepped closer. "I have no reason to besmirch your good name. However, I should point out to you, since no one has already, that Mr. James Theodore Fennington is a cad and a wastrel. Never mind that he is a well-known rake and a voracious gambler."

She clapped her hands to her cheeks. "Oh! You are a horrid, horrid man." She glanced over her shoulder, as if looking for a means of escape. "If you dare touch me again or come any closer, I will scream."

Tears rolled down her face and Stephen instantly felt ashamed. Splaying his hands in the air, he heaved a sigh. "I won't touch you. In fact, I have no desire to touch you."

He shook his head at the sound of her gasp. "That is, we seemed to have gotten off on the wrong foot. Let me introduce myself." He gave a deep bow. "Your servant, Lord Stephen Clearbrook."

A small squeak emerged from the girl's throat, which in

seconds became a full bellow of laughter. "My servant? Good gracious, you are my worst nightmare, sir."

Stephen's head snapped to attention and he narrowed his eyes on the female. Was she mad as well as stupid? Irritation flowed through his veins. No woman had ever laughed at him except his sister, and for her he made allowances because she loved him. He stared back in contempt, waiting for Miss Shelby to compose herself.

The look on her face quickly changed back to one of horror.

Exasperated, Stephen tried to soothe her. "I have no reason to touch you, Miss Shelby . . . at least not yet."

Wide-eyed, she hastened to her trunk as if the ornate piece of luggage would save her. "Stay away from me."

"I daresay, *Miss Elizabeth Shelby*, if you are who you say you are, then we have more important matters to discuss than the question of servant and master."

Two delicate brows drew together. "We do, do we? Well I must say, you are full of surprises today. But believe me, I am in no mood to amuse you any further. I have other matters to attend to. I thank you again for saving me from that fall, but let me remind you, your gentlemanly act does not give you the right to take over my life."

To his continued surprise, the woman turned her back on him and began tugging at her trunk, muttering something about too many gowns. Stephen stood rooted in place and watched in silent amusement. She dragged the trunk about a foot before she was panting heavily.

"And where do you think you are going now?"

She sank onto her trunk and glared at him. "Obviously my plans have changed. But I warn you, your lordship, I may seem meek, but I am not about to sit here and take your insults any longer. If you were a gentleman, you would leave."

A gentleman? The devil of it was that that's precisely what had thrown him into this fix in the first place.

Rising from her seat, she pointed a small white finger at him. He almost laughed, thinking her actions more like his sister's. Emily would adore her.

"Leave me alone. Do you hear me? If you ever dare to interfere in my life again—"

"Interfere in your life? Dear woman, you were the one who came toppling from the sky, throwing me to the ground as if you were an anchor shot from the upstairs window."

Anchor? How apropos, he thought grimly, the realization of the situation slowly penetrating his brain.

At least the female had the grace to flush. "Well yes," she said meekly, "that was rather unwise of me. I should have waited until everyone had left."

Stephen swallowed a growl of anger. The impudence of the chit. She could have been killed!

"And I do appreciate your saving my life and taking the fall for me, my lord"—her eyes narrowed into slits of rage—"but since you have also ruined my life, I would say we are dead even. So it only signifies that we leave it at that."

Ruined her life? Stephen's lips curled. This was the end of his playing the controlled gentleman. "Miss Shelby, *dead even* will never describe the situation that is between us."

"Us?" she hissed. "There is no *us*."

He almost felt more sorry for her than he did for himself. Almost. "I have something I need to say, madam, and whether you like it or not, you must hear it from me first."

Her chin lifted, completely negating any first impression Stephen had of fragility. "Say it and be done," she said in a clipped tone. "I never want to see you again."

A twisted smile flashed across his face. It was clear that this woman would never go along with her father's edicts. As long as he gave the chit his side of things, she would be on his side faster than the Prince Regent could spend a guinea. It was to her benefit that they agreed on a plan.

"Well, Miss Shelby, not seeing me again may be a bit hard to arrange."

"Oh, say what you will and be done with it!"

"Ah, I see you two have already met. Capital! Capital!"

Stephen groaned at the sound of William Shelby's deep voice projecting from the darkness. Within an instant, the portly silhouette emerged from behind the wisteria.

As Shelby came into full view, the man's silent glare

bored a hole through any hope of Stephen extricating himself from this unseemly union. Whether his daughter agreed to the marriage or not, Stephen knew without a doubt that Shelby would make certain it went on as planned.

"Papa!"

Elizabeth hurried toward her father, her heart jumping out of her chest. Milli stood beside him, her eyes wide. Did their father know this man?

Elizabeth stiffened suddenly. The trunk? Could her papa see it in the shadows?

Standing beside her father, she tightened her hold on her cloak, trying to hide the rip in her gown. If her father had any idea she was planning a trip to Gretna Green, she would be locked away in the country for a year. Not that her papa didn't love her, but he was as strict as Caesar when it came to disobedience.

"Lizzie, my love. Milli mentioned you were going for a walk to help your headache. But I daresay it is too late for you to be out here alone without an escort, ball or not. I know you were not feeling well, but how fortunate you have met up with Lord Stephen Clearbrook. Has he told you the news?"

Elizabeth's brows furrowed in confusion when the lord purposely moved away from her trunk, removing her father's gaze from the evidence of her elopement. What was this man about now? He was not trying to save her from her father's wrath, was he?

"What news, Papa?" she asked, feeling oddly grateful to Lord Stephen Clearbrook.

"You tell her, your lordship?" William Shelby said, rubbing a hand over his chin as Milli opened her mouth and closed it again.

"No," was the curt reply as the lord crossed his arms over his chest, staring back at Elizabeth.

Elizabeth looked from one man to another, an uneasy feeling settling in the pit of her stomach. The icy brittleness hanging in the air had nothing to do with the weather. Murmured voices from the ballroom floated to her ears, a dim reminder of the party still taking place.

William Shelby stared hard at the hovering gentleman and Lord Stephen glared back at her father.

A rush of blood drummed through Elizabeth's veins. The two had obviously met before and whatever had happened at their last meeting was not finished.

"Tell me what?" she asked hesitantly.

William Shelby's face instantly changed, his frown lifting, only to be replaced by a tight smile. He stepped closer to Lord Stephen and had the effrontery to slap the man on the shoulder as if his lordship were his long lost son.

"Why, Lizzie dear, his lordship here has asked for your hand in marriage. And I have accepted."

Elizabeth felt the world tilt beneath her. "W-what?"

Stephen looked at this woman and for not the first time that evening felt a wave of pity for her. She was as headstrong as a mule, but she had to be or her father would have pushed her along life's path without a thought to what she wanted.

But her stubbornness didn't seem to be working for her now, for William Shelby had decided his daughter's fate as much as the man had decided Stephen's. Well, not precisely. Stephen had done it to himself. This girl was the man's daughter, a circumstance she could never change.

Shelby cleared his throat, slipping a hand between the buttons of his snug waistcoat, his militant stance more like that of Napoleon Bonaparte issuing an order than that of a doting father. "I have accepted, Elizabeth."

Stephen frowned. No woman deserved such a cold introduction to her future, especially one's own daughter.

"I see." Miss Shelby shifted a daring look in Stephen's direction, then turned to Milli. "The spectacles, Milli."

Milli frowned and fished in her pocket for her sister's spectacles, giving them to her. Anger flashed in Miss Shelby's blue eyes as she put on the ugly eyewear.

Stephen felt an instant warming toward the girl. Or was it respect? Dash it, but those spectacles were repulsive, and it seemed she thought to scare him off with them. How many females would try that on an unwanted suitor? Not many.

"Take those silly things off your nose, Lizzie. I won't have you acting like some insipid bluestocking."

Miss Shelby pursed her lips and swiped the spectacles off her face, stuffing them into her cloak. Stephen's amused gaze riveted on the creamy expanse of her neck and followed her hand.

He abruptly put a stop to his wayward thoughts. Thunderation! She was a rich termagant, too tall for his liking, and her father was greed incarnate. It was a blasted nightmare.

"I suppose he is tolerable, Papa," Miss Shelby replied, lifting her head. "He is definitely a muscled sort of brute. Has a good set of teeth. A thick brown-black mane of hair."

Stephen perceived a slight mist forming in the lady's eyes and his gut clenched. She was more sensitive than she let on.

She deserved better. But Stephen was an honorable man. He paid his debts. He would not back out of this arrangement if it killed him. He swallowed, feeling like a boy cornered after stealing from the baker. However, this was more than cakes at stake. This was both their lives.

"Of course, Papa," she continued. "I take it this man has a title worthy of your money, does he not?"

Shelby grunted uncomfortably. "He don't come from livestock, Lizzie. He is the fourth son of a duke. And you will desist with this incorrigible behavior. Do you hear me?"

The lady seemed deaf to her father's command, for she forged on, her lower lip quivering, something William Shelby did not seem to see or want to see.

"Ah, sired from a duke," she said softly. "And the fourth son. My, how honored I am." She batted her eyes and gave Stephen a deep curtsy that made him feel about an inch tall.

She darted a sweet glance toward her father. "I daresay he needed a tidy little sum to get him through life, and he came to you offering himself as a prize for your eldest daughter?"

William's thick lips curled into a real smile. "Well yes, poppet. It did go something like that."

Dark blue eyes shot toward Stephen. "Then I daresay he will have his money's worth, will he not? You will give my husband a good sum for the use of his lordly title?"

Stephen bit back an oath, wanting to strangle the girl. She was making it sound as if she had been bought. This was ridiculous. But before he could utter a single word on his behalf, William Shelby fell into the trap.

"That's the way of it, Lizzie. I am to provide him with a great sum when you are wed. But perhaps I should leave you two alone for a few minutes."

"But, Papa," Milli interrupted.

"Millicent, go back inside and get your hot chocolate."

Milli gave her father a swift salute. "*Certainement, Napoleon!*" With a sour grimace, the girl disappeared beyond the trees, marching toward the servants' entrance.

Ignoring Milli, William continued, looking toward his eldest daughter. "Knew you had a headache and wanted to clear your mind. A walk will do that, but next time, Lizzie, you must take an escort."

He gave a hearty chuckle. "Milli mentioned you were out here alone. Girl does have a vivid imagination though. Never know what's true or not. In fact, I had better leave you two alone and see what havoc she's raising in the kitchen."

He turned toward Stephen. "No need to worry about the announcement. I will send the notice to the *Gazette* immediately. All Town will be abuzz. You are staying here for the night?"

"I am," Stephen answered, his jaw tight.

"Ah, then, until tomorrow." Shelby bent forward and gave his daughter a peck on the cheek. "See you in the morning, Lizzie."

A sweet concerto filled the air while Stephen and Elizabeth watched in shocked silence as the man disappeared from sight. "How lucky I am." Miss Shelby's quivering voice broke through the stillness. "And you, Lord Stephen Clearbrook, was it not you who mentioned something about a thief? How many heiresses have you sought out?" Her blue eyes glittered with unshed tears—tears she had obviously held back from her father.

An unwelcome blush stole across Stephen's cheeks. "It was not like that at all."

By heaven, he would like to call Shelby out for this.

She gave a laugh that sounded more like a sob. "Ah, I see. But then what makes you believe you are any different than Mr. Fennington? You have no quizzing glass, is that it? Oh no, of course, you are far above such things, are you not? You have no need to use any type of spectacles at all, do you?"

"You have no idea what I need, madam."

"Oh, but you are mistaken. You may have saved me from my father's wrath by keeping him away from my trunk, but if you had not interfered, that trunk and I would have been long gone by now. So, do not tell me I have no idea what you need."

"Indeed," he said, his lips thinning, barely following the thread of her conversation. "What is it that I need, Miss Shelby?"

"Money, my lord. My father's detestable money."

Chapter Five

*E*lizabeth paced the length of her father's bedchambers, seething with indignation at the night's folly.

Lord Stephen Clearbrook! The hateful, arrogant man! She would never marry him. Not if he were the last man in England.

Granted, the man might have a title, not to mention the face and figure of a god, but that meant absolutely nothing. He was a penniless thief and would never have her heart. And if she had anything to say about it, he would never have her father's money either.

"He is a despicable man, Papa, and I will not have it. I will not marry him!"

William Shelby turned from the fire, his deep gray eyes filled with sympathy and something more—grim determination.

An icy finger of despair slid down Elizabeth's spine. She had seen that calculating look on his face many times before when he was involved in the most ruthless of business ventures. It meant no shortcuts, no leniency, no giving in, and cursed be the man or woman who dared to stop him from achieving his goal.

"Papa . . . please . . . I beg you, do not do this to me."

Her father glanced back into the crackling fire, dipping his hands toward the hearth for warmth. "I know how you are feeling, poppet. But believe me, this is for the best. We could always look for an earl or a marquess or, by Jove, even a duke. But this is enough. More than I had ever hoped for."

With a tired sigh, he turned back to her, stuffing his

chubby hands into his pockets. "I ain't one to be greedy, Lizzie. But the man's the fourth son of a duke. Don't you see? Your children will be able to hold their heads up in Society and never have to prove themselves to the world."

Elizabeth's heart tripped. "But I do not love him, Papa. And the man does not love me." *He loves another.*

Her father shook his head. "I will not go back on my decision. It's as good as done. I've already sent the notice to the papers. Told my friends. In fact, many of Lord Harmstead's guests know all about it by now."

Elizabeth grabbed the back of a chair, her fingers digging into the cushion. And what about Mr. Fennington? To let him wallow in her wake seemed too heartless to contemplate. She should have made her plans sooner.

"But, Papa, to marry a man I do not love?"

"Not another word about it." Her father cut the air with his hand, giving her his back as he moved toward the bedside table to pour himself a glass of wine.

Elizabeth stood, shocked. The man she had loved all her life was dismissing her plea as though they were speaking of something as mundane as what entree was to be served at supper. She felt as if he had ripped her heart out of her chest and stamped on it.

"The deed is done, Lizzie. Lord Stephen is a fine fellow. Fine on the eyes, too. Can't deny that. Got you a prime gentleman, I have. Strong muscled, dresses with elegance, but not a bit of the fop in him.

"Ain't one of those stuffy fellows. He was at Waterloo and I have heard of some mighty fine things he did there. Fine officer. Saved Wellington's life. Caught a ball right through the leg for him. Threw himself in the line of fire."

Elizabeth's eyes riveted on her father's face and Lord Stephen instantly jumped a few notches in her estimation. "He saved Wellington's life?"

"Indeed, he did. I have my sources. But keep your lips shut on that, my girl. Covert information, don't you know."

He laughed. "I daresay, maybe this will make you feel better. Heard that Lady Odette had her cap set for him. Wasn't she the one who gave you all that trouble in Bath?"

Elizabeth's stomach rolled. Her father might think he was planning the union with her best interests at heart, but she should be able to choose her own husband.

"You have a prize there, my girl. Handsome as one of those Greek gods you and Milli read about." William Shelby puffed out his chest and took a swallow of his wine. "Yes, indeed. Should have handsome children, too. Imagine, they will be nieces and nephews to a real duke. By Jove, this is famous."

Elizabeth stood in mute horror as his glass clanked on the table beside him. He wasn't going to change his mind. It was useless talking to him.

"The thing is, Lizzie, you couldn't get much higher than that unless you married into the king's family itself."

A metallic taste seeped into Elizabeth's mouth and she realized she had bitten the inside of her cheek. The blood from her cheek sat on the tip of her tongue, but she felt as if it had leaked from her heart. No, she would not marry this lord.

She backed up toward the door, not able to say another word. Her father was not going to listen to her. He had sold her to the highest bidder, Lord Stephen Clearbrook, the son of a duke.

With a pang she realized that there was no way to escape from this horrible nightmare, not unless Mr. Fennington came through for her. And he would. She would make certain he would.

Stephen had tossed and turned all night hoping the entire escapade at the gaming table a dream, but now, standing in Lord Harmstead's breakfast room, he felt his insides curl in disgust at the thought of what he had done. His entire future had been played out in a few turns of a hand.

He forced a cool smile as he greeted the guests roaming about the sideboard for their food. By the smug look on some, he could tell they had already heard the news. His gaze immediately shifted to that little minx Milli who seemed as innocent as a kitten, sitting off in the far corner of the room watching him. She gave him a sly wink. The impudent chit.

And where was her elder sister? Still sleeping?

He recalled the embarrassment on Miss Elizabeth Shelby's face when her father had announced the marriage, and at that moment he had actually felt sorry for her.

Though the moonlight had played up the blue in her eyes, he had gathered his wits this morning, coming to the conclusion that she was a boring bluestocking with plain features and a tongue as sharp as a knife.

Just what he needed—a nagging, detestable female. And in those ugly spectacles she looked like some fifty-year-old spinster. If the predicament had involved someone besides himself, he would have thought it all rather amusing.

Yet the plain fact of the matter was he was stuck with the chit. His family would no doubt disapprove and he couldn't blame them, especially since there was the small fact that Miss Shelby wanted nothing to do with him at all.

And the truth was, he didn't want her either. He wanted Lady Odette. But the thought that Miss Shelby would choose Fennington over him vexed him more than the thought of her being his wife. The little idiot. She had no idea of the depths of that man's depravity.

Hiding a scowl, Stephen threw some eggs and kippers onto his plate, keeping up a conversation with Lord Maverly to his left.

"In for the hunt tomorrow?" the baron asked.

Stephen slapped a piece of bread onto his eggs. Hunt? He didn't need a hunt because he had already been the hunted. He had planned to stay at Harmstead to woo Lady Odette. He had danced with her last year at Almack's and although he hadn't known her long or well, he thought her charming and sensitive. He had been hoping that this Season he could ask her to be his wife. But those plans had changed.

"Won't be staying. Leaving today as a matter of fact."

"Ah, yes. Heard you came up to scratch with Shelby. Lucky man. There was many a gentleman wanting to be in your shoes. Man is as rich as the king, they say."

The baron lowered his voice as he placed some butter onto his plate. "Daughter isn't much to look at. A bit on the tall side, but who cares about that? Marriage to her will give you plenty of blunt at the gaming tables now, eh?"

Stephen's mouth hardened as he turned toward the man. It was one thing talking about money, another talking about money and a lady at the same time. "Utter another word about my fiancée and I will see you at dawn."

Mavernly's plate clanked against the sideboard, and his cheeks turned ashen. "No harm meant. Smart as a whip, they say—er, pretty blue eyes, too. And being tall can be an attribute—"

Stephen's glare turned to ice, his voice to barely a whisper. "You have one minute to depart from my side, and if I catch sight of you any time during my short stay here, you will call your second. Am I making myself clear?"

The man swallowed. "P-perfectly." He set his plate off to the side. "Not hungry anyway. Digestion problem." And then he was gone.

Clenching his plate in his hand, Stephen turned and bumped into the loveliest lady he had ever laid eyes upon. His tongue stuck to the roof of his mouth. He stared into two celestial pools of emerald green, vowing that no matter what, he would never again enter into a card game with high stakes.

"Good morning, Lady Odette. Up early, I see." Hell's bells. He could have been waking up to *this* every morning instead of the sharp point of that female's tongue.

They stood alone at the buffet table. Her hands, white and elegant, fisted at her sides. Tension crackled between them.

The statuesque figure lifted her delicate chin and flicked a pair of long, dark lashes at him that made Stephen want to haul her toward him and kiss her. She was beauty itself. He could have had all this if he had not been such a fool.

"Good morning?" she answered tartly, yet her smile was as sweet as honey. "I do not see what a good morning it is when one has been played the fool," she hissed between her berry lips.

So she had heard. What did he expect? That a miracle would occur? Stephen's mouth thinned as he looked into those hard emerald jewels, his throat tightening with regret.

"I beg your forgiveness, but my circumstances have changed. I would give anything not to have hurt you."

Honor demanded he not tell Odette of the exact circumstances surrounding his engagement. And though he did not particularly care for Miss Shelby, he did not feel the engagement her fault. It was that greedy unfeeling father of hers who wanted a title so badly he bartered away his daughter like chattel.

Odette dropped her gaze to the cherry tarts on the sideboard, hiding her scowl. "Cherries give me hives, you know."

He wanted to sweep her into his arms and soothe her ailing heart. She couldn't even look at him she was so hurt. He thought he heard her sniff. He had no idea it was the grinding of her teeth.

More people were quickly moving into the breakfast room, and he knew he needed to distance himself from the lady. He gave her a slight bow. "Your servant, madam."

He turned to leave but stopped short when she rested an elegant hand upon his arm. "Lord Stephen." Her face softened, and his heart gave a kick. She was lovely when she smiled.

She turned and grabbed a plate of eggs and bread. "I am always ravenous in the morning." Her eyes twinkled and before she walked away, she slipped a note into his hand. "Good-bye, my lord. Or should I say, au revoir."

Heart thumping, Stephen took a seat, realizing she had written the note before she entered the breakfast room. With the eagerness of a little boy, he peeked at the small piece of paper in his hand. *My lord, if you find you need to see me again after you are wed, you know where to find me.*

He immediately lifted his gaze across the table to find Lady Odette smiling his way. An uncomfortable heat rippled through him. Why, the shameless strumpet. She was no lady at all. How could he have been so wrong about her? Would she have done the same thing if he had married her?

"Excuse me. May I pass, please?"

Stephen turned at the sound of the husky voice behind him. It was Miss Shelby, and she was trying to squeeze past his chair on the way to the sideboard. He looked to her left and saw a hoard of murmuring dowagers peering her way. The pinkness of Miss Shelby's cheeks told him she was as embarrassed as he was.

A combination of pity and protectiveness surged through him.

Miss Shelby looked younger today. More vulnerable. Her blue eyes looked red and puffy. But her figure was given full advantage in the light and by heaven, she was not at all plain, and not much taller than most women in the room.

He distinctly recalled holding her supple form when she had fallen on top of him, and he caught himself smiling at the memory of one creamy calf shimmering in the moonlight.

"And good morning to you. If it is not the lady of travels and adventure."

Her face colored a deep red as he stood and moved his chair in for her to scoot by.

"My father knows nothing of that . . . that arrangement," she hissed, "and I would advise you to say nothing as well."

His interest was piqued at her audacity in telling him what to do. He leaned over as if to help her through the crowd, whispering into her swanlike neck. "If we are to become man and wife, madam, I would advise you not to advise me."

"Truly, you are a beast," she said as she smiled sweetly, glancing over her shoulder at the exact moment her father strutted into the room.

"Ah, my lord," William Shelby greeted loudly, "Elizabeth, good morning to you both."

"Good morning, Papa."

Stephen watched Miss Shelby's mouth thin with displeasure as she hastened to the sideboard, gathering her food and ignoring her father's smile.

It was about a minute before Stephen spoke. "Shelby."

Stephen towered over the man by at least a head. But what the rich cit lost in height, he made up in cleverness. And sad to say, cards as well.

"My lord," Shelby went on, "I was wondering if I might have a word with you before you depart."

Stephen's gaze traveled over the room, settling on Elizabeth taking a seat one over from Lady Odette—a seat very far away from him. Those amazing blue eyes locked onto his face and he felt an instant heat in his belly.

Was he attracted to the girl? Plague take it. Every passing second, Miss Shelby reminded him more and more of his sister Emily and her spirit.

And then there was Lady Odette with the deceitful emerald eyes. He was glad he had discovered her true nature now. His life would have been a living hell. What kind of stupid dreams had he been spinning in his head?

"My Lord?"

Stephen shifted his attention back to the portly man beside him. "Perhaps later we can have a word in the library."

"Splendid." Shelby proposed a time to meet and slapped Stephen on the back, as if dismissing him, then piled three buttered scones on top his plate and moved toward the cherry tarts.

Elizabeth could barely control the spasmodic trembling inside her, she was so angry. She had seen the letter in his lordship's hand. She also knew what Lady Odette was like. It didn't take a goose to figure out what was going on. If Lady Odette dared put one finger on her intended she would—

Good heavens! What was she thinking? She almost giggled to herself, glancing at Lord Stephen taking the seat beside her.

Why was he moving near her? Her heart twisted. For appearances, of course. Well after she was done with him, he would not wish to be within ten feet of her, let alone be her husband.

She would make him so fearful to be near her, not even half of her papa's money would entice him to marry her. Of course, when the engagement was broken he could go back to that strumpet Odette and she could go back to Mr. Fennington.

"Let us have a toast to the new couple," Lord Harmstead suddenly announced, standing beside William Shelby. "Champagne for everyone."

Five liveried footmen marched into the room with glasses of champagne set on silver trays. A rumble of voices filled the air, and all eyes were on Elizabeth and Lord Stephen.

It seemed barely anyone had slept in this morning, and Elizabeth had never felt so embarrassed in her life. They must all know by now that their union was not a love match but a marriage of convenience.

Hot color crept up her neck, and her chest tightened. All she wanted to do was run from the room. She started to rise but a strong hand stopped her, gripping her wrist.

Elizabeth locked gazes with the man beside her as he raised his glass with his free hand.

"To my beautiful fiancée. A diamond of the first water."

Shocked at the insistent squeeze on her arm, Elizabeth lifted her other hand from her lap, gave a sweet smile, and lowered her eyes demurely.

A roar of approval rang throughout the room. Even Odette gave a clap of her hands, but to Elizabeth the lady's burning glare did not go unnoticed. Tears of humiliation filled Elizabeth's eyes, though everyone seemed to think they were tears of joy as another roar of approval sounded.

But to her amazement, Lord Stephen seemed to have deduced the reason for the tears. He was now frowning at her with those solemn brown eyes. His thumb played at the underside of her wrist before he let her go. "Elizabeth," he said in a pitying tone.

She ignored him and, feeling reckless, downed her drink in less than a minute, and asked for another. Ha, see how he likes a wife who drinks, she thought, feeling a buzz in her head.

How dared he call her beautiful and make fun of her? She would not marry this brute. Mr. Fennington loved her. This man would never see what she was made of. All he wanted was Odette. Well, let him have her . . . after the engagement was broken!

The talk soon moved from the engaged couple to the day's festivities at the Harmstead mansion and all that was planned.

Elizabeth sank into her chair, wishing the floor would swallow her whole and spit her up on the other side of England.

Thank goodness she would be leaving this place shortly and traveling to London. As soon as her father found lodging they would be off to Town. Her father had promised her a night at the opera while showing her and Milli the sights.

Elizabeth held the empty champagne glass between her fingers, ignoring the handsome man beside her and the smell of his bayberry soap. She wondered if he ever looked ugly. Maybe she could prolong the engagement for at least a year. Yes, that would surely give her time to think. She was ready to rise when suddenly one of the servants slipped a note beside her plate.

She grabbed the piece of paper and tucked it between the folds of her morning gown. Hope sprang inside her. There could only be one person who would send her a note.

"More champagne, Miss?"

"Y-yes, please." As the servant poured her another glass, something made the hairs on the back of her neck stand on end. Lord Stephen was scowling at her.

"I think you have had enough champagne, *Elizabeth*."

She blinked. "We are not married yet, my lord," she said through clenched teeth, "so do not try your heavy hand with me."

His eyes darkened as she stood to retrieve a piece of bread from the sideboard. She bit her lip and hurriedly opened the letter. It was from him! Mr. J. T. Fennington.

Her eyes quickly scanned his words. He was going to see her soon. Her heart fluttered like a butterfly in spring. He truly did love her.

"A love note, Miss Shelby?"

Elizabeth jumped at the sound of the silky whisper sliding along her back. "No," she said curtly. "It's a note from my long lost aunt."

The man's lips thinned, a sign she should have recognized immediately, because the next thing she knew, he was escorting her into the hall toward a small alcove behind the stairs.

The remaining guests in the breakfast room smiled as if they knew the couple needed to be alone. All except Mr. William Shelby whose worried eyes were pinned on his daughter.

"I forbid you to meet with that man," Lord Stephen replied. His breath was hot against her cheek as he cornered her against the wall. "Is that understood, Miss Shelby?"

So, he knew what was in the note, did he? His face was within an inch of hers and her heart pounded with the challenge of defying him. There was something boyish about his expression that made him seem less dangerous than he tried to appear. In fact, at the moment she would have thought him extremely appealing if it were not for him telling her what to do.

"Oh, you forbid me, do you?" She shot him a withering stare. Good gracious, she was feeling quite dizzy.

Taut lips stretched across a perfectly chiseled chin. "If you dare go against my wishes, you won't like it at all."

Elizabeth had the audacity to laugh, shaking her head, causing tendrils of soft wheat-colored hair to fall about her face. She knew she had probably had too much champagne but she really didn't care. He was a beast with thoughts only for himself. Her knight in shining armor was Mr. Fennington, who loved her for what she was, not her father's money.

Stephen stared in amazement at the woman before him. The girl was half drunk. With those dancing blue eyes, rosy cheeks, and her disarrayed hair, she looked beguiling. The thought unnerved him, especially when he peered over his shoulder at the sound of clapping heels coming their way.

Lord Githers and Mr. Blundly had stopped and were now staring at Miss Shelby as if she were a prize for the hunt. In fact, they seemed to notice the same thing Stephen had. Miss Shelby was enchanting and she didn't even know it.

A giggle escaped her lips and Stephen stiffened.

Blundly lifted his brow. "Quite a catch, is she not?" Interested dark eyes traveled along Elizabeth's person. "Well done, my lord."

Stephen wanted to yank the man by his cravat, but he didn't need a scandal. Instead he gave the men his iciest glare and they spun on their heels, back down the hall.

"You need a cup of tea, Elizabeth. Come sit down."

She was still giggling as they reentered the breakfast room. Stephen kept a smile in place, though beneath his cool demeanor he fought against the insane notion of throwing the confounded female into the nearest lake.

Her reaction to drinking was uncanny. His sister was like that. One glass of wine, and she was a bowl full of jelly. It would do him well to remember that fact, he thought as he swallowed hard, feeling her soft body swaying against his.

He caught a whiff of fine French perfume. He shifted uncomfortably, taking in the creamy whiteness of Miss Shelby's swanlike throat. What the deuce was wrong with him?

When he woke this morning he thought he was in love with Odette, and now he was becoming quite fond of a blue-eyed, sharp-tongued, crazy woman who only yesterday had dropped from the sky to meet her lover.

He took a seat near the bay window, away from the crowd. "I'm going to get you a cup of tea," he said abruptly. "Wait right here."

"I'd like a doll . . . a doll of cream," she said with a hiccup.

He smiled. "A dollop of cream?"

She frowned. "That's what I said."

He was back in a minute with her tea but stopped short when he noted Odette in conversation with Miss Shelby.

"Elizabeth, dear, you must let me congratulate you on your catch. You have come a long way from Miss Horatio's Seminary, have you not? Of course, with your papa's money, you probably could have set your cap for the Duke of Elbourne himself . . . if he were not married, that is."

All color left Elizabeth's face. Stephen was oddly disappointed when she did not give Lady Odette her due.

"But then I hear the duke has no need for money and is

set up quite nicely. Quite nicely, indeed. Now, Lord Stephen is another matter, is he not? But I do believe your father's money might even set him up higher than his brother."

The last remark seemed to make Elizabeth's hands tremble. Stephen felt a fierce roar in his belly at the way Lady Odette was babbling on about William Shelby's finances and Elizabeth.

It was obvious the conversation had filtered to some other parts of the room as well. William Shelby's eldest daughter sat in mortification, too choked to speak. Stephen realized that the champagne had mangled her brain or she would have had her wits about her and given the entire room something to talk about.

"Of course, many people have a marriage of convenience and things have a habit of working out," Odette went on, softly patting Elizabeth's shoulder in a pitying manner.

At that precise moment Odette tilted her head in Stephen's direction. Whether she had known he was standing there or not, she had taken advantage of the situation to humiliate Elizabeth even more.

"Money is good for some things, Miss Shelby," she said, her chin lifting, along with her skirts, "but it cannot make a princess out of a bluestocking."

A female titter from the corner of the room sent up a gasp of disapproval from one of the ancient dowagers. But it didn't signify. The damage had been done.

Stephen glared at Odette as the harpy stepped aside to speak with a nearby earl. The little witch! Thank goodness he had never asked the chit to marry him.

Concealing the anger boiling beneath his skin, Stephen strolled forward and handed Elizabeth her tea. For the first time in the last twenty-four hours he was glad Shelby had whipped him at cards. He would rather have an honest female like Elizabeth Shelby at his side than a two-faced shrew.

Stephen watched as Elizabeth's face became a ghostly white and her breath came out in little pants of distress. Would she swoon and give Odette's cutting remarks more power than they had? If she did, this incident would become the Season's *on-dit*.

Honor demanded he do something quick. But one thing he decided there and then was that this would be the last time she sipped champagne in the presence of anybody but himself!

With an easy grace, he leaned over and took hold of Miss Shelby's hand. "Ah, my love, you must ready yourself for the journey to London. I cannot bear to be without your company and have asked your father if your family would do me the honor of becoming the guests of the duke and my family at the Elbourne townhouse."

The cessation of voices allowed the sound of forks clanking against plates to echo throughout the room, followed by dead silence.

Inwardly cursing, Stephen was more aware than ever that everyone in the breakfast salon had been paying attention to the scene between Lady Odette and Miss Shelby.

Smiling like a besotted lover, he kissed his betrothed's hand. "My love, perhaps you should return to your chambers and rest before the journey."

Lady Odette's emerald eyes narrowed into slits as she turned on her heels and left. Elizabeth's blue gaze widened. She managed a smile as Stephen escorted her back to her father.

After a few minutes of polite conversation, Stephen made his excuses, bowed, and departed from the room. He stopped short when he found Milli waiting for him down the hall.

Huge gray eyes locked onto his face. "I do believe I'm beginning to like you, you know. But do not try to best me with your acting . . . or Lizzie, your lordship. She's not stupid."

Stephen's mouth dropped open in surprise at the girl's frank assessment of his conduct in the breakfast room. Before he could say anything in his defense, the little elf turned, gave him a saucy wink over her shoulder, and hurried upstairs.

Chapter Six

*E*lizabeth stood gazing out the window of Lord Harm-stead's library, blinking against the afternoon sky. Her head hurt as though someone had taken a hammer to it. The champagne had been too much, too quick—and so had Lord Stephen Clearbrook.

"Did you see what he did at breakfast, Papa?" She turned to her father. "Did you? He acted as if . . . as if he loved me."

Elizabeth was both furious and touched at Lord Stephen Clearbrook's behavior this morning. She could very well see how he had saved Wellington's life. The man was no coward.

That point was proved when he acted the hero this morning, saving her from an embarrassing scene. Although making that ludicrous announcement was akin to professing his love for her, the two of them were definitely not a love match.

Yet she couldn't deny the spark of warmth that had swept through her when he pressed his lips lightly to her hand. She would not think about that. Nor would she think about the way his eyes had devoured her with such tenderness that she wanted to cry.

No, she didn't want to think of him having any heart at all. She wanted him to be a callous man whom she could distance herself from. Even heroes were callous at times.

But he had not been callous, her heart whispered.

Whether he pitied her or not, he was a fiend with feelings, she told herself. Feelings that could charm a woman into a rake's lair with one blink of his devastating smile.

However, *she* would not be Lord Stephen's woman. Why, when he had pulled her into the hall after she received that note from Mr. Fennington, the circumstance had not affected her at all!

Oh maybe she had enjoyed his nearness a tad more than she would admit. But who wouldn't? Those chocolate brown eyes had probably swept many a lady off her feet. Yet she was no simpering female and even heroes had their flaws. She would never forget the fact he only wanted to marry her for money.

"He is a gentleman, Lizzie. Knew that the moment I clapped eyes on the fellow."

Elizabeth stared at her father, her mind working furiously to extricate herself from this absurd situation. "Of course he's a gentleman; he's the son of a duke."

"But that ain't precisely what I meant. You must see that honor is as much a part of Lord Stephen Clearbrook as breathing. It's a code the man lives by. All the men in the Elbourne family live by it. His three brothers are very highly thought of, my dear. You should be pleased to be marrying into such a family."

There was a bit of reproach in his tone and Elizabeth tried to mentally count to ten. Honor? Forget about the man's past. What kind of honor was it when a man married a woman for her father's money?

This conversation was getting her nowhere.

"Well, if you ask me," Milli piped in from across the room where she sat on a leather chair, swinging her slippers across the rug, "I believe his lordship would die for Lizzie if he had to. Now that would be real love, would it not?"

"Millicent, please do not tell me that you are falling for the man's charms," Elizabeth said, pinching the bridge of her nose. This was the outside of enough.

"Oh, but I like him regardless," her sister said, jumping off the chair. "An hour ago I saw him in the hall, and he gave me a sack of candy, whether I became his sister-in-law or not."

Elizabeth groaned. The charms of this rake were never ending.

"He may be handsome, Lizzie, but he's not the smartest man on earth," Milli added thoughtfully. "He treats me as if I were only twelve. Can you believe that? I will be fifteen next month."

"Fifteen?" William Shelby replied with a frown.

Elizabeth was surprised at Milli's defense of the handsome lord. Though Milli was smaller than girls her age, she made up in spirit for what she lacked in height. Brown locks coiled about her face and down her back in a childlike innocence that made most people think she was younger than she was. No wonder Lord Stephen had given her candy.

"See, Papa," Elizabeth said with a hopeful edge to her voice. "The man cannot be serious about wanting to marry me if he made that comment to Milli about her possibly not being his sister-in-law."

William Shelby lifted a bushy brow. "Depend upon it. His lordship is very serious. Do not shame him or me by insisting on breaking this engagement. The announcement has been sent to the papers. As a gentleman of breeding, he ain't one to rescind his offer and I will not let you reject it."

Elizabeth felt her frustration rising. She could not marry the man. He would never love her. Lord Stephen Clearbrook would have his flirts in London like many gentlemen of the *ton*, and as this morning had proved, the man could charm a flea.

Besides, if the man continued his obnoxiously nice behavior, she could very well learn to like him and would that not put her in a precarious situation?

Elizabeth scrambled for anything that could thwart this marriage. "But what if after a time, he does not want me . . . and he asks *me* to break the engagement?"

William Shelby smiled. "Want you? How could he not want you, my dear?"

He wants Lady Odette, that's why. He would never look twice at me if I were not an heiress.

How such a war hero could suggest a marriage between Elizabeth and him was a puzzle to her, but then again, men were so different from women, nothing surprised her anymore.

Her heart gave a little twist of regret at her monetary circumstances. She would never be certain about anything because of the money attached to her name.

"But it's obvious he wants your money, Papa, not me."

Shelby stuffed a hand inside his waistcoat pocket. "And who with any brains would not want my money, poppet. But rest assured, the man wants you, too. All is well. Now run along with your sister and see to your packing. It seems we are going to be the guests of the duke while we are in Town."

Milli twirled about the room like a ballerina. "Goodness gracious, I have never met a duke. Is he as handsome as Lord Stephen?"

Elizabeth gritted her teeth. No one was as handsome as Lord Stephen Clearbrook, she decided, but that was beside the point. She had to make her plans. First, she must post a letter to Mr. Fennington telling him of her lodgings while in London, then she would ready herself for the journey to the duke's home.

As soon as her father and Milli left the library, she asked one of the servants for paper and pen. It would do no good to write her missive in her bedchamber. There was no telling what Milli would convey to her father, let alone what the abigail would pass on to William Shelby, since he paid the girl's wages.

After Lord Harmstead's servant opened the writing desk in the corner of the room and set Elizabeth up with what she needed, she took her leave. Alone now, Elizabeth slipped on her spectacles and sighed as she dipped the pen into the ink and pressed the point of the quill to the paper. She had just finished signing her name when the door opened.

"Hard at work, Miss Shelby?"

The deep baritone voice slammed into her ears like an icy polar wind. She jumped from her chair, almost turning over the inkwell. "Er, you . . . you surprised me."

"Evidently." Lord Stephen's sharp gaze swung to the letter on the desk. "An avid writer as well as a traveler, I see."

She hurriedly stood in front of the desk, hiding the evidence. "I may be the daughter of a businessman, my lord, but I assure you, I have been educated in all things. I speak three different languages, I draw, I play the pianoforte and the harp, and I know well how to sit a horse."

"So I have heard." His brown eyes glinted with amusement. "You are well educated in the English language as well, I see. Have you any other attributes I should know about?"

Warm brown eyes traveled from her face to the tip of her slippers and back again.

A blush swept across her cheeks and she cleared her throat. "As you must know, my lord, I find this situation intolerable."

He cocked a dark brow at her candid remark. "And pray tell me, Miss Shelby, do you always speak your mind?"

He strode toward her, his cool gaze locking on the desk.

She moved a bit more, trying to block his view. "Well not always, my lord."

She watched in horror as his long limbs quickly ate up the distance between them. Her heart beat faster. Good heavens. He looked like a determined tiger treading through the jungle in one of those books she had read in her father's library.

He stopped and tilted his head to the writing desk behind her, his lips curling into a wry smile. "So, Miss Shelby, who is to be the recipient of your wonderful pen?"

Distinctly recalling his words about having no contact with Mr. Fennington, she swallowed past the lump in her throat and managed a smile. "A sick friend."

He pursed his lips, moving within a hair's breadth of her. He smelled of shaving soap and fine leather, very male scents that were starting to annoy her because they did silly things to her stomach.

"A sick friend?" he repeated. "How very noble of you."

He snaked his hand around her and when she realized his intent, she spun about and snatched the letter off the desk, but not before he caught a piece of it too.

The letter ripped in half.

"Look what you did!" Her cry of protest covered the relief she felt at holding the top half of the letter with Fennington's name on it.

He glared at his half of the letter. "Yours forever . . . Elizabeth?"

The words were pushed through locked teeth. Elizabeth gulped. To lie or not to lie, that was the question.

"Miss Shelby." He planted his very large hands on top of the desk and glared at her. "I have given you fair warning, have I not?"

She took a hesitant step away from his formidable form. "We are not married. And lord or not, I take no orders from you."

He seemed to have trouble speaking.

Finally, after wiping a stiff hand over his face, he took a deep breath and crumpled his half of the letter in his fist, stuffing the remnants of the missive into the palm of her hand.

"Have you no brains at all? Mr. Fennington is a thief and a rake. He will probably never marry you. His plans are to blackmail your father into buying him off." His lips thinned when he realized that his fingers were still touching hers.

Stepping back, he slipped his hand into his coat pocket. "You may depend upon it. He will ruin your good name in the process. Is that what you want?"

Elizabeth gasped in outrage. "Of course not. What you say is not true!" Her hands shook with fury as she balled the two halves of the letter in her hand.

"It is true, madam. Every hellish word of it."

"How dare you use that tone of voice with me. You . . . you liar. You, sir, are no gentleman."

His eyes flashed. "He chased after my sister one hour before her marriage. He even tried to kidnap her with plans of taking her to the border. Believe my words or not, it doesn't change the fact that the man is a weasel, unfit to marry any lady, rich or poor."

Elizabeth felt the slap to her heart as if he had physically given her the blow himself. This man was lying. "I do not believe you." Her knees felt wobbly. She sank onto the writing chair beside her and held back tears of frustration, not daring to let this man know how much he affected her.

He stood back, crossing his arms against his chest, his dark eyes pinning her to the seat. "Oh believe me, Miss Shelby, it is all true."

Even with that aristocratic glare, she was intensely conscious of the man, but she would never tell him that.

His jacket fit him as if he were royalty. His neckcloth was folded in simple lines, as if he had not a care in the world and cared even less about what the world thought of him. His breeches fit him to perfection, accentuating his powerfully muscled form. And his confidence vexed her to no end.

Was there nothing that irked him, besides her? Even his manner this morning, to save her from an embarrassing scene, was perfection itself. But she was not of his caliber. Even Fennington had that stupid quizzing glass. And she her spectacles. They were made for each other.

"You will not contact Mr. Fennington, is that clear?"

Her eyes were cold as she gathered her strength and rose from the chair. "No."

He unfolded his arms and came toward her. "No?"

She skirted the chair, pushing it in front of her. Well what did she expect? He had demanded instant obedience and she had flung her defiance in his face. He did have his pride, but confound him, so did she. "I said no."

He took another warning step toward her. Not knowing what made her do it, she picked up the pen in the inkwell and pointed it at him. "Not another step, I tell you."

He laughed at her then, as if she were nothing more than a stupid little rich girl spoiled by her father's money. He reminded her of Lady Odette. Odette always laughed at her, too.

The girl would spread falsehoods about her father, whisper about Elizabeth's ugly face and the spectacles she wore, toy with her self-esteem, and tell her she was nothing without her money—just as she had at breakfast. Odette called her homely, with no prospects for the future—no prospects except marriage to an old man with a title who would have a host of gambling debts a mile long.

And now this man was laughing at her, too.

Elizabeth pushed down the bile creeping up her throat. She would not be laughed at. Mr. Fennington never laughed at her.

"Will you spear my heart with that pen, Miss Shelby?"

"You have no heart, my lord, or you would never have broken mine."

He frowned then, his gaze softening. But she had no wish for his pity. *Never.*

"You have a smudge of ink on your nose," he said, half-smiling.

Oh, the injustice of having such a handsome face. It was not fair. Not fair at all. Fury almost choked her from saying anything more, but she did.

"And . . . and you are too clean, my lord!"

With a jerk of her wrist, she flipped a spray of ink his way, splattering that all too perfect white shirt and cravat as if they had been trampled on the battlefield.

His eyes rounded in shock, for it looked as though he had been shot at point-blank range.

With a muffled groan, she ran for the door.

"Why, you little spitfire," he shouted, taking a step in her direction. The next moment he stopped abruptly and looked down at his chest, his lips curving into a full-fledged smile.

And then he did the most outrageous thing. He laughed.

An hour later Stephen stood inside the library, rubbing a finger over the ink stain on the writing desk. He had already changed his shirt and had delivered Lord Harmstead his apologies for his clumsiness, offering to pay for the damages. Harmstead would not hear of it.

"Afternoon, my lord."

Stephen looked up as William Shelby walked into the room. "Shelby," he said dryly.

It was all Stephen could do not to give the man the facer he deserved. Did Shelby think once of his daughter's pain? Did the man think he could make her love Stephen just because he was a lord? Hell's teeth, it was an intolerable way to treat a lady.

Barely able to stop from grinding his teeth, Stephen waited patiently for the discussion that was to come. The man stuffed his hand into his waistcoat pocket and closed the door with a satisfied smile.

Stephen was instantly reminded of Cook fattening up the goose before the kill on Christmas morning. The conversation moved quickly from the weather to Elizabeth's future.

"Now as I see it, my lord, wooing my little Lizzie through the Season is out. It ain't that I don't want her to have a bit of fun, but it don't signify since you made your feelings known in the breakfast room."

Grinning, Shelby exposed a set of crooked yellow teeth, giving the appearance of a man quite proud of catching a lord for his daughter. "You must see that by now everyone believes that this is a love match. It don't matter if it isn't, just that everyone believes it. Better this way, you know."

Trying to ignore the man's pompous speech, Stephen stared at the ink staining his two fingernails. He felt a smile tugging at the corners of his mouth as he vividly recalled a pair of fiery blue eyes. So he was too clean, was he?

"But I must make one thing clear, my lord. You must never let Elizabeth know I traded her for a debt you owed. Women get these fanciful thoughts, don't you know."

Stephen looked up from his fingers. "Fanciful thoughts?"

The man shifted uncomfortably. "She believes you sought her out for my money, of course."

"Now let me see if I have this straight," Stephen said, his gaze flat and unreadable. "You want your daughter to believe I needed funds so badly that I sought to wed her and procure your money in the process."

Shelby's eyes lit with approval. "Yes, yes, precisely. Thought we already agreed upon that."

"However, I am not to tell her I lost at the gaming table with you, and that you, the wonderful loving father that you are, fobbed her off on me."

Stephen was grateful to see that at least Shelby's cheeks had pinkened. What kind of father was this man? Elizabeth certainly deserved better and so did little Milli.

Stephen's protective instincts took over again. "Listen

here, Shelby, I don't like being a party to manipulation. Why not tell your daughter the truth? That I lost at a game of cards and you offered her as a way to release me from debt. It isn't as if she doesn't know you want a titled son-in-law."

Shelby grimaced. "Are you mad? If I tell her I wagered her on a debt owed to me, there's no telling what she would do. The girl's as impulsive as Napoleon entering Russia."

Stephen had to admit she was that. And if he told Shelby's daughter the truth, perhaps he could sway things his way. However, honor demanded he pay his debt, and telling Miss Shelby the truth would hurt her deeply. Though Stephen didn't love the girl, he was not an ogre. Her father had done enough damage in that department.

Hurting a female to gain one's independence was something a weasel would do—someone like Fennington. Two orbs of baby blue came to Stephen's mind and he frowned at their innocence. The thought of Fennington running away with Elizabeth Shelby chewed at Stephen's conscience like a dog at a bone. "You can still stop this insane wedding, Shelby. Call it off."

"No, your lordship. I am not going to do that. Already sent the announcements."

"Announcements can be rescinded."

"The fact of the matter is, I have no wish to see it done and you owe me a good sum."

Stephen's temper flared. "I can have that money in a week and you know it. Would you cast your daughter into a fire where she would get burned? Because that's exactly what you are doing! I certainly don't love her. And she certainly doesn't love me."

She loves another, he thought grimly.

"Love will come," Shelby said, pulling out a cigar and tapping it against his palm.

Stephen let out a snort of disgust. "You're mad. She wants nothing to do with me."

The portly man paused, then tilted his head back as though he were looking at Stephen for the first time. "If I didn't know better, I would say you cared for my girl."

Stephen glowered at the man. "I care for most human beings, Shelby." *Most, but not all, including that despicable Fennington character your stubborn daughter believes she is in love with.*

"Well then this should be most advantageous to you, I believe. In exchange for my daughter I will relieve you of all your outstanding debts. And don't forget, I am returning Creighton Hall to you. An added bonus, don't you think?"

"How convenient for you, sir, that I have a few measly debts you can pay. What a doting father-in-law."

The man flushed as if he were being complimented. "We will get along nicely, my lord. Uh, Stephen. May I call you by your Christian name, seeing that we are to be family?"

No, he wanted to shout. We are not going to be family or friends.

"I realize you must not bother your brother, the duke, about your debts, seeing as they can cause families such trouble. So I decided to take it upon myself since you are to be my son-in-law. I ain't one to shrug off my duty. I informed Harmstead I would be sending him a new desk within the week."

That comment drew Stephen's attention. "You what?"

"I'm sending the man a new desk within the week. You should be more careful with your writing instruments, my lord."

Stephen wanted to knock the man's smiling eyes out of his blasted head.

"Oh, did I forget to mention that after you are married, you will have a new townhouse as well? One in St. James. No need to thank me. Father's duty and what not." The man puffed out his chest. "I will reside next door to continue my services on your behalf. Don't want my grandchildren to go without, you know."

"Your grandchildren? Do you believe I will not be able to fend for my own children, sir?"

Shelby's forehead wrinkled in confusion. "Oh, oh. No need to get fussy about it. I ain't one to allow my family to suffer. We can keep the money under our hats, you know."

Stephen wanted to pick the man up and throw him out the window. And by Jove in his wilder days he might have done just that. But in those days he was always approaching his father or his brother Roderick with a bill or two. He had stopped applying to his family for money when his father had died. Except, he thought with a scowl, for last week with Roderick.

He had finally decided to take control of his own life and stop depending on his family to extricate him from unseemly situations. That was the precise reason he had gone into the business venture with Brule.

Stephen clasped his hands behind his back. "You, sir, may see me marry your daughter. You may bestow upon both of us your blessing. And you may return Creighton Hall to the bosom of my family. But fiend seize it, as to other favors, you will curtail your flow of money my way. Is that clear?"

The man raised a chubby hand to his neck and pulled at his cravat, surveying Stephen with an approving eye. "Indeed, my lord. Knew you were a man with a spine. That's what my little poppet needs. A little bending of her will and she will be fine. Of course, a mere present of something on her birthday or the birth of a grandchild isn't charity, you know. I do hope I will be able to offer my monetary services. And of course, there is the dowry." He raised a proud brow.

"The dowry?" Stephen spat out, his jaw stiffening with rage. "How very convenient."

Without another word, he spun on his heels, barely able to control his fury. Any father who would give away his daughter to a stranger was half out of his mind.

"But where are you going, my lord? We have not set the date for the wedding or considered the other matters we need to attend to."

Stephen stopped and glared at the closed door. There would be no wedding if it were up to him. If he had known that this pompous idiot was to be his father-in-law, he would never have had a drink in his life.

"We will pack and depart tomorrow," the man went on. "If that is soon enough."

Stephen whirled around. "Soon enough for what?"

"You have invited my family to the Elbourne townhouse, my lord. Have you forgotten?"

The devil. Yes, he had forgotten. Roderick would spear him alive. "No, of course not. I am departing today to ready things." *For my new maddening family*, he thought with a grimace. Jupiter and Zeus, this entire week was incredible.

"Capital, my lord. We will not be late. Depend upon it."

Stephen resisted slamming the door behind him as he departed from the room. He ordered his horse to be ready in one hour for the ride back to London to inform his family of his upcoming nuptials. Ha! Would they not be surprised?

He climbed the stairs to his chambers and paused when he saw a train of maids departing from one of the bedchambers. He winced as high-pitched screams burst from beyond the door.

"My face! My arms! Oh, what is happening to me? I look like a squished strawberry. And it itches! Every part of my person itches! Gracious, you peagoose, get me something! Anything! Now!"

To his astonishment, Millicent Shelby came running from the room, her breath coming out in little gasps, her face pale.

Stephen took hold of her shoulders and frowned. "What the deuce is going on in there?"

Milli swallowed, her eyes bugging out of their sockets. "It's Lady Odette."

"I know very well who it is, but what has happened?"

Milli pulled away. "Why, do you love her or something?"

Stephen's lips twitched. "You are too young to ask such a question."

"But my skin! Look at it! Dooooooo something!" Odette's squeal continued to rise in pitch. "Father said you had a way of healing even the sickest of animals. Do something before I burst!"

"Take this, Odette. It will make you feel so much better."

The sound of Elizabeth's husky voice floated out the door, sending Stephen's head snapping up. His glance swung back to Milli's guilty expression. "Well?"

Milli shrugged, looking at the floor. "I did not think she was very allergic, you know. Besides"—Milli raised her head, lowering her voice—"she is such an odious creature anyway."

Her eyes smiled appreciatively. "Odious Odette. That does have a certain ring to it, does it not? Who would think cherries would do such a thing to the human body?"

Milli turned to leave, but not before Stephen grabbed her shoulder and spun her around. "You minx. You gave Lady Odette cherries and she reacted quite violently, is that it?"

"I, uh, added a little juice to her hot chocolate."

"But she ate breakfast with us this morning."

"The chocolate was sent up later to her room. She reacted to the cherries most horridly, but how was I supposed to know that?"

A glint of amusement flashed in Milli's gray eyes, and Stephen stared back at her, speechless.

"You see, my lord, Odette's skin has taken on a rather mottled look. Her throat is swollen and her eyes as well. But Lizzie will care for her, as always."

"Lizzie?"

"Yes, but you must not tell a soul about the cherry juice. My father will lock me in my room for a month."

And rightly so, Stephen thought grimly. "What is your sister doing in there? Can they not send for a doctor?"

"A doctor? Lizzie is far better than any of those bloodletters. She will care for Lady Odette, but I can tell you it is beyond my comprehension why."

Though Stephen's feelings for Odette had been lost completely the moment he had seen her true character, Stephen could not condone what Milli had done.

"A stunt like that could have killed her," he said sharply. "Why did you do such a terrible thing?"

Milli tilted her head back to look him straight in the eye. "I know I was wrong, but she made Elizabeth cry, and if you dare make Elizabeth cry, I will do something more horrid to you. Like . . . like poisonous mushrooms!"

"You will, will you?"

"Yes, I most certainly will."

He blinked. Well at least Elizabeth had one person to defend her.

"Milli, is that you outside that door? For heaven's sake, stop dawdling and fetch me some of that lotion from the housekeeper."

The door eased opened and Stephen came face to face with Elizabeth. Her hair was flying every which way as she held her spectacles to her breast. "My lord!"

His respect grew for this woman every minute he was with her. "I was wondering if I might be of some help," he said. "The lady sounds as if she is dying."

Milli let out a snort behind him.

"She is not dying, my lord. It seems you have been taken in by my sister's theatrics again." Ignoring him, she urged her sister down the hall. "The lotion and be quick."

The door started to close and another squeal hit both their ears. "Elizabeth! Hurry! There is another bump bursting out on my elbow as we speak."

"I am coming, Odette. Do not scream. It will only make things worse."

Stephen stood immobilized as the door shut in his face. What kind of woman was this? She was taking care of the one person who had hurt her, and now she acted as if it had never happened. And . . . she had literally shut the blasted door in his face.

Though his admiration and respect for her had heightened, he knew that it would never do to marry the girl. Their union would be a complete and utter failure.

Marriages of convenience usually were failures unless there were some hard and fast rules in the union. A mistress. A turned eye. A series of parties and balls which neither attended with the other. Oh, he knew some couples who lived like that and thought it grand. But deep down he knew they were only fooling themselves, like his own father and mother had done.

Stephen wanted love in a marriage. Not duty and half-truths. It seemed he had been far off the mark with Lady Odette, but if Elizabeth thought herself in love with Mr. Fennington, there could be no hope for their future at all.

*   *   *

Later that evening Elizabeth was too exhausted to eat. She went to her room, changed, and hopped straight into bed. Pulling the covers over herself, she wondered if Lord Stephen had left for London. He had looked so ridiculously handsome standing outside Lady Odette's door she thought she would swoon. But he was not there for her. He was there over concern for Odette.

Something deep in her heart began to ache. Would anybody ever care for her and come to her door when she was ill? She wondered if Mr. Fennington would take her limp hand in his, not leaving her side until she regained her strength.

Warm brown eyes dotted with gold suddenly popped into her head. Her throat tightened with dread. Lord Stephen only pitied her. "Well good riddance. I hate him."

"You do?"

Elizabeth jerked upward. "Millicent Harriet, what are you doing hiding behind those curtains? I have not set eyes on you since you delivered that lotion for Lady Odette."

Milli inched forward. "Did she . . . did she die?"

Elizabeth narrowed her eyes on her sister's shaking hands. "Of course she did not die."

"Truly, or are you just humoring me?"

"Milli, what did you do?"

"Oh!" Milli fell onto the bed with her hands to her face. "Death is but a flight into another world where time stops and then begins again. Death be gone and never come again to this precious world—"

"Milli!" Elizabeth was too tired to attend to her sister's theatrics.

Milli raised her head. "You are humoring me, dearest. She did die. I knew it! I killed her! Will they hang me? Will she have flowers on her grave? Will Father be mad?"

Elizabeth slipped out of bed and lit a lone candle from the embers in the fire. Pulling her sister off her bed, she took Milli by the shoulders and gently shook her.

"Tell me, Millicent."

"He made me do it."

"*He? He* made you do what?"

"Put the cherries in her drink."

"You put the cherries in Lady Odette's hot chocolate?"

Milli kept her face to the floor. "H-he made me."

Trying to keep her anger at bay, Elizabeth combed Milli's hair with her hand. What type of blackguard would have a girl do his dirty work? Odette might have asked for much while staying at Harmstead Hall, but she did not deserve this. "Who, dear?"

"Lord Stephen Clearbrook."

Elizabeth's hand dropped to her side like a lead ball. "His lordship?"

Milli nodded again, her head to the floor.

Elizabeth saw red. The wretch! Just because the odious lady snuffed Lord Stephen's advances, he decided to take his revenge in the meanest, most despicable way. How dare he stand by that door and ask her if she needed any help! This only solidified her plans to reunite with Mr. Fennington.

"You must never listen to that man again. Promise me."

Milli raised her eyes in confusion and frowned. "But—"

"No." Elizabeth did not wait for an answer. All she saw was how perfect Lord Stephen appeared with his simple cravat and perfectly fitting breeches and wide strong shoulders.

How perfection could be so deceiving!

For a man to save Wellington's life one day and do such a dastardly deed the next was inconceivable. Did he think by hurting Odette he would move up in her estimation? Oh, she didn't know what to believe. But she would not be fooled. No, she would make her plans accordingly.

And to think that she was going to apologize for spraying him with the ink. She had never attacked a person before in her life, but that man brought out the worst in her. She must not let this marriage take place.

Chapter Seven

*S*tephen was back in London sitting at White's, caressing a glass of untouched brandy as he explained his situation to his brothers.

"You what?" the Duke of Elbourne shouted.

Stephen set his glass down and pressed his fingers to his eyes. "Thunderation, keep it down. These are not intricate military plans I am explaining to you, Roderick. I lost the blasted hand and now it seems I am engaged to Miss Elizabeth Shelby of Portsmouth. Her family should be arriving tomorrow to stay at your townhouse." He lifted his head, letting out a twisted smile. "Hope you don't mind, your dukeness."

"Don't mind?" Roderick snapped, throwing a hand through his blue-black hair.

His brother Clayton grabbed Stephen by the arm. "Have you gone mad? You cannot marry a girl you don't know."

"How kind of you to give me such wonderful information," Stephen said, knowing that even though Clayton was two years his senior, it did not signify in the least. "Why did I not think of that before? The size of your peabrain never ceases to amaze me. Must be those violet blue eyes of yours, all beauty and no brains."

Clayton's lips thinned. "I would not be speaking of brains at a time like this."

"Ask me if I am surprised," Marcus said, downing a glass of port. "Because I'm not."

Scowling, Stephen spun the glass between his thumb and forefinger. By Jove, only a year younger than Roderick,

Marcus looked like the duke with his dark hair and gray eyes, and he was acting just as pompously.

"You have been gambling for high stakes the past three years, little brother," Marcus went on. "Drinking too."

Stephen looked away. Unfortunately, Marcus was correct. The past three years, since he had had the argument with his father that sent the duke galloping through the fields and falling off his horse to his death, he had been drinking to excess.

The drinking had not ceased when he returned from Waterloo. Memories had haunted him of that day he stabbed the Frenchie and the dying man fell into his arms, asking him to pray for his two motherless baby sons who were now without a family to fend for them. Hell, yes, the past three years had been too long indeed.

But had those years of guilt been long enough to wash away the pain? Had they been long enough to forget the way he had lashed out at his father for the man's treatment of the duchess and then had his father died because of it? Had those years seen enough gambling and drinking to turn his life around?

Lord help him, he didn't know any more.

"Stephen, Marcus asked you a question." Roderick cuffed his brother on the shoulder, obviously annoyed at the entire situation. "Can this idiotic engagement be withdrawn?"

Stephen shook his head. "I was without the required payment at the time. It was cash on the table. I knew it. Shelby knew it. I fear the man had already chosen me to be his daughter's husband. I had already fallen into the trap before I knew what was happening. He wanted a titled gentleman."

Clayton smiled and leaned down to look his brother in the eye. "No offense, dear brother, but you are only the fourth son of a duke. Shelby should have chosen dear Roderick here if he wanted a grand title. Why, the Duke of Elbourne is as pompous as they get. Except for Prinny, that is."

Stephen's lips curled into a wry twist. "What a nice thing to say, especially since he is already married. It seems Marcus and you would have been better prizes."

Clayton frowned. "I daresay. Let's not get any ideas."

Roderick frowned. "You cannot be serious about this," he said to Stephen.

"Serious? I am deadly serious. There is naught for me to do about it. If the announcement did not make it into the papers today, it will be there tomorrow. I shan't jilt the girl now."

"Oh ho." Clayton slapped a hand against the table. "So you have an eye for the silly female in question?"

Stephen shot him an icy glare. "She may be headstrong but she is not silly."

Roderick began to smile. "Is she as pretty as her father?"

Clayton and Marcus let out a snort of laughter.

"I hope not," Clayton uttered. "Does she have any teeth?"

Marcus laughed again.

Stephen's grip on his glass tightened. He wished he had not said a thing to his brothers. "I will not discuss Miss Shelby and if you know what is good for you, neither will you."

The brothers closed their mouths and narrowed their eyes.

"Can we not buy this fellow off?" Roderick asked grimly.

Stephen shook his head, recalling the set of innocent blue eyes that had glared at him with such contempt in the library. He remembered the tears earlier that day. But it was that steadfast gaze staring back at him last night, when Miss Shelby was caring for Lady Odette, that pierced his soul.

Miss Shelby was a sensitive creature, with more heart than most women he knew. He could not humiliate her. Not now. Not ever.

"Money will not win Shelby over. He is determined to see his daughter married to a lord. Can you believe Fennington has been hounding her?"

Roderick raised a stern brow. "Not that idiot!"

"Does he still carry that infernal quizzing glass?" Marcus asked, his eyes narrowing. "What an abomination."

Stephen nodded. "Afraid so."

He did not tell them his fiancée thought herself in love

with the fool or that she had made plans to run away to Gretna Green with him.

"Then it seems unless a miracle happens, our poor brother here is to be wed as soon as that special license becomes available."

Stephen ground his teeth at Clayton's remark. Miracles were things he did not believe in these days, at least for him.

William Shelby's coach rolled steadily along the country road on its way to the Elbourne townhouse in Mayfair. Elizabeth stared out the window, her temper still in full boil after Milli's remark concerning Lord Stephen and the cherry juice the girl had poured into Odette's chocolate.

"That was very kind of you to care for Lady Odette, my dear," her father announced.

William Shelby had been trying to gain her attention for the last half hour, but Elizabeth was so mad at him she could spit. She finally looked at him, knowing Milli was asleep, bundled in the blanket beside her.

"How could you continue this charade with . . . with that man?" she whispered in a raw tone.

She really wanted to say, *How could you make me marry a man who would intentionally make another woman ill by throwing cherry juice in her drink? How could you make me marry a man when I want another? How could you ruin my life?*

Shelby shifted uncomfortably in his seat. "Now, Lizzie, you cannot stay angry with me for the rest of your life."

She stiffened and shifted her gaze to the window. They were coming into London. "Then do not make me marry this man."

William Shelby sighed and folded his hands across his lap. "This is for the best, poppet. He is a good man."

"Good man? He is a bounder and a cad."

Milli peeked out from beneath her blanket and frowned.

"My Egypt is so ill, I fear I may die as well."

Stephen's mother, now Lady Bringston, a duchess who had married a marquess, glanced up at the youngest of her four sons. Her violet eyes pooled with tears as she sat in the drawing room of the Elbourne townhouse holding her fluffy white feline to her breast. "You know, one would think it was . . . but oh, no, it could not be. There are no male cats on our estates. Besides, Egypt stays inside."

Barely glancing at his mother or even hearing her words, Stephen paced the room, raising a hand to smooth the knot of muscles in his neck. His thoughts were on the Shelbys.

"I do wish Bringston were here. He would know what to do."

"What was that, Mother?" What in the world was she talking about? Was she crying over Bringston?

"Nothing, dear."

Stephen walked into the hall, then back into the drawing room. Roderick and his wife had prior engagements and had gone out for the day, but the duke had given Stephen strict orders to stay at the townhouse to await his unwanted guests—otherwise the guests would not be staying.

"I am so happy you have found someone to spend the rest of your life with, dear. I own I was worried about that gambling habit of yours."

Stephen peered out the window. "Yes, well my games of high stakes are behind me." *And so is my life*, he thought grimly. His mother was delighted to discover he was finally marrying. The lady had no idea he had been bamboozled into the wedding. He fought back a grimace.

"I fear I must look like something Egypt brought in from the garden," the lady said. "I should freshen up a bit. If your guests arrive before I return, you can have them shown to their rooms. And don't forget, Lord Stonebridge and your sister will be arriving soon."

Stephen had discovered only late last night that his sister would be staying at the duke's home too, though she would be confined to the house. The doctor had said her pains were coming too early for the baby to be delivered. Fearing for his wife's health, Stonebridge had insisted on moving her into the Elbourne townhouse so she would be in better company when the baby arrived.

Stephen turned suddenly at the sound of dragging feet and a loud sniff. "Mother, are you ill?"

The lady had neared the door. She shook her head and gave a sob. "It's . . . my poor . . . Egypt." Clutching the cat, she hastened from the room.

With a pang, Stephen realized his mother was worried about Egypt's condition and, the idiot that he was, he hadn't been listening to anything she had said in the last half hour unless it had pertained to him.

To his dismay, he was stopped from running after her by the butler's announcement of the arrival of William Shelby and his family. Not a minute later his sister arrived and the introductions were made.

Stephen thought Elizabeth Shelby looked pale and worn. It seemed she showed all outward signs of his innermost feelings.

As soon as the guests were shown to their bedchambers, he went in search of his mother but to no avail. An hour later the Shelbys rejoined him in the drawing room.

"Lord Stephen," Shelby said, his eyes taking in the room, "the duke has a fine home here. Not as grand as the one I have in Bath, but fine indeed. I am looking for a house here in London near St. James. Actually two. Would you know of any?"

A muscle ticked on the side of Stephen's jaw and he refrained from answering. *Two townhouses directly beside each other,* he thought. *That would be the day, when he let his father-in-law live next door!*

Out of the corner of his eye, Stephen watched Elizabeth's face grow taut as she walked toward the bay window looking out onto the street. She was as embarrassed as he at her father's words. But she carried herself with such an inner grace it touched him. It also intrigued him that she had barely met his sister before the two were acting like the best of friends.

Unfortunately Emily had already retired to her chambers for a rest. Lord Stonebridge was nowhere to be found as well. He was probably hovering over Emily, treating her as if she were as fragile as the blue china cup Shelby was holding. That left Stephen as the sole person to receive and entertain the three Shelbys.

"Oh, Papa," Milli said, frowning. "I would like to return to my bedchambers. I do feel a headache coming on." Her body instantly went limp and she fell on top of the sofa with a plop.

Concerned, Stephen shot from his seat. "Is she ill? Should I fetch a doctor?" He turned when he heard muffled laughter coming from the other side of the room. "You find your sister's ill health funny, Miss Shelby?"

Blue eyes twinkled back at him. "Oh no, my lord."

"But I do have a headache," Milli said, sitting up. "A horrid one."

"Very well, dear," Shelby said as Stephen pulled the bell cord. "Follow the servant to your chambers."

Milli obviously sighed with relief when the maid immediately entered. The girl departed from the room, almost running. "It hurts something terribly. Could be a bout of apoplexy!"

"Well," Shelby said, patting his belly and exchanging suggestive looks with his daughter and Stephen. "Must rest before the meal, you know."

He left before Elizabeth could say a word. She turned three shades of pink and dropped her gaze to the floor. "I am tired as well, my lord. If you would please excuse me."

Stephen came up behind her and placed his hand on her arm. "I'm sorry you find yourself backed into a corner, Miss Shelby. If there is anything I could do—"

She turned around so fast it took him off guard. "Do? Are you playing some sort of hideous joke? Anything you could do? Have you not done enough? Why, poor Lady Odette suffered terribly after you left! Do you have any kind of conscience at all?"

Stephen stiffened, mystified at her outburst. Was this little wren standing up for the vulture that had clawed her heart out at breakfast the other day? Lady Odette was a sly female, and he, for one, was glad he had discovered the truth in time.

"I do believe the lady in question will mend."

"Oh, I cannot believe you would do that to her!"

Stephen blinked. What kind of thanks was this when he had pulled her out of a disagreeable situation that morning? He had all but worshipped at Miss Shelby's feet, and she was throwing it back at him as if he were nothing.

"She offended you, madam. My future wife. How could I not?"

Shocked, he watched her face turn a deep shade of purple. "I will never marry you. Never!"

Stephen's stunned gaze followed her backside as she swept from the room.

"Well, well, what have we here?"

Milli came to a dead stop. She had been dancing in the ballroom by herself, pretending she was a beautiful ballerina when the most handsome man appeared before her like a prince in a fairy tale. "Who are you?"

"Your servant, Lord Marcus Clearbrook, mademoiselle. And you?"

"Miss Millicent Shelby."

His black brows lifted. "Ah, Miss Shelby. Your sister is going to marry my brother, is she not?"

There was something hard in his voice that set Milli's teeth on edge. "Elizabeth is very pretty."

"Indeed."

"And very smart."

"Indeed."

"And very rich!"

His eyes darkened. "Indeed," he drawled.

"Oh you think I am a child, but I'm not. I'm fourteen and going to be fifteen next month."

His lips curved into a mischievous grin. "Indeed. Well, little ballerina, when you are out may I ask you for a dance?"

Her bottom lip trembled. He was making fun of her. "*Indeed* not. You are too stuffy, by far. Why, you are nothing like your brother at all. He is everything that is proper." She brushed past him and heard him chuckle.

"Good-bye, my little ballerina. I will be looking forward to that dance in a few years."

Before he could say another word, she ran into the hall and disappeared.

"I see you have met my sister," Elizabeth said, walking into the ballroom.

The man turned. "I beg your pardon. You must be my brother's fiancée, Miss Elizabeth Shelby. I'm Lord Marcus Clearbrook. You must know I never meant to hurt the child."

Elizabeth saw the guilt in his eyes and tried to reassure him. One never knew with Milli. "Of course you didn't. I fear my family gave her too much leeway growing up. My father was always away on business, and I was at a seminary for young ladies in Bath and—" She stopped, realizing she was rambling. "How I do go on. You must think me quite silly."

Lord Marcus smiled. "Not at all. I must say, my brother did well to snatch you from the pool of marriageable females."

Elizabeth blushed. "You are too kind. If you would forgive me, I must see to Milli."

Marcus took her hand, bowed, and kissed the tip of her fingers. "Your servant, madam."

At that precise moment, Stephen stood covertly on the stairs, his dark gaze settling on his brother.

After Elizabeth departed, Marcus stepped out of the ballroom and lifted his gaze. "Ah, Stephen, I daresay you are wondering what just took place here. You should have made yourself known."

Stephen's heels clapped down the stairs. "You kissed her hand is what took place. And I also saw your gaze attached to her like one of those foxed dandies at Prinny's last ball."

The gleam in Marcus's eyes did nothing to alleviate Stephen's misgivings.

"She is much prettier than you described. Those blue eyes pierced my heart like cupid's arrow. You'd best be careful and not leave her to her own devices when Mother starts dragging her to all the balls this Season. And if you somehow disengage yourself from her, I would be very interested."

For not the first time Stephen felt a spurt of jealousy toward a man who had paid his attentions to Elizabeth. But this was Marcus. "Shut up, or I may have to box you one."

The light in Marcus's eyes turned dangerous. "If it comes to that, then I suppose you want her after all. But I will be there if you discard her. By Jove, you had me believing she was an ogress. I think she is the loveliest of creatures, and if you dare jilt her, I will be the one boxing your ears."

His words were said between clenched teeth as he turned down the hall, leaving Stephen glaring at his back.

"I think he loves her," Milli said in a somber tone as she came out of her hiding place behind the gigantic Chinese urn near the bottom of the steps.

Stephen glanced over his shoulder. "He does not love her. And I ought to take you over my knee for eavesdropping."

Milli's eyes rounded. "Pooh. You would do no such thing. But I hazard to say if you found Elizabeth kissing Marcus back, you just might do that to her."

Stephen let out an exasperated groan as the girl turned and fled down the hall in a wake of lavender bouquet.

"Why me?" he said to the urn.

"You say something, Stephen?"

Stephen looked up to see his brother-in-law starting down the stairs. "Say something? No. It was the urn, you see. It gives advice to stupid, idiotic rakes such as I."

"Ah, I see. Hearing voices? Never one to give advice, but since you helped me in my struggle to make off with your sister, I will give you a good piece of counsel before you marry."

"And what, pray tell, is that?"

"Stop speaking to urns, you idiot. Down a few bottles at White's. Fall flat on your face if you like, but don't go mad until after the ceremony. Take it from me, until you get that ceremony over with, you never know what can befall an engagement. I should know." Stonebridge's gaze sparkled with amusement.

"Très amusant," Stephen said, retreating down the hall. "Sometimes I wonder why Emily married you at all."

"She loves me, Stephen. She loves me."

Stephen's lips thinned as he turned the corner into the library. The trouble was, something inside him wanted Elizabeth to love him, too, and if that wasn't more idiotic than talking to an urn, he didn't know what was.

The sky was overcast and a low rumble boomed in the distance as Elizabeth entered the gardens behind the townhouse. She was at a loss as to Milli's whereabouts and decided to look for the girl along the garden paths when she heard someone sobbing. She quickly turned the corner and found herself standing over a handsomely dressed woman sitting on a stone bench, holding one very fluffy white cat that looked as if had been pampered every day of its fat little life.

"Forgive me. I didn't mean to intrude."

Violet blue eyes met Elizabeth's and the lady sniffed. "There is nothing to forgive, my dear. Poor Egypt is dying."

Elizabeth tilted her head toward the bench. "May I?"

The lady nodded. "You must be Miss Shelby. I am Lady Bringston, Stephen's mother. Forgive me for not greeting you, but my—" she sobbed, "my poor dear is so listless, I cannot leave her. And I cannot see anyone, I am so filled with grief."

Elizabeth sat beside the older woman and petted the cat. She calmly made her own introductions to the lady and continued to stroke the animal's soft fur. After a moment, she pulled out a handkerchief from her skirt pocket and handed it to Stephen's mother. "Your Grace."

"Thank you, my dear." The lady blew her nose. "Never have one when I need it, you know. And you do not have to bother saying 'Your Grace' with me. You will be my daughter-in-law soon. Besides, I am Lady Bringston, a marchioness now." Another sniff. "Oh, how I do wish my husband were here."

Elizabeth didn't know quite what to say. "I find having a

handkerchief on one's person at all times comes in very handy."

The lady smiled. "You are so very right, my dear. I knew my Stephen would not choose some insipid girl to be his wife."

No, he chose some insipid girl with money.

Feeling her heart clench, Elizabeth avoided the lady's intent gaze and turned her attention toward Egypt.

"May I take a look at your cat? I have had some experience with animals. Perhaps I could help."

The lady's gaze looked hopeful. Thunder boomed in the distance. "You have? Well, my dear, take her." She set the cat in Elizabeth's lap. "Egypt is the most darling of creatures. If Bringston were here, he would know what to do."

"He knows about animals?" Elizabeth asked, as she stroked Egypt and poked at the feline's body checking for any signs of disease.

"Yes, and a dear he is. I should have traveled with him to his estates and to see his mother, but, oh she is so jealous of me, you see, I refused. What a goosecap I was . . . ."

Elizabeth felt Egypt's stomach and smiled.

Stephen stepped into the gardens, searching for his mother. It had been hours since he had seen her. He wanted to tell her about Egypt. A servant mentioned she had ventured outside. The wind had picked up and the clouds were beginning to groan.

A slight sprinkle of rain hit his face and he wiped it away with his hand. A woman's excited shout stabbed the air and he spun to his left, only to see his mother standing half outside the door to the kitchen, her body assaulted by a strong gust of wind, plastering her skirts against her legs.

"Mother," he said, striding toward her.

"Oh, Stephen. Is she not wonderful?" His mother threw out her arms and hugged him, squeezing him so hard he stepped back and took hold of her shoulders.

"Who?" His mother had been missing Bringston so much perhaps she had snapped.

For years after his father's death Stephen had tried to

comfort his mother. She had loved the duke and when he had died, she had fallen apart. But Stephen could never forgive his father for not loving this woman. And that made Stephen's own situation more difficult. He was going to have to marry a woman who did not love him. And at this point, he had no idea exactly what he felt for Miss Shelby. It was an insufferable situation.

"Why, your dear Elizabeth," his mother answered. The rain fell lightly against their faces. "You are marrying the sweetest girl on the face of this earth—besides your sister, of course."

Stephen stood, dumbfounded.

"Come, take a look." His mother dragged him out of the rain and into the kitchen. "Are they not beautiful?"

Stephen's stunned gaze shifted to the corner of the room. There sat Egypt, licking her litter of four tiny kittens. No, it was five, including one little ball off to the side.

Kneeling on the floor was Elizabeth, her gown damp and dirty from whatever ministrations she had had to deliver. Her spectacles were on the table, resting beside a crumpled handkerchief.

Stephen's stomach clenched at the sight. The lady was enchanting. Unaware he was watching, she picked up the stray kitten and pressed it against her cheek.

"There now. You'll be safe and warm with your mama. You've had a harrowing day, but all is well, my sweet."

Stephen felt another spurt of jealousy. He knew instantly that Elizabeth Shelby would make a fantastic mother. His heart gave a kick and he could not take his eyes off her.

Then he saw the most incredible thing. His mother, who was known to be quite fastidious, knelt down beside Elizabeth and started talking to the kittens.

"You vexatious creatures. What a scare you gave me." She picked up a wet ball of fur and turned. "Come here, Stephen."

Elizabeth glanced over her shoulder and a blush swept across her face as she took in her own appearance. "Oh!"

"La, my dear, Stephen does not care a whit what you look like. He loves you." The lady smiled dreamily. "Love is what truly matters in marriage. And I have found it with Bringston."

Elizabeth eyed Stephen with such horror he felt about an inch high. It was obvious she was thinking about what his mother had said and she quickly dropped her gaze. "I must ready myself for dinner."

The older lady looked up. "Have them send you some hot water for a bath. Stephen will see to your every need, won't you, my dear? Why you kept this girl a secret I'll never know."

Elizabeth stood and brushed the dust from her skirt. She hurried across the kitchen. Stephen followed. He took her elbow, gently pulling her closer to him.

She halted. "Yes, my lord?"

He lifted her chin with his finger. "Thank you."

She looked away, the painful gaze spearing his heart. Did she love that weasel Fennington so?

"You're welcome. But truly, I must ready myself for dinner. Pray excuse me."

"I will see to your every need, of course," he said more sharply than intended. She gasped and fled from his arms. "What the hell is wrong with me?" he murmured, glaring at the floor.

"Confound it, do not speak to your feet."

Stephen looked up to find Stonebridge smiling at him. "What the deuce are you talking about?"

"My wife may fear it runs in the family, talking to one's feet and what not. Can you not see that I have enough to worry about? When will you learn to stop this nonsense?"

Stephen's fist clenched. "Oh, go to the devil."

"Oh, but I've been there—before I married your sister, that is. And I can tell you something, until you face the devils inside yourself, you won't have any peace at all."

Chapter Eight

The weather was horrid as Elizabeth slowly made her way down to dinner. Sheets of rain fell from the sky while the wind howled against the walls of Elbourne Hall, making travel all but impossible. She knew that any guests who had been invited this evening would not be coming. Only an idiot would dare to step outside on a night like this.

She drew in a deep breath and tried to calm her pounding heart. She had already made the acquaintance of the duke, but it was his intense gaze that unnerved her. He didn't seem happy about her engagement to his brother.

She shouldn't care, but she did. Of course, Lord Marcus seemed kind and so did his brother Lord Clayton.

She felt a little lift, recalling the moment she had met the duke's wife and his sister. The duchess, Jane, as she asked to be called, since they were to be family, had been all smiles, making her feel as welcome as Lady Emily, a dear lady whom Elizabeth felt at home with the moment she met her.

But a sister was one thing, a brother who was a duke was something altogether different. What had Stephen told him? Or was it the plain fact that she was not of the illustrious *ton*—that is, without her father's money?

Only minutes ago she had discovered that she would be alone tonight with the Clearbrook family. Milli was exhausted and had pleaded a headache. Her father had done the same, begging to be excused. The journey in the coach always tired him out.

She regretted speaking to him with such anger about his

plans to wed her to his lordship, but it was her life and she should decide her destiny, not him.

Her thoughts turned to Stephen, and despite herself her heart began to soften.

She certainly didn't want to recall the loving way he looked at his mother as she cared for the kittens. *But the cherry episode still lay deep in her mind, refusing to be settled.* How could a man be so two-faced?

Milli could not have been wrong about the incident with Odette, could she?

And yet, no matter what, Elizabeth couldn't control her attraction to the man. His charm was like a spell and she found herself beginning to like him. If that were not maddening, she didn't know what was.

Although his mother had said he was an impulsive child, the love in the lady's voice had not been lost on Elizabeth, and she had instantly felt a prickle of regret at the way she had treated him that day in the library. The man was an absolute enigma.

"Good evening," Stephen's mother announced, her steps quickening as she drew up beside Elizabeth in the hall. "Did the servants bring you hot water for a bath? Is there aught else I can do for you? I will never be able to thank you."

Elizabeth laughed. "I did nothing but help Egypt with her kittens. Please do not make me some kind of saint."

The lady raised an elegant brow. "I will never forget your kindness, Elizabeth. If you ever have need, please feel free to come to me. But I am so sorry your family is under the weather this evening."

The lady waved her hand toward the dining room, her eyes sparkling, no doubt because of her new kittens. "La, I fear it will be a bit informal tonight with our tight little group. None of our guests will wish to travel."

As they entered the room, the gathering turned their way.

Elizabeth saw Stephen's expression tighten and a lump formed in her throat. The two middle brothers gave a warm smile of welcome. The Duke of Elbourne nodded grimly. The young duchess flashed a quick glare at the duke before she took Elizabeth's hand in a warm welcome.

Stephen stepped away from his stiff position at the window and walked toward her. "You look enchanting. I'm sorry your father and Millicent are unwell. Is there anything I could do to make them more comfortable?"

Elizabeth managed a smile, knowing the young duchess was taking in the scene with a calculating eye. "They are resting comfortably, thank you."

Silence fell over the room like an ominous black cloud.

"My dear," the duchess added gracefully, still holding Elizabeth's hand, "you are already acquainted with Lady Emily and her husband Lord Stonebridge?"

Forcing another smile, Elizabeth was soon drawn into an easy conversation with Stephen's sister. The rest of the family began to chat among themselves and the awkward moment was over.

"I hear you saved Egypt from certain death," Lady Emily said, laughing as she patted her round belly, walking near the window to peer out at the storm.

Elizabeth flushed at the candid remark, knowing the lady was referring to her delicate condition. But it seemed no one considered the comment scandalous since Lady Emily happened to be surrounded by family.

However, Elizabeth immediately detected the note of worry on Lord Stonebridge's face as he followed his wife with eaglelike eyes, and she sympathized with him. Many ladies died during childbirth. Her own mother had died giving birth to Milli, had she not?

"Little Egypt is doing quite well," Elizabeth offered. "But I own the entire day has been a great surprise to your mother."

Lady Emily grinned. "Yes, but I daresay a delightful surprise. She needs some diversion with Lord Bringston away."

A thunderclap shook the mansion and Elizabeth flinched. The room darkened as the candles flickered eerily on the tables.

Lady Emily winced and Elizabeth stared at her thoughtfully.

"I hope you like roasted duck with lemon sauce, sweetheart."

Stephen's silky voice broke into Elizabeth's keen scrutiny of his sister. A small shiver worked its way up her back as he took that moment to come up beside her. "It is one of Cook's specialties."

Sweetheart? Her stomach flip-flopped like a dying fish on a pier at the sound of the endearment passing his lips. His charm was never ending. The rogue.

"I have never had it with lemon sauce before, my lord."

Like a besotted suitor, he guided her to her seat, whispering in her ear, "Then we will have something to talk about later, won't we?"

His warm breath fanned her face, and she stared helplessly at the table. Why was he doing this to her?

"Stephen, dear," his mother said as he took his seat, "you must be our escort tomorrow to the dressmaker's. Elizabeth will need a new wardrobe. One never has enough gowns, you know."

Elizabeth looked up, dumbfounded at the lady's suggestion. "But my father has always seen that I have the best in gowns."

Stephen raised a brow in her direction and picked up his wineglass. "Alas, he will not be the one to care for you when we are married. In fact, after we are wed I have made it clear to your father that he will pay for nothing."

The duke seemed to choke on his food. Elizabeth blinked.

Lady Emily smiled. "Miss Shelby, Mother tells me we are to have an engagement ball in two weeks. It will be an extravagant affair. Of course, I won't be able to come, but I will be settled in my chambers, sending spies for all the details."

"An engagement ball?" Stephen exchanged confused glances with his mother and Elizabeth.

Engagement ball? If Elizabeth were not so horrified by the information, she would have laughed at her fiancé's reaction. Was he too embarrassed to be seen with her? And what of his family? Did everyone but the duke think it a love match?

For a time the conversation revolved around the ball and

the upcoming festivities. Through it all, Elizabeth felt like a fraud. How much longer was this to go on?

After dinner the ladies departed to the drawing room, leaving the men to their port. Almost immediately Stephen's mother withdrew to the kitchen, wanting to look in on Egypt.

Elizabeth continued to converse with Lady Emily, who was quickly showing signs of fatigue.

"Mother was beside herself until you came, Miss Shelby. We are all so thankful that you turned up when you did."

Elizabeth smiled. "I did not deliver the kittens. Egypt did all the work. I just helped make her comfortable."

Eyes twinkling, Lady Emily wiggled her large stomach into a comfortable position as she sat on the sofa. "Hmmmm, imagine if Egypt started having those kittens on Mama's lap? I doubt any of us would have slept the night." She chuckled and immediately winced as she moved again.

Elizabeth looked at her thoughtfully, not for the first time that evening. "Speaking of sleeping, are you sleeping well, considering?"

"As a matter of fact, no. My back hurts like the devil."

Elizabeth burst forth with laughter.

"The question is, are you sleeping well, Miss Shelby?" the lady asked suddenly, her expression keen.

Elizabeth blushed. How could she tell this woman that her cherished brother had made a deal with her father? Money in exchange for the use of his title. There was no love at all.

"You are not in love with my brother, are you?"

"I, er, think him very handsome."

"I see. It is a marriage of convenience then." Lady Emily sank against the cushions. "What kind of scrape did my brother fall into now?"

Elizabeth turned a frowning gaze toward the flames leaping in the hearth. Thunder shook the mansion, rattling the windowpanes. "I imagine he was eager for my father's money."

"No," the lady said vehemently, "Stephen could have come to Roderick for that. Or at least Marcus or Clayton."

Elizabeth wondered how much Lady Emily knew of her brother. "Perhaps he was tired of coming to his family for aid."

Lady Emily paused as she placed her hands on her stomach. "So you find him handsome? What about charming?"

Charming? Of course he was charming. He also had a vengeful streak that marred his perfection.

Elizabeth stood, walking closer to the fire. "Your brother has his charms." She stopped and turned to face Lady Emily. "But I don't want to marry him for that or for his title. My father wanted this marriage. Do you hate me for that?"

"Of course I don't hate you. I gather your father wanted a title for you. It is not as uncommon as you think."

"Not for me." *I want to marry someone who loves me for myself.* But when she tried to picture Mr. Fennington's face, Stephen's chiseled profile came into view.

"Oh!"

Elizabeth's head snapped up at Lady Emily's shriek. The lady squeezed her eyes shut, and her lips were turning white with pain.

"How long have the pains been coming?" Elizabeth asked, hastening to the lady's side. She grabbed Lady Emily's wrist and felt her pulse.

Lady Emily spoke through clenched teeth. "Oh, for the past four hours, I believe. They were only minor irritations. I never thought they meant anything. The doctor said I might have pains off and on and should stay off my feet but I never thought . . . oh my, is it to happen tonight?"

Her face turned ashen as she sought Elizabeth's hand and squeezed. Violet eyes filled with fear when they met Elizabeth's gaze. "I am to have this baby next month. Not now."

The rain slapped hard against the windows of the drawing room, reminding them both of the inclement weather. "Oh, dear heaven. I don't want my baby to die. The doctor won't be able to travel in this. What I am to do? My husband is usually as calm as a duck on water, but since I have been with child the man has been an intolerable nuisance."

They both let out hesitant laughs.

"A baby takes its time, Lady Emily. Just take some deep calming breaths and everything will be fine."

Elizabeth kept glancing at the door. She needed to contact Lord Stonebridge. Wanted to scream his name. He seemed to be a man who could do just about anything. He would drag the doctor through sleet and hail to attend to his wife if need be.

Lady Emily took another breath and seemed to relax for at least a few seconds. "Yes, yes, I feel better now."

Elizabeth patted the lady's hand. "Now you are going to have a few minutes between pains, but when they start to come faster it will be harder to speak. But when it is all over you will hold a beautiful baby in your arms and all will be well."

Elizabeth prayed she was right. For years she had read books in her father's library on a surgeon's life and practice. The information had become quite helpful with her medical treatments, especially with animals. But when it came to giving birth to a human baby, well she certainly was not qualified to be involved in that. It just was not done.

Lady Emily nodded as she bit her lip and passed through another contraction.

Elizabeth straightened. "I must fetch your husband now. He will know what to do."

Lady Emily squeezed Elizabeth's hand and shook her head. "I don't know if that's a good idea. I love him, but he is an absolute idiot when it comes to things like this."

"He will do what he needs to do, believe me."

"No, you do not understand."

The fear Elizabeth saw in the lady's face turned her heart.

"I cannot see a doctor coming out in a night like this. My husband will go for him, but I cannot take the chance he will be caught in this terrible storm. He can send a footman. Yet what if this babe does not wait?" Lady Emily's face turned white as another contraction passed.

She swallowed and dropped her hand against her side as she tried to relax. "You are my only hope until the doctor comes," she said, the tears rising to her lids. "The men in this house are healthy male specimens who have seen more blood on the battlefield than I care to know about, but believe me, they are entirely useless with something like this. It scares them witless."

Elizabeth did not believe all of them would be useless. For some reason she thought Stephen would not be a veritable ninny.

"Am I intruding?"

Both ladies' heads jerked up as Stephen wandered into the room, his dark eyes narrowing on his sister's pale face.

Elizabeth knew she was doomed to help. She nodded to the lady, receiving a half-smile in return as another pain started.

"No, my lord. You are just in time to help with the birth of your niece or nephew."

Stephen's stunned gaze shot to Elizabeth. "Well you can simply tell my sister she cannot have the baby now. It is not time!"

Veritable ninny, no. Ninny, yes. Elizabeth's eyes flashed as she stalked toward him. "She is having the baby *now*. I will need your help, do you understand?"

The man who was never at a loss for words seemed mute.

"Very good." Elizabeth could not think of his nearness, could not think of their engagement, she could only think of the babe that was to be born. Another life. "Your first duty is to take care of the men in this house, especially Lord Stonebridge, and make certain he does not interfere. And don't let him fetch the doctor himself."

Stephen nodded grimly, the fear in his eyes matching the fear in Elizabeth's heart. But she would never dare show what she felt, not in front of Lady Emily.

"My dear, I believe it is time we retreat to our chambers. You have been looking quite peaked—" Lord Stonebridge had entered the room and upon seeing his lovely wife writhing in pain, his eyes went wide with shock.

"Confound it! Someone do something!"

He ran to Lady Emily's side while she tried to tell her husband everything would be fine. He insisted on going for the doctor, but she asked him not to leave her. She told him the weather was impossible anyway. Another pain came and Lord Stonebridge seemed to be in more pain than his wife.

Elizabeth looked on in despair as the man squeezed his wife's hand until it turned blue. Saints above, this was going to be one *long* night.

She gave a sharp glance toward Stephen, telling him to take the earl out of the room, in addition to giving him a mental list of everything she would need. It took a moment for Stephen to gather his wits before he dragged Stonebridge from his wife's side.

Elizabeth glanced back at Lady Emily and smiled. "Do you think you could make it to your bedchamber between pains."

Lady Emily's violet eyes danced. "Do you think I can get past my husband before he throws me into his arms and drops me down the stairs?"

Both women laughed and Elizabeth knew she had found a friend.

"Well what the devil is taking so long?" Lord Stonebridge shouted as he paced up and down the drawing room rug like some caged animal ready to pounce at the smallest sound.

"Not to worry. Miss Shelby is with Emily, trying to make her as comfortable as possible," Stephen said as he handed the father-to-be another glass of brandy. "The maids are willing to step in if the time comes. Many of them have helped deliver children."

The earl spun around. "Miss Shelby? She's a gently bred lady! And the maids? Confound it! You should have let *me* go for the doctor. That footman you sent won't be back for hours."

The duke stepped in, a frown marring his dark features. "There is not one single carriage out in this horrid weather, Jared. And if you dare try to leave, I will tie you down. You know I can do it. Do you hear me? I don't want this baby born without a father."

Stonebridge hurled his glass into the fire. "I cannot bear this waiting!"

Stephen's brown eyes flashed with amusement. "Speaking to the fire now, are we? I thought we had a little talk about that."

The earl lifted his head and grinned. "So we did."

Stephen slapped his brother-in-law on the shoulder and sat him down for another game of chess. But the truth was, he was scared too. Yet if anyone could calm Emily down, it was Elizabeth. She was reliable and confident, two factors lacking in most of the eligible females of the *ton*.

The earl's queen shot across the room, startling Stephen.

"Confound it," Stonebridge shouted. "We've been in this blasted room for over four hours!"

Roderick, Clayton, and Marcus glanced up, then went back to their card game. Their mother, Lady Bringston, was flitting about outside Emily's bedchamber, trying to be helpful. *Elizabeth*, for that is how Stephen thought of her now, was trying to calm down Stephen's mother as much as she was Emily.

William Shelby had made an appearance, then taken to his bed, assuring everyone that his eldest daughter had the healing touch, and even though she had never delivered a babe before, she would rise to the occasion. It was a shocking statement to make of a gently bred female, but for some absurd reason Stephen did not doubt Elizabeth's capability.

It was an hour later when the doctor came rushing past the door and was barely out of his damp coat before the earl had pounced on the man, shouting for him to hurry to his wife.

Stephen and the duke had to physically pull Stonebridge back to the drawing room and leave the doctor to his work.

But for an unguarded moment, Stephen had caught a glimpse of Elizabeth standing outside Emily's chambers, looking understandably relieved as she issued orders to a maid. He never thought he had seen a more beautiful woman in his life than his fiancée in her disheveled state. Her sleeves were rolled up to her elbows, wisps of wheat-colored hair curled around the nape of her neck, and sweat blotted her temples. Something warm swelled in his chest at the sight of her coaxing his mother to take a glass of ratafia as they waited outside Emily's room.

"Women have babies all the time, Jared," Stephen said, back in the drawing room.

"Well, confound it. This is my woman," the earl ground out. "I don't know what I would do if anything should happen to her."

Stephen detected a slight mist in the earl's eyes, and an ache grew in his chest. He had a sudden desire for what this man had. He wanted a woman to love and a woman to love him back. He wanted a child to love, a family to cherish. Dash it all. He wanted Miss Elizabeth Shelby.

"The doctor made it on time. He knows what he's about," the duke added with the voice of authority. "You have nothing to worry about. Besides, Emily is as strong as a horse."

Stonebridge's head snapped up, his eyes sparkling. "I don't think your sister would take kindly to being likened to a horse."

Stephen bent over the fire to see if he could rescue the queen that had been thrown near the smoking embers. "No," he smiled, "don't think she would, Roderick."

"Hello."

All heads turned toward Milli who had entered the drawing room. Her head was a tangle of dark brown curls framing two wide gray eyes.

"Ah, our little ballerina," Marcus said, his eyes smiling.

Milli lifted her chin. "I know you will excuse me for barging in on you, but I want you all to know that my sister Elizabeth is better than most doctors."

Stephen's eyes twinkled at the girl's boldness. "Thank you, Milli. But the doctor has arrived, and at present, your sister is caring for my mother. Now, perhaps it is time you retire. Rest assured, you will be notified of everything in the morning."

Milli colored. "Well, I am only trying to put you all at ease, for Lizzie told me that sometimes men are such babies in times like these."

Marcus coughed. "I believe Stephen is right, my little ballerina. You should take yourself to bed immediately."

Milli's eyes flashed. "Women do know some things. Why, I'll have you know that Lizzie delivered Mr. Fennington's puppies last month and a prime lot they were."

Lord Stonebridge shot from his chair. "She what?"

Stephen clenched his teeth. King George, this was all he needed tonight. The thought of Elizabeth inside Fennington's home made him want to call the man out. But bringing up Fennington's name to Stonebridge on the night of his babe's birth was outside of enough.

"The puppies were so cute," Milli went on, taking the earl's question as interest in her continuing the conversation. "But I was not supposed to tell anyone about that."

She frowned when her comments were answered with a brittle silence. The five gentlemen were now staring at her as if she wore nothing at all. She swallowed uncomfortably.

"You see, Elizabeth has a liking for Mr. Fennington. Why, she would have run off to Gretna Green with him if it were not for—"

Stephen was across the room in three quick strides and barely caught the girl by her shoulders, spinning her toward the door before she could finish.

"If not for what?" Lord Stonebridge asked sharply.

Stephen did not want Elizabeth's name dragged through the gutter with that cad. "Milli has quite an imagination, do you not?" he said to the girl.

Milli pursed her lips, as if she finally realized something was wrong. "La, she did not marry Mr. Fennington. But as in the Shakespearean tragedy, she wanted to." And like the little actress Milli was, she fell against Stephen, a limp hand to her forehead. " 'Parting is such sweet sorrow—' "

"That is enough, Millicent."

The girl blinked as Stephen escorted her into the hall. "But I had such an audience. Did you see the way they stared at me?"

To Stephen's disgust, the audience followed.

"What is this about Fennington?" Stonebridge growled.

Before Stephen could say another word, he was saved by the wail of a newborn babe. Stonebridge rushed past him like a horse running at Newmarket.

Elizabeth came down the stairs, smiling as she took both of the earl's hands in a tight grip. "It's a boy. A healthy boy."

"A boy," the earl murmured, choking back tears as he ran up the stairs. "Did you hear that, gentlemen? I have a son!"

The men whooped with glee, returning to the drawing room to toast the earl's new heir.

But Stephen stayed rooted to the floor, staring at Elizabeth. Her honey-colored locks spilled down her back and across her face, shimmering against the candlelight. Her face was as flushed as an English rose. But it was her engaging smile that tripped his heart and sucked him in like an undercurrent.

"A boy!" Milli ran upstairs to take a look at the child, passing her sister. "Oh, how wonderful. A boy!"

Elizabeth's smile faltered and she stumbled on the steps, obviously tired and worn, her bottom lip trembling. "Your mother was so worried. But I think she is fine now."

"Thank you." Stephen stepped forward and caught her in his arms. "You must be exhausted."

To Stephen's surprise, her face crumpled and she buried her face in his shoulder with a small, choking sob.

"Ah, Elizabeth," he said into her hair, inhaling the sweet scent of her. "Don't cry. You did a wonderful job."

Her body fell limp against his. Stephen swept her into his arms and called for the servants to send up hot water for a bath. He strode into her chambers and sank into a nearby chair, settling her on his lap with her face still pressed against his cravat.

Heaven above, she felt so good in his arms. "You did wonderfully. The baby is healthy? My sister is well?"

She nodded. He patted her shoulder awkwardly. "Well, then, what have you to cry about? The doctor came in time, did he not?" Another sob broke from her throat.

"Elizabeth." He kissed the soft skin beneath her ear.

She shook her head, sniffing back her tears. "Y-you don't understand."

He stiffened, instantly thinking of Milli's outburst downstairs. "If you're crying over that Fennington fool—"

Her eyes widened. "Oh! How could you say such a thing?"

She shot off his lap, wiping the tears from her face. "L-leave, before I scream."

He stiffened. "Scream? You must be joking."

"I am not j-joking." Her teeth started to chatter and she sank against her bed with a hiccuping sob.

Milli came running into the room and glared at him. "What have you done to my sister?"

Stephen took one last look at Elizabeth, turned, and strode from the room.

Chapter Nine

"*H*e weighs hardly anything at all," Stephen said as he sat on a bedside chair in Emily's chambers, holding the newborn in his arms. "The little imp. Richard is a fine name, Em."

Emily sank against her pillow and smiled as she picked at her breakfast. "He may be small, but he has terrific lungs. My only concern was getting him into the world. Once he was here, I knew all would be fine. Elizabeth was wonderful, trying to soothe my nerves when I was in so much pain. I don't know what I would have done without her before the doctor arrived. But I must say, you amaze me. When did you ever hold a baby?"

The baby cooed and Stephen softly patted the blanketed bundle. Elizabeth was wonderful. He never should have brought up Fennington's name last evening. It had ruined everything.

"Don't you know, my friend Harry has had three of these. I am not without some education, Em. In fact, I have held some of Pearson's brood when they were only weeks old."

Emily paused. "Hmmmm. If I didn't know better, I would think you wanted one of those little imps."

Stephen stood, smiling as he rocked the baby in his arms. "One thing at a time."

"Have you seen Jared about this morning?" Emily asked.

Stephen grimaced. "Your husband, madam, is inspecting the baby linens for cleanliness as we speak. The man is a veritable ninny when it comes to you and this babe."

"Yes, he is," Emily sighed, her lips curving upward.

Stephen's brows snapped together. "The man is also giving me advice that I would rather shove . . . oh, never mind."
The baby snuggled closer to Stephen's chest and let out a
whimpering cry. "Jupiter, Em. He . . . the . . . my chest is
soaked."

Emily laughed. "So much for bravery. Call in Betsy, the
nanny. She will change him. No need for a soldier like you
to attend to such a dastardly job. Uncles do not attend to
such weighty matters of everyday life. Clayton certainly
would never do it. I am not certain about Marcus or Roderick either."

Stephen's dark eyes danced. "You underestimate me. If I
can ride into battle, I can certainly change a wee little infant.
Just watch me and see how it is done by a master. But you
are not to tell a soul, mind you. I would never live it down."

Elizabeth stood in the hall, unexpectedly overhearing the
conversation between brother and sister while catching a
glimpse of Stephen holding the baby.

"By Jove, Em, I didn't know a little thing could do so
much damage. Er, perhaps we should call in Betsy after all."

Elizabeth's heart swelled with tenderness for the man.
This was the real Stephen Clearbrook. A man who loved his
sister, his family, his nephew. For a moment last night he
had almost led her to believe a marriage between them
would work.

But he didn't love her. He was a man who needed her father's money. It was done all the time. The birth of his
nephew was the joy she had seen in his eyes, not anything to
do with herself. Her happiness had been shattered the
minute he had mentioned Fennington's name.

Tears pricked the back of her lids as she fought the emotions swirling inside her. As quietly as she could, she turned
and made her way back to her room.

His charm was her undoing. Lord Stephen had wrapped
himself around her heart, and she didn't know how to extricate him.

With just one smile from that rogue, her insides melted
like snow on a summer day. And when he held her last night,
her thoughts had spun like a windmill, making her forget the

incident with Lady Odette. But the more she dwelled on it, the more she thought that perhaps Milli had misunderstood his instructions about Odette's drink. None of it made sense.

Still, his charms were so remarkable he could hide almost any flaw in his character and it would be hard to detect.

But there was one thing she would never forget. He wanted to marry her for her father's money and there was no changing that undeniable fact, charm or not.

Closing the door to her room, Elizabeth sat at a small corner desk and penned a letter to Mr. Fennington. She would post it when she went into Town. After last night and especially this morning, she knew she had to do something. She had tried to keep her distance from Stephen, but it was all for naught because nearness or not, she still wanted him to love her. Seeing him holding the baby so tenderly touched her deeply. She had to leave.

"What are you doing?" Milli popped her head into the room.

Elizabeth quickly stuffed the letter into the drawer and turned to her sister. "I am writing a letter, Miss Nosy."

The girl peeked over Elizabeth's shoulder. "To whom?"

Elizabeth knew that Milli had taken a liking to Stephen, and the girl could easily drop a hint to that very man a letter was being sent to Mr. Fennington and *that* would ruin everything.

"It's none of your affair to whom I write, Milli. But since our visit to the dressmaker's has been postponed for at least a few days, you might want to set aside some time and do the same. I would think your friend Grace would like to hear from you."

"Yes, she is so lonely since her parents died. I shall write to her." Milli paused. "Good gracious, what is that horrid squeaking?"

Elizabeth tipped her head to listen, her eyes twinkling. "I do believe that is Lady Bringston singing. The woman hovers over that baby as if it were her own. Lord Stonebridge has begged me to ride with his mother-in-law somewhere before she drives him insane. But for now, we are stuck here, so you had best gather your writing utensils and go to work."

Milli's lids fluttered closed as she fell onto the bed with a silly smile. "The dressmaker. How utterly romantic. More romantic than writing letters. Perhaps Lord Stephen will see you in a gown of gold and fall to his knees, begging for a scrap of your love."

Elizabeth doubted she would ever see the handsome lord on his knees for anybody, let alone her. He had too much pride.

"Someday your acting will cause you trouble, Milli. Mark my words."

Fine gray eyes stared back at Elizabeth. "Someday I will marry a prince who has fallen in love with me at first sight."

"If you want a prince, you had best practice those dancing lessons Papa paid for *and* practice your writing."

"Dancing?" Milli frowned and slid off the bed, heading for the door. "I am not a ballerina, you know. Oh, by the way, the duke was wondering how well you knew Mr. Fennington. He believes the man is only after money from rich heiresses, and he is very concerned about your relationship with the man, even though you are engaged to his handsome brother. And Lord Stonebridge—well, he evidently *loathes* the man."

Elizabeth's face colored. "What did you say to the duke?"

Milli huffed. "Well, I certainly did not tell him you fell out of that tree and onto his brother while you waited for Mr. Fennington to sweep you into the carriage and ride to Gretna Green, if that is what you meant."

"Millicent, sometimes I would like to throttle you."

Milli laughed, running from the room. "But you would have to catch me first."

Elizabeth pulled out her letter and stuffed it into her reticule. Obviously this household had something against Mr. Fennington. And how could she believe anything Lord Stephen said? She would have asked Emily if her condition were not so delicate. The lady would surely know if the stories were true.

But Elizabeth knew Mr. Fennington to be a fine man. He loved her. He did not love her money. Now Lord Stephen Clearbrook, with his devil-may-care attitude, wanted only her money. That charm of his was lethal to her well-being. Love was what mattered most in a marriage. Love and truth.

Scowling, Stephen stood in the library and threw one boot onto the hearthstone, nursing a glass of sherry in his hand while Roderick hovered over him like some vulture picking at his prey.

"And another thing, if you were not so thick in the skull, you would see what a gem you have on your hands."

Stephen's cool gaze lifted. "Gem or not, Your Grace, I should be the one to choose my own wife."

"Who the hell cares what you want? Do you have any idea how well she handled the situation with Emily? You cannot jilt her."

"You think I don't know what Miss Shelby did by keeping Emily calm until the doctor arrived? I am not stupid!"

"Hell's teeth. Can you not even call the lady by her Christian name? You are engaged!"

Stephen knew very well he was still engaged to the lady. The problem was she was in love with someone else. "Elizabeth. There! Are you satisfied?"

He folded his body into the nearby chair, his gaze hard and unforgiving as he stared into the flames.

Roderick slapped the fireplace mantel with his hand. "If I were not your brother, I would call you out."

Stephen slowly lifted his head. "Why the devil don't you, then? It would make my life easier."

The duke's eyes turned black. "You hurt that innocent angel and you will answer to me."

Stephen laughed. "Oh, this is grand. She now has you in her corner, too. As well as Clayton and Marcus."

His gallant brothers had made a point of pulling him aside after breakfast, telling him he was one lucky fellow to have a woman with a head on her shoulders.

"Why do you dislike her so?"

Stephen's lips thinned. "You don't understand, do you?"

"You were always the cocky child, Stephen. It's time you took responsibility for your actions."

Stephen shot from his seat, his finger stabbing the air. "Oh, I see. You wish to become my father, telling me what to do. Well don't you dare try to interfere in my life. I can handle everything myself. As a matter of fact, if I ever come to you asking for money or a favor again, you may well deduce that I am at death's door with a bayonet in my back."

"Then I give you fair warning," the duke replied, his tone sharp, "you'd best not hurt that girl."

"Yes, you have already told me you were her champion. Well, hell, Roderick. Where was Mother's champion when she needed him?"

"What the blazes are you talking about?"

"Don't be an idiot! Where was Mother's help when she married our father? Where the hell was the love he was supposed to give her? Were you too blind to see how it was? How could she have fallen in love with a man who did not love her? Did you know her heart ached for his love every day he lived with her?"

Roderick's face paled. "Let it go, Stephen."

"Truly, do you think me a peagoose? Ask Mother if you do not believe me. But believe this, I will not enter into a marriage without love between both parties. I will not enter into a life like mother did and while the time away with a broken heart. Do you take my meaning?"

"I take your meaning, little brother. The question is, do you take mine?"

"Indeed, Roderick. I have eyes and ears. But do not fight me on this. You have a wife who loves you. How dare you interfere in my life."

"No, Stephen. That is where you are wrong. It is two lives—yours and Elizabeth's."

Stephen knew Roderick was right. And plague take it, if he were not a gentleman he would leave for the Continent first thing tomorrow morning. But truth be told, he was falling for Miss Elizabeth Shelby, and the crux of the matter was, the lady could not stand the sight of him.

*   *   *

A week later, with the duchess by her side, Elizabeth stood inside a fitting room at the dressmaker's shop and bit back a groan of discomfort as the French seamstress pinned and tucked her until she felt like an overstuffed sofa cushion.

"You will look wonderful in silvers and blues," the dressmaker said, her smiling eyes taking in Elizabeth's proportions. "For the engagement ball you will be a diamond of the first water."

"We have postponed the ball for another week, but we must have these gowns as soon as possible," Jane added as she stood beside the dressmaker, offering her own opinions on more gowns for Elizabeth.

Elizabeth managed a smile. *Her engagement ball.* The entire situation with Lord Stephen was making her extremely nervous. Something had to be done soon.

The young duchess gave her a sly wink. "I know you are tired, dear, but if we want Emily to have any peace at all, we must keep my mother-in-law away from the house as long as possible. I declare, Jared was ready to throw his fist through the wall. My dear mother-in-law has been cooing and fluttering about that baby as if it were one of Egypt's kittens."

Elizabeth chuckled, recalling one of the kittens that was to be given to Milli when it was ready to leave the litter. The kitten was solid black with almond-shaped amber eyes and a speck of white at the end of its tail. Milli called it Cleopatra. The name suited the small feline perfectly. The kitten already acted as if it were queen of the litter, making its own way in the world.

"I cannot believe your mother-in-law wants to go on with the engagement ball," Elizabeth said to the young duchess as the dressmaker finished and left the room. "Two weeks from now seems barely enough time to prepare after all that has happened."

Jane laughed. "The preparations will keep her entertained while her husband is away. She misses him so much.

It seems there has been some trouble at one of his estates and he will be gone away longer than he predicted."

Milli ducked her head inside the fitting room. "*Excusez-moi*, but if you hurry back into your things, Lizzie, maybe I can show you what I found out here. It's simply enchanting!"

The duchess laughed as Milli skipped back into the shop. "She's a wonderful girl, Elizabeth. Go on and get dressed. I'll try to keep my mother-in-law busy on the other side of the shop."

Elizabeth finished dressing and tried to compose herself as she left the fitting room to search for her sister.

"Oh, Lizzie, look here," Milli proclaimed. "You must have this silver-blue ribbon to go with that matching material over there. It will go so well with your eyes. Stephen will simply die when he sees you in it." The girl's eyes fluttered closed, as if she were caught in a delicious dream.

"I thought you were on my side! And he is Lord Stephen Clearbrook to you."

Milli picked up a handful of buttons. "I am on your side. But as to Mr. Fennington, I believe Lady Emily is correct. I now have proof he is a villain. Lady Emily has confirmed it."

"What has Lady Emily got to do with this?" Elizabeth replied, lowering her voice.

"She told me that Mr. Fennington broke into her chambers one night, intending to carry her away to Gretna Green."

Elizabeth felt her heart sink. "And?"

"And her four brothers found the man, right there in her chambers! Truly, I am not fibbing, Lizzie. Lady Emily told me so. Needless to say, Mr. Fennington wiggled his way out of that mess and into another when he tried to kidnap Lady Emily just before her wedding took place. Luckily, her brothers found him again before Lord Stonebridge appeared, and they tied Fennington up until after the ceremony."

Elizabeth did not realize she was wringing her hands around the silver ribbon until Milli gave a deliberate swoon over the counter and closed her eyes.

"Lord Stonebridge," Milli said, opening one eye, "wanted to draw and quarter the man, but Lady Emily asked that he be deposited in the nearby village and left alone. She spared his life. What a saint."

Milli opened the other eye and peered across the room past the window where the youngest of the Clearbrook brothers waited for the women. "I have been thinking it over—your marriage, that is," Milli continued, "and I believe you should marry Lord Stephen Clearbrook instead. He is as handsome as any prince. And agreeable, too."

"Agreeable? After what he did to Lady Odette. How can you say such a thing?"

Milli had the grace to blush. "Well, he is not the ogre you think, Lizzie. I may have overreacted a bit."

Elizabeth's stomach twisted. "Milli?"

Milli chewed her lip and shot a wary glance toward the man outside. "He had nothing to do with Lady Odette's drink. She treated you horridly, so I put the cherries in her drink all by myself. It was later when I thought of Lord Stephen. I thought . . . well, thought you would be flattered that he liked you enough to seek a tiny bit of revenge against Odette. So I said he did it!"

"Oh Millicent, how could you?"

"She was mean to you in Bath."

Elizabeth put a hand to her cheek. "And all this time I thought he had done such a despicable thing. I had my doubts, but—" Her lips thinned as she glared at her sister. "You had best apologize to the man."

"Me?" Milli looked up horrified. "Apologize to *him*?"

"Yes, and do it now before his mother steps outside."

"B-but he has no idea what I said."

"That's all the more reason to apologize."

Milli's lips tightened. "If he beats me, I will blame you."

"You deserve a beating, young lady. Now, go to it."

Elizabeth watched as Milli stomped across the room and out the door. The bell chimed as the door closed and

Stephen looked up from the walk, making his way toward Milli.

"Pssst. Miss Shelby."

Elizabeth jumped. She glanced over her shoulder, behind the bolt of green muslin, and her mouth dropped open in shock.

"Elizabeth, I must speak with you."

"Mr. Fennington, what in the world are you doing here?"

The man had wedged himself between the bolts of material and the small dressing room, his blond head peeking over the lace.

The word "coward" came to mind as Elizabeth paused and surveyed the man as if it were their first meeting. After Milli's assessment, Elizabeth had begun to rethink her own plans and her heart. Perhaps this man was not who she thought he was. Perhaps he did want her papa's money and did not love her at all.

"Mr. Fennington, I cannot come to you," she said, lowering her voice. "It is not proper."

"I cannot very well talk to you in the open when he"—the man tilted his head toward the window—"is guarding the door."

"*He* is not guarding the door," Elizabeth said hotly, stalking toward the cowardly man, more aware than ever that he was a fraud. "*He* is waiting until we finish our shopping."

"Well, then." Before Elizabeth knew what had happened, Mr. Fennington had grabbed her hand and hauled her into the nearby dressing room. "Dearest Elizabeth, you must speak with me."

The door clicked closed behind him.

Elizabeth's eyes narrowed in contempt. "This is most improper. How on earth did you slip inside here without anyone seeing you for that matter?"

He smiled, drawing nearer, swinging that ugly quizzing glass in his hand. "My dear, a few coins dropped here and there, and even a shop girl will do anything I ask."

Elizabeth backed up against the wall, not liking the way he was staring at her. It was clear to her now. This man would do anything for her papa's money, even challenge the wrath of all the Clearbrook brothers to obtain his goal. But he was a coward, all the same.

"I have to go," she said, lifting her chin and reaching for the door. "The ladies will be looking for me."

With a low laugh, Fennington threw his arms on each side of her head, caging her in. "The ladies are too busy. That shop girl is showing them every silk and muslin in the place."

Elizabeth felt the heat of the room envelop her as his sour breath hit her. She should never have made this man's acquaintance. She had been stupid. All Milli's stories of knights in shining armor, begging for her love, were idiotic dreams. Nothing like that would ever happen to her.

Fennington seemed to detect her wary feelings and he pressed a rough cheek against hers. "My dear girl. Have you forgotten how we were to escape to Gretna Green to be wed?"

Elizabeth pushed her hands against his chest. "I really should go. They will be wondering where I am."

"They are all a bunch of fools, my dear."

Elizabeth gasped when he pressed a heavy hand to her cheek.

"I cannot marry you," she said coolly.

He cupped her chin in a firm hold, his eyes daring her to refuse him. "And pray, why not?"

"Papa has made an agreement with Lord Stephen Clearbrook. The announcement has been sent. You must have seen it."

"Clearbrook, bah!" He jerked out a flask and took a swig.

Elizabeth slipped from his hold, eyeing the quizzing glass clanking against the metal container. "Good gracious, Mr. Fennington, are you foxed?"

"I am not foxed. Just a man in love." He grabbed hold of her waist, pushing her firmly against the wall.

"Mr. Fennington, please!"

"Very well, Elizabeth, if you insist." Before Elizabeth had time to think, the man closed his slimy lips over her mouth.

*   *   *

Stephen wanted to wring the girl's neck. "So your sister has believed all this time that I wanted to poison Lady Odette?"

Milli shrugged. "Poison is not the exact word I would use."

"Giving a lady a concoction that could give her a rash and kill her is what I consider poison, young lady."

He took hold of Milli's elbow and escorted her to his carriage. "Get inside." Letting out a mumbled curse, he turned to his thickset footman. "Keep an eye on her for me, Henry. If she leaves this carriage, you no longer have a position."

The man crossed one beefy arm over the other. "Yes, m'lord."

Stephen stalked back into the dressmaker's shop. The chime tinkled above the door as the shopgirl ushered him toward the back where his mother and Jane were conversing with the owner.

"No, I do believe a light blue silk with a delicate lace about the arm would be quite the thing for her."

"Mother."

The lady glanced over her shoulder. "What do you think, Stephen? Light blue or forest green for Elizabeth's ball gown?"

"Light blue," he snapped without needing to think twice. "Speaking of Elizabeth, where is she?" he asked impatiently.

His mother pursed her lips in concern. "Why, I have no idea. Jane, dear, did you see where she went?"

The young duchess frowned. "She left the fitting room, but I didn't see her after that. Maybe she is with Milli."

The thought that Elizabeth had left took hold of Stephen's heart and squeezed. "Millicent is in the carriage," he said, a rush of blood drumming to his head, "and as far as I can see, Elizabeth is nowhere in this blasted shop."

"Perhaps she returned to one of the fitting rooms," the dressmaker said, her smile faltering at the lord's dark face.

"Was she being fitted for another gown, then?" Stephen asked, almost blushing at the thought of barging in on his intended.

"I do not believe so. There's no need to worry. But since her sister ventured outside for a breath of air, perhaps—"

Before the lady could finish, the bell above the door jingled. Milli burst into the shop with Henry attached to her sleeve. "My lord!"

Excusing himself from the ladies, Stephen gritted his teeth as he approached the red-faced footman. "Henry?"

"Said her sister was in trouble, my lord. Started screaming like a banshee, she did. Heads were turning and I ain't one to hold the ladies against their will."

Stephen nodded a smile in the direction of the two ladies who were thankfully far enough away, unable to hear the conversation. His slight gesture let them know the situation was nothing to concern themselves with. A moment later he glared back at Milli as she dragged him across the shop.

"What is it?" he hissed.

"He was hiding over there," she said in a hoarse whisper.

"Who?" Stephen snapped, his patience all but gone.

Milli slapped his arm. "Mr. Fennington, of course! Who else?"

Chapter Ten

"**M**r. Fennington?" Stephen snatched Milli's wrist and tilted a steely gaze toward Henry. "Return her to the carriage and this time do not listen to a single word she has to say. If she screams, tell anybody that asks she is as mad as the king."

Henry nodded.

Milli stomped her foot. "I tell you, I saw him!"

A muscle twitched dangerously in Stephen's cheek as he crossed his arms over his chest. "And why did you not tell me this earlier?"

"Well," she chewed her lip, "I thought perhaps you could rescue Lizzie after a time, you see. Like one of those knights who comes to rescue the princess. If Mr. Fennington had his way with Lizzie, you could call the man out and be the hero."

Every muscle in Stephen's body went taut. *If Mr. Fennington had his way?* For some idiotic reason Stephen was beginning to believe Milli's story. It was that flash of worry in her gray eyes that did it. In one swift move, he picked her up and shoved her toward Henry. "If Fennington has hurt her, you will not be able to sit down for a year, young lady."

Milli's eyes filled with tears. "I am fourteen, don't you know? You cannot do that. And, well, the man is such a complete idiot, I daresay he won't do anything at all except wave that monstrous quizzing glass about his head and tell Lizzie how much he loves her and what not."

She leaned forward, her eyes flashing. "But I thought one good blow from you and Lizzie would swoon at your feet."

Stephen fought the urge to take the girl over his knee. "Where are they?"

Milli pointed toward the fitting room. "I think they are in there."

Stephen exchanged glances with his footman. "Forget what I said earlier. Bar the blasted door after I go in."

Milli's face lit with awe as she was dropped from the footman's hold. "Is it to be a mill then? It will be the first real fight I have ever seen. Of course, in the Tragedy of—"

"Millicent!" Stephen threw the girl his iciest glare. "If you have any sense at all, hold your tongue. You are to stay over there with my mother and the duchess or I'll have your hide. And do not tell them a thing about Fennington. They are searching the patterns as we speak, thinking your sister outside for a breath of air or perhaps trying on another gown."

Milli frowned. "You think he will hurt Lizzie?"

Stephen did not answer. He strode toward the small dressing room hidden behind the shelves of material. The memories of Fennington manhandling his sister in another shop invaded his mind. He felt his control slipping. The thought of that maniac's hands on Elizabeth sent his blood pumping.

But the sudden notion that Milli was hamming him about the entire scene like some Greek tragedy did cross his mind. Instead of flinging the dressing room door open like a madman, he knocked. "Elizabeth?"

When no one answered, formality gave way to instinct and he swung open the door. His gaze fell upon Elizabeth's white face. Fennington was directly behind her, that monstrous quizzing glass hanging between two white fingers.

Stephen had two disturbing questions bouncing about in his brain. One, was Elizabeth running away with this man? And two, was she afraid of him catching her with her lover? He tried to banish the incriminating thoughts from his mind as he glared at Fennington, whose face had turned the color of curdled milk.

Yet the man had the audacity to raise that stupid quizzing

glass and stare through it as if he were at a dinner party. "Alas, my lord, we meet again."

Stephen strode forward, touching the lady's shocked features with the ends of his fingers. "Elizabeth?"

Wary blue eyes locked with his. "Do not hurt him," she whispered hesitantly. "I beg you."

She must have seen the danger flashing in his eyes for he dropped her chin, his hands growing stiff at his sides. So she cared for the man, did she? "Get in the carriage, Elizabeth."

She frowned and looked back at Mr. Fennington, regret shimmering her eyes. She blinked, drawing her chin upward. "I am not leaving you two alone."

Heaven help him! She was worse than Milli. "Get in the carriage." Stephen ground out the words, barely checking himself from throwing her over his shoulder and taking her there himself.

She opened her mouth to reply, but he roughly drew her toward him and kissed her instead. It was a kiss of danger and intrigue. A kiss that said she was his, and not Fennington's. A kiss that left her breathless, weakening her defenses. As she grew slack in his arms, he directed her toward the door.

She was his, and he was not about to let her go. She would love him if it took an entire lifetime.

"How romantic," Fennington said, pushing himself off the wall as Elizabeth exited the room. "Too bad she prefers me instead."

That was the last thing the man said before Stephen drilled his fist into Fennington's face.

Two weeks later, Elizabeth sat in her room readying herself for her engagement ball. She frowned as she stared into the looking glass. Since the incident at the dressmaker's, she had avoided Lord Stephen at all costs. To him, his kiss had branded her like a prized horse.

That's all she was to him, a prize that had been won. A sack of money that sealed his future. Yet she had to admit, for a few maddening seconds she had felt wanted, cherished, even loved.

But she was a fool to think of love because Lord Stephen had avoided her too, giving her only a polite hello and good-bye at meal times and barely engaging in conversation even when prompted. He left for the club every evening and returned home after she retired.

The entire family felt the tension, but their futile attempts at bringing the couple together had made things far worse instead of better.

A few days earlier, William Shelby had been called out of town on business. He would not be at the ball to stand up with her.

Elizabeth felt so alone and abandoned. What would her future hold here? How could she attend the engagement ball? How could she not? Mr. Fennington was obviously no longer part of her plan. And although her mind had been working furiously to find a way out of her predicament, it was to no avail.

"He will sweep you off your feet and into the gardens, Lizzie."

Milli had not stopped her tirade of romantic dreams since she entered five minutes ago. It was the last thing Elizabeth needed right now, because whether she wanted it or not, she was falling in love with Lord Stephen Clearbrook.

Fennington meant nothing to her now. He was a weasel, just as Lord Stephen had informed her. However, she would never tell the handsome lord that he had been correct in his assessment of her former suitor. Her pride was already at a low point. Besides, had she not already decided the kiss at the dressmaker's shop was one of ownership, not love?

"And then he will kiss you, Lizzie, and you will melt into his arms and run off together into the moonlight."

Elizabeth rolled her eyes at her sister's swoon. Milli pulled a strand of hair from her forehead as she drew in an audible sigh.

There was a knock on the door and Milli jumped off the bed.

"Do you mind if I come in?" Lady Emily peeked into the room, looking radiant in a lavender gown.

"Not at all," Elizabeth said, guiding the woman to the

chair near the hearth. "But if you wanted to see me, I could have come to you. You should rest as much as you can."

Lady Emily smiled. "It has been three weeks since I gave birth. Besides, I had to get away from my husband for a few minutes, at least. Can you believe he thinks I'm as fragile as a china teapot? But in truth, I believe he misses his little girl. Gabrielle, his daughter from his previous marriage, is staying with his aunt in the country. He was to fetch her last week, but the poor thing had the sniffles." The lady glanced into the fire and sighed. "I do miss her, too, but with the new babe being so small, we must take every precaution."

Elizabeth sensed the lady wanted to tell her more. She looked up at Milli, tilting a glance toward the door. "Millicent, do you not have something to do?"

Milli frowned. "Oh very well, I'll leave you two to talk about men, but I will return, never fear."

Both ladies laughed as Milli withdrew from the room.

Emily held out her hands toward Elizabeth. "I know I have said this a hundred times, but my dear Elizabeth, I can never thank you enough for what you did for me that night."

Elizabeth blushed, feeling the warmth of Emily's grip. "I was only doing what anyone would do in that situation. The doctor came and all was well."

The lady shook her head. "Oh, you silly girl. That is not true. You were marvelously calm throughout everything. However, that is beside the point. I am here on a mission." She dropped Elizabeth's hands and bade her to pull up a chair beside her. "I am here to help you capture my brother's eye and his heart."

Elizabeth stared back, too shocked to speak.

"I know it is a marriage of convenience you are to enter into, but I can see my brother is bordering on, well, let's just say, something else?"

Elizabeth's eyes widened. "Something else?" Was there a slim possibility the lady was speaking of love?

"You are a smart woman, Elizabeth, but the Clearbrook men are as stubborn as old hens. Still, a woman in love might be able to bait one of them to come out of their nest of safety, if you know what I mean."

Elizabeth managed a smile. "You are too optimistic. Your brother does not love me. He only wants my father's money."

Emily's gaze did not waver. "You are wrong about the money. Not Stephen. He could have gone to my brothers for a loan. No. Marrying you involved something much more complicated. But that is neither here nor there. I have called the maid to fetch the scissors. You will have to let me get to work."

Elizabeth backed up. "Now, Emily, let's not be so hasty."

Emily laughed. "Hasty? Goodness, Elizabeth, it is not as if I wish to cut off your head. Only a snip here and there and you will look like an angel. Mama has a taste for clothes, but when it comes to hair, she doesn't know a thing. That French sweep on your head does not do you justice. We need to shape your locks about your face, accentuate your eyes." She paused and smiled. "When I'm done, Stephen will fall all over you like a lion who hasn't eaten for a month."

A few minutes later Elizabeth reluctantly took a seat and let Lady Emily go to work. By the time the lady was finished, Elizabeth had a head of springy brown curls that framed her face, making her look quite the thing. Blond streaks added depth to her new locks, a natural highlighting that had been hidden.

After the maid left with the scissors and iron, Emily smiled, quite pleased with herself. "Well, what do you think?"

Elizabeth touched her hair, not able to believe the change in her appearance. Her hair had been too heavy to curl before. But now the difference was unbelievable. She looked—well, pretty. "You think your brother likes me a little?" she asked meekly, lifting her eyes in the mirror to lock with Emily's.

Emily leaned forward. "Of course he does. And after tonight, who knows what he will do."

The muscles of Elizabeth's throat tightened. Did she want Stephen to love her? Would she follow through with this sham of a marriage?

She looked back at her reflection. The haircut accentuated her eyes, along with the silver blue of her gown. A small part of her wanted Stephen to notice her tonight—truly notice her.

"There is one thing you must do tonight," Emily announced.

"What?" she asked, trying to hide her emotions.

"You must dance with all my brothers at least twice and above all, avoid dancing with Stephen if you can, except, that is, for your opening dance. I have spoken to Marcus, Clayton, and Roderick. They are quite in agreement with me."

Emily's eyes twinkled. "Of course, Stephen has no idea we have this all planned to the letter. And besides my brothers, you must flirt with the most eligible rakes that my horrid siblings will provide for you."

Elizabeth could not hold back her laugh. "You are a wicked sister. Your brother will think me a terrible flirt."

"No, he will think you the most beautiful woman in the room, and he will eventually come to your aid, whisking you into the gardens for a kiss."

"But it seems so dishonest. I cannot do such a thing."

"Oh yes, you can. Do you want him to fall madly in love with you or not?"

Elizabeth's heart skipped. "Yes, yes, I do. I believe I'm starting to fall in love with the fiend myself."

Emily laughed. "Very well, then. Let's get to work."

"Who the devil is that dancing with her now?"

Stephen paced the back of the ballroom, keeping his fiancée in sight at all times. She had taken his breath away when he had seen her descending the stairs, looking like a princess with her soft golden-brown curls framing those deep blue eyes. He wanted to comb his hands through her locks and sweep her into his arms.

And when he had dropped his gaze to the low cut of her silver-blue gown, which displayed her feminine curves, he had gulped back an audible groan.

Her snow white skin looked soft and delicate. But it was

those eyes. Their innocence had reeled him in. They were quite the loveliest pair of eyes he had ever seen.

The duke raised a black brow and leaned against the wall. "Don't you recognize your own brother Marcus?"

Stephen stopped, barely able to see the couple across the ballroom, the lighting from the crystal chandeliers was so dim. "This is their second dance together and a waltz at that. What is the man thinking?"

Roderick cleared his throat and smiled.

"And what is so funny?" Stephen asked. "I seemed to recall you being a bit addlebrained when Jane had you running around in circles. If I recall correctly, you claimed you didn't love her."

"That was long ago." The duke's voice was dangerously low. "If you dare remind her, I will hang you by your toes."

Stephen felt a bit of satisfaction at his brother's reaction. At least Roderick wasn't smiling anymore. Stephen certainly wasn't. This was the first time a woman had turned his life completely upside down.

Oh, it was more than the idiotic wager that made him feel stupid, it was Elizabeth Shelby herself.

She was different from the usual ladies he favored. He found himself intrigued, and yes, maybe a little bit in love. The thought unnerved him, since it was obvious the female loathed him. Besides, she still seemed to have a liking for that weasel Fennington.

"I believe I will have a go at your beautiful fiancée."

Stephen had no time to answer before the duke pushed himself off the wall and moved across the floor, claiming Elizabeth for the next dance. Following that set, Clayton took the blue-eyed siren in his arms. Stephen also noted, with a spurt of jealousy, that his brother looked to be acting all too familiarly with her. It wasn't hard in the dim light to see that Elizabeth was laughing at something he said. Her face positively glowed.

Stephen raised himself on his toes. Thunderation! What the deuce was going on here? Clayton seemed to be lowering his lips to her neck. He had best be whispering. The music stopped and Stephen started toward Elizabeth. He should have kept her shackled to his side all night. And why was Clayton introducing her to Lord Pool? The man was a first class rake!

"Ah, there you are, Stephen. I was just saying to Lady Roberts how lucky you were to find such a level-headed beauty."

Stephen halted. It was all he could do not to shake his mother off his arm. He watched in alarmed silence as Pool escorted Elizabeth to the refreshment table.

Stephen's animosity toward the man rose to an extreme when he saw Pool's gaze sink from Elizabeth's face to other delectable portions of her anatomy. He would kill the man!

"Do you not think it would be wonderful, my dear?"

Stephen was pulled away from his thoughts at the sound of his mother's question. Obviously, he had missed something here.

He could only smile at the ladies who surrounded him. "Delightful," he replied woodenly, peering across the dance floor to where Pool had led Elizabeth once again.

"Splendid! I told Mr. Shelby you would have no problem with it, considering that he said you already had the special license. Next week is a perfect time for a wedding."

Stephen's head spun back to the conversation. "Wedding?"

The ladies laughed as if Stephen were teasing them. But his mother knew better. The lady pulled him aside. "You just agreed to be wed next week. I had no idea you were not listening, but there is no way to run from it now. The information will spread in minutes." She sighed, her gaze flipping across the floor to Elizabeth. "I daresay you two lovebirds cannot wait to be wed."

Stephen stood dumbfounded. *Married next week?*

His gaze was glued to Elizabeth as he marched across the room, determined to hold onto his fiancée until the night ended. He had only danced with her once.

Something inside him turned warm at the thought of holding her, kissing her lips, pressing her soft body to his.

Perhaps next week was not too soon after all.

Chapter Eleven

*L*ord Stephen was incensed.

Elizabeth could see it in those sable brown eyes as he drew nearer to her. His gait across the dance floor was determined, like that of a man in battle, skilled and powerful, yet intelligent and quick. At that moment she knew that indeed this was a man who could easily have saved Wellington's life.

The daunting notion sent a slight shiver through her.

Good gracious. She had unleashed a veritable tiger.

Evidently, the man's sister had known exactly what she had been doing, but now Elizabeth was not quite so sure she should have complied with the lady's wishes. Guilt played havoc with her stomach. What on earth had she done?

Swallowing, she turned to Lord Clayton standing beside her.

"Not to worry, my dear. He is as gentle as a lamb."

Elizabeth brought a shaky hand to her bosom. "But he seems, um . . . rather determined. Perhaps after our first dance, I should have paid more attention to him."

She grabbed Clayton's arm. "Oh, my lord, do take me outside before he comes."

Clayton took pity on her, ushering her aside.

"Listen to me," he said as they walked beyond the French windows onto the terrace, "you cannot have a man's heart if you keep brushing him aside. I know my brother, and he will come around. But you must be strong."

"I am strong. But he does not love me. I cannot change that fact." And it hurts too much to bear.

Clayton laughed, tucking a wayward curl behind her ear. "You are such an innocent."

Elizabeth looked up into his eyes and smiled. He was like a brother to her, the brother she never had. "It is so embarrassing to love a man when he does not return that love."

"What? He adores you. And against my better judgment, I would advise you to maneuver him into the gardens before the night is out."

Her brows lifted and she cleared her throat. "Do you truly think that a viable option?"

"Think what a viable option?"

Stephen stepped through the doors, gently taking hold of Elizabeth's arm, shooting his brother an icy glare.

Clayton's smiling eyes fell on Elizabeth's face. "I was speaking of the gardens, little brother."

Elizabeth felt the grip on her arm tighten.

Music drifted in the background, but all she heard was the thumping of her heart. Was Stephen jealous?

"The gardens?" Stephen said, his voice holding a note of warning. "No one will be taking Elizabeth into the gardens unless it is me. Is that understood, *brother*?"

Clayton gave them both a formal bow. "Understood all too clearly, *brother*." And with those final words, Clayton retreated into the ballroom, stopping to pull Milli from behind the curtains. "You little minx. Marcus told me about you."

Elizabeth would have laughed as she watched Milli's face turn white the moment Clayton gave away her hiding place, but her own face paled as she turned to the man beside her. Her heart beat faster as she felt the tension between them grow.

"Your lordship, perhaps a bit of punch—"

Stephen tipped her chin, making her look at him. His eyes impaled hers. "I believe our Christian names are in order since we will be married within the week."

Elizabeth blinked. "Within the week?"

"We are to be wed next week. I have the special license."

Her tongue grew thick, her mind spinning. "A special license?"

His finger trailed a path along her neck, and she thought he would hear her heart pounding outside her chest. What was he doing to her? She was falling under his spell, and she knew if she let this continue, she was doomed. She glanced over his shoulder, hoping for a sign of one of his brothers.

"Ah, searching for a knight in all his chain mail to rescue you, my dear?" He whispered the words along her neck as he tugged her deeper into the gardens.

She dug her heels into the graveled path, knowing that if she moved any further beyond the ballroom, there was no turning back. "I, uh, have a bit of a chill. Perhaps we should turn back and you could fetch my shawl for me."

The man had the audacity to laugh.

"What?" she asked sharply. "Is there a problem with a woman being chilled?"

"Chilled or scared?"

Elizabeth took a step back. His intense gaze seemed to be peering into her soul, searching for her dreams, searching every nook and cranny where her most private thoughts were hidden. It was unnerving. She glanced around her.

Rosebushes, trees, and the dark.

No, she did not want to walk any further into the gardens with this man. Her heart could stand only so much pain.

Before she had a chance to run, he took hold of her hands. "Elizabeth, don't be frightened."

"I . . . don't fear you, my lord."

"Stephen," he said, his tone a caressing command.

"Stephen," she said softly. How many times had she repeated his name in her head? A hundred? A thousand?

He pulled her closer, his breath soft and sweet against her face. "Tell me, how did a beautiful woman such as you slip away from rakes like me and never get caught . . . until now?"

His hand swept up to touch her cheek. The strain between them began to fall away like the leaves of autumn, making her vulnerable to his charms. She swayed against him, knowing he had already wormed his way into her heart.

"Elizabeth." His lips brushed hers in a tender kiss.

When he gently pulled away, she was unable to explain

the feelings whirling through her mind. No man had ever kissed her so lovingly, including Mr. Fennington.

She loved this man. It was more than the kiss. It was something he had touched in her soul. Oh, yes, his charms had doomed any resistance she had ever tried to exert, and being a war hero only enhanced his appeal. But it was when she had seen him holding that baby she knew her fate was sealed.

Stephen stared down at the woman in his arms. What was she thinking? Did she love him? Or did she still love Fennington? Would he have a marriage like his parents'?

He had no wish to play games with this innocent. He had to know if there was a chance of having some kind of happiness in their future. He had to know her feelings toward him.

"Elizabeth, do you think you could ever find it in your heart to love me?"

He was pleased when she smiled at him, her teeth glimmering against the glow of the moon. "Love you?"

He noted a slight chip on one of her bottom teeth. So the lady was not so perfect after all. He lifted her hands to his lips, kissing them. "Am I so hard to love?"

Her bottom lip trembled as she spoke, "I think I'm falling in love with you . . . Stephen." Her whispered words were husky and low, like smoke twirling in the night.

His chest tightened when his glance slid to the creamy skin of her neck. Who would have believed his night of gambling would come to this? This wonderful woman was kind, intelligent, and most of all, she loved him. What more could he ask?

"You are beautiful, Elizabeth."

Tears sprang to her eyes, and he took that moment to kiss her again. The taste of her, the smell of her, the touch of her was his undoing. They fit together so perfectly, he thought he was dreaming. Her lips were as soft as the rose petals in spring. Salty tears of happiness rolled down her cheeks. His heart leapt as he pulled her into his arms, drawing her further into the garden.

Elizabeth felt alive for the first time in years. Stephen's

tender concern for her was another point in his favor. And this was the man she was to marry.

Marry. The word whirled through her mind, curling around her heart like a whisper of heaven.

Resting her head against his shoulder, she closed her eyes, letting him slide her onto his lap as he took a seat on a bench in a far corner of the garden.

"Elizabeth, sweetheart."

She opened her eyes and lifted her head.

Every muscle in her body stiffened.

For there, behind a large oak, stood Mr. Fennington, his frown carved into his face like the knots of the ancient tree that shadowed him.

Stephen's hands froze on Elizabeth's stiff form. Guilt flooded him. What had he done?

"Forgive me."

He placed her beside him, his breathing labored. "My instincts ran away with me, Elizabeth. I beg your pardon."

From what he could see from the moonlight, her face was as white as his cravat. He felt like the worst rake in London.

"Elizabeth, say something. Please."

Her hand was clammy, and she seemed frightened out of her wits. He had pushed her too far. She was not a lady of the night or some lonely widow. She was an innocent, and dash it all, she was to be his wife. He had moved too quickly.

Wide blue eyes stared up at him as she pulled her hands from his grip. "You have no need to ask my forgiveness, my lord," she said all too coolly.

My lord, he thought with a grimace.

"I . . . that is, we must return to the ball." She blinked rapidly, wringing her hands on her lap.

"You are fine then? You do not hate me?"

She gave a hesitant laugh and stood, stepping into the full light of the moon. "We must go back."

He nodded, knowing he would have to control himself until the wedding. "I promise you, you will have no need to fear me."

If she could have turned whiter than before, she did. Stephen felt as if someone had kicked him in the stomach.

Cursing himself for his hasty actions, he took her arm, sensing her uneasiness. "Let us return and see what fools my brothers have made of themselves."

Her laugh was forced, and he wondered if he had ruined everything. He would keep his distance from her, giving her room to breathe. He realized, with an intensity he couldn't explain, that he wanted this woman for his wife, for his lover, for the mother of his children. He wanted her, and by heaven, nothing was going to stop him from having her. Not even himself.

Minutes later, Elizabeth stood in the ballroom, speaking to Stephen's mother. But her fear Mr. Fennington would somehow make an unannounced appearance was like a noose about her neck. The very sight of the man in the gardens made her throat constrict until she felt faint.

The crowd had pushed in around her, the gentlemen asking for a dance, the dowagers wanting to know where she had bought her gown. But to her surprise, none of Stephen's brothers had come to her rescue, not even Stephen.

Her fiancé had left her like a cold fish after he had kissed her. He must have been having second thoughts about their marriage. She was not a good kisser, she knew that. She hadn't the experience. Yet if was there was any chance at all that he might love her, she had to rid herself of Mr. Fennington.

She thought she had made it perfectly clear that she was not interested in the man. She had no idea what had happened between Stephen and him at the dressmaker's that day, but upon her exit, she had thought she heard a groan of pain.

Yet, when Stephen had hopped in the carriage, he seemed not the least bit breathless, and his ensemble was in perfect condition. However, the hardness in his eyes alone had betrayed his emotions. He had been angry. And rightly so.

Somehow she would have to make Mr. Fennington see that she meant what she said. Knowing the fool, he probably thought she would slip from the ball to see him, and drat the man, she would have to do just that to set him straight.

Within minutes she had made her way past the French windows and returned to the gardens. The music slowly dropped to a low murmur while a cool breeze fingered through the trees. She knew Mr. Fennington would eventually find her. But as it was now, she could not have the odious man intruding into her life anymore.

She was about to give up her search when a cold hand clamped over her mouth, and she was dragged behind the bushes. She fought against the body that held her.

"Miss Shelby, Elizabeth, it's me."

Her mouth thinned in anger when Mr. Fennington released her and she spun around. "Why did you do that? I am perfectly capable of speaking to you without being accosted."

"I received your letter to come and fetch you."

Elizabeth stilled. *The letter?* He had received the letter she had posted before the shopping excursion. How long ago was that? "Well, it does not signify. I've changed my mind. In fact, I already gave you a piece of my mind at the dressmaker's."

He grabbed hold of her shoulders. "You cannot change your mind."

"Let me go. You're hurting me."

Reluctantly, he stepped back. "Beg your pardon. It's just that I love you so much, I can never think of letting you go."

Maybe she had misjudged him. "Mr. Fennington, I don't want to hurt you, but you must see that what we had was a silly infatuation and nothing more. It is entirely my fault for leading you to believe I would marry you, and I pray you will forgive me, but I can see that we would no longer suit."

"Forgive you," he hissed. "Why? Because you have fallen in love with a lord like your father wanted you to." A low rumble of laughter released from his chest. "Oh, this is too much."

A wave of uneasiness coursed through her. "This is my engagement ball," she uttered, afraid now that people might hear them. "I cannot be away any longer. Someone will miss me."

His sudden hold on her arm startled her. "You think that handsome lord loves you? What kind of innocent are you?"

Elizabeth tried to wiggle out of his grip but found herself being dragged further into the bushes.

"Mr. Fennington. I have tried to be nice to you, but it seems clear to me that you do not understand the word 'no.'"

"I heard and saw everything, *Miss Shelby.* The words of your undying love. The way he kissed you, as if you were the only woman he loved. But the fact of the matter is, he never told you he loved you. His latest flirt is that new opera singer. It's not as if his brothers don't know it. How can you be so naive? His kisses were nothing more than a ploy to marry you without a fight."

"I—I don't believe you." But her heart began to slowly crack. Stephen had never declared his love for her. And she, fool that she was, had declared her love for him like some silly child.

"Tell me, whose kiss did you like best, Lord Stephen Clearbrook's or mine?"

Elizabeth stared back in alarm at Fennington's twisted smile. "I need to return to the ballroom. Now if you will please unhand me, sir."

Before she could finish, he pushed his lips onto hers. "You will never be free of me, Elizabeth Shelby. How do you think your lord will feel when he discovers you have been meeting with your long lost lover?"

The crunch of gravel sounded behind her, followed by a low, familiar voice. "I would think the man would not be favorable to the idea, would you, *Miss Shelby*?"

Elizabeth spun around and gasped in horror as Stephen's towering silhouette appeared before them. He took another step into the moonlight and the tautness of his face was quite clear. Disgust glimmered in his eyes as he tilted his head toward the ballroom. "Return to your engagement ball, Miss Shelby."

"It . . . well, this is not what it seems."

His black brows narrowed. "To the ballroom, Miss Shelby. Or need I carry you back?"

She clenched her teeth, trying to stem the flow of tears.

Avoiding the gazes of both men, she walked back toward the music, her eyes barely able to see where she was going.

A few seconds after Elizabeth slipped into the ballroom, she was stopped by Lady Bringston. "Elizabeth, dear, have you been introduced to the Duke of Wellington?"

Elizabeth looked up, startled to see the war hero standing beside her. "Forgive me, Your Grace. I have been busy with the other guests."

She blushed as the man took his hand in hers. "Miss Shelby, delighted to meet you. And there is nothing to forgive. My congratulations on your upcoming marriage." He gave her a wink and leaned forward. "Hope you won't forbid your gentleman to play cards with me now and then? Not like some of those wives I hear about?"

Forbid Stephen to play cards? She could never forbid Stephen anything. The idea was ludicrous. Almost as ludicrous as a knight in shining armor coming to her rescue. Besides, she would never be his wife, so what did it matter?

She laughed, displaying a merriment she did not feel.

But inside, she was numb to the world. Hot tears bubbled up her throat.

She had made such a fool of herself. She hoped Stephen did not hate her. Perhaps she could explain. But would he believe her? Could she ever win back his trust?

"You will regret this," Fennington said, reeling back and holding his nose.

Stephen was almost enjoying himself. If it were not for the sight of Fennington kissing his intended, a facer to Fennington's idiotic quizzing glass and what was behind it would have made his day. "You dare come within twenty feet of Miss Shelby and I will hang you by your nails. Do you understand me?"

Fennington wiped his bloody nose with his sleeve. "She loves me, you know. How do you intend to stop that? Beat the girl?"

Did Elizabeth still pine over this idiotic fool? "Are you waiting for another blow to your head, Fennington? Or will you be on your way?"

Fennington ground his teeth and picked up his quizzing glass. "You think yourself better than I, do you? You think you deserve Shelby's money more than me?"

He gave a muffled laugh. "Why, you are just like the rest of us. Ain't no difference. Money is money. No two ways about it. You sold your soul. But she won't love you, just remember that. Those were my lips she tasted last, not yours."

"One more word and I will kill you." Stephen's voice was dangerously low. "You are lucky to get off with your nose still attached. But never fear, this is not finished."

Fennington opened his mouth, then shut it. Stephen didn't wait. Anger took hold where his patience left off. He took the man by his pants and flung him across a pair of thorny rosebushes. Fennington rolled off them, groaning as he scrambled onto his hands and knees, hastening toward the exit in the back.

Stephen watched in silence as the man climbed over the wall and disappeared into the night.

Sold his soul. The words echoed in the hollow crevices of Stephen's entire being. When he had seen Elizabeth in Fennington's arms, he had been ready to kill the man.

Had she been lying to him all along?

He stalked back to the ballroom, intending to seek her out and finish this once and for all. He gave a start when he saw Wellington as her dance partner.

"Your eyes are about to fall out of their sockets, little brother," Roderick said, strolling in from the gardens.

Stephen scowled. "I suppose you heard everything?"

Roderick's smile never reached his eyes. "I say we haul the man off to America. Send him as an indentured servant or something to that effect."

"It sounds as if you hate Fennington more than I do. But America won't do. It will have to be Australia."

Roderick glanced across the dance floor. "He almost took away our sister, and now he's after your bride. Could I dislike the man more than I do?"

Stephen's eyes glittered from beneath the crystal chandeliers as he watched Wellington take the honor of escorting Elizabeth into the supper room. Thunderation, he could not very well push the war hero aside. "No, but I aim to have him pressed into service with His Majesty's Navy." He turned a grim countenance toward his brother as they made toward the exit to supper. "What say you to that?"

Roderick raised a calculating brow. "Done."

Stephen was about to enter into the specifics when he detected Lady Odette coming his way. "Who the devil invited her?"

Roderick looked up and frowned. "Mother, I suppose."

"Hell's teeth. You escort her into supper then. I cannot very well do it at my engagement ball. But drat it all, Wellington has Elizabeth on his arm, engagement or not."

Roderick shook his head. "This is your problem, not mine. Besides, I see my sweet duchess trying to attract my attention. Duty calls. Must go."

"Coward."

Roderick smiled over his shoulder. "Been called worse, you know." He smiled. "By my darling wife, no less. It would not do to make her wait. No telling what she will call me then."

"I'll call you something before the night is out," Stephen said between his teeth a second before Lady Odette and her father approached.

Elizabeth watched over the rim of her wineglass as her fiancé spoke with Lady Odette—at their engagement supper, no less! Obviously the lady had fully recovered from her cherry incident. At that moment Elizabeth wished she had a bowl full of cherries to push down the lady's throat. The thought instantly horrified her. What was happening to her?

"He's as angry as Napoleon when the man lost the war."

Elizabeth glanced up to find Lord Marcus hovering over her, his eyes alight with mischief as he spoke about his brother.

Wellington had excused himself to take part in a conversation about the Peninsular Wars with some of the eager gentlemen who had served beneath him but had never made his acquaintance. Elizabeth had been honored when England's hero had taken her to supper. Yet she had seen the teasing sparkle in his eyes. The man seemed to be waiting for her fiancée's next move, and he laughed when he saw Stephen stiffen. Wellington thought the reaction jealousy. Elizabeth knew otherwise.

"Anger is not what I would wish for in a future husband," she said to Marcus.

Stephen's brother shrugged, picking up a plate of peas and ham. "He is to be married. That would anger any man if he did not want it."

"I see," she said tightly.

"Do you?" Marcus peered over his shoulder and smiled. "Don't be too hard on him. He believes in love from both sides. He saw what happened in my parents' marriage. My father gave my mother every convenience. The only thing lacking was love."

"Your parents entered into a marriage of convenience?"

"In a way." He glanced affectionately toward his mother. "My mother loved my father, but the love was never returned. You see, he had always loved another."

Elizabeth frowned. And she had loved Mr. Fennington, or thought she had. That had been her biggest mistake. And now Stephen thought she still loved the fool.

Marcus set his plate down and took Elizabeth's free hand in his. "You must be patient. He will come around."

Her heart stumbled. Come around to what? Love? Trust? She slipped her hand from Marcus's gentle grip, angry at herself for thinking such things, and doubly angry at herself for falling in love with his handsome brother.

"You must forgive me, but I have a horrid headache. I will return as soon as possible."

Before Marcus could speak, she hastened from his side in search of the exit, knowing very well she could not leave for the entire night. She spent a half hour in her chambers, wishing she could start the evening over.

After returning to the ballroom, she managed to keep a smile on her face as she made the acquaintance of many of the guests, avoiding Stephen and his cool assessing gaze. No one seemed to notice the tension between the engaged couple, no one except the Clearbrook brothers, who were eyeing Stephen with contempt.

She finally made it to her bedchamber two hours later without speaking to Stephen again and fought back the tears. Could she ever convince Stephen they could escape his parents' fate? Probably not. Could he ever love her after the last incident with Fennington? She didn't know.

Her life was spinning out of control, and if her father did not come back soon, she was going to go mad.

She would speak to her papa. Tell him how miserable the situation was. He loved her. He had always wanted the best for her. This wedding could not take place as things stood now. It could not.

Chapter Twelve

"*I*mpossible! You will marry Lord Stephen Clearbrook and that is final!" William Shelby wiped a crumpled handkerchief across his forehead and lowered his voice. "Lizzie, don't be stubborn. The arrangements have been made."

Elizabeth took an agitated turn about her father's spacious bedchamber. Her life was shattering into a million pieces and he was doing nothing about it.

William Shelby had returned from Portsmouth the day after the engagement ball. It was nigh onto impossible to change his mind, but it was her life that was hanging in the balance . . . and her broken heart.

"But, Papa, I do not love him."

She wondered if she truly knew what love was. She had not loved Mr. Fennington and thought she had. And Stephen believed she still did.

"Fustian, child. Love will come in time."

"But he loves another!" There. It was out. Lord Stephen Clearbrook loved Lady Odette.

"Posh! Don't believe it. Anyway, if you do not love him, then why care if he loves another?"

She wanted to stamp her foot. "But I want to marry for love. You of all people should know about love, Papa. You loved Mama."

He slowly shook his head and turned away.

Elizabeth went to him, resting a hand on his shoulder. "Oh, Papa. I don't know what came over me. I did not mean to bring Mother into our conversation. Please forgive me."

He gently took her hand and guided her toward a green-striped wing chair. "Sit down, Lizzie. It's time you heard this from my lips before you hear it from another."

Elizabeth regarded his pale face with a hint of alarm. "What? What is it?"

"Now, poppet, I don't know how to say this without hurting you, but you must not think less of your mother," he pulled nervously at his neckcloth, "or, I hope, of me."

Anxiety spurted through her veins. "What?"

He sat down opposite her, his hands hanging between his knees, the handkerchief pulled taut. "It's like this, Lizzie . . ."

He avoided her gaze, staring absently across the room, wetting his lips. "When I was married to your mother, I had a friend on the other side of town."

"A friend?" After a tense pause, she rose swiftly from her seat, knowing what was coming next. No, her father loved her mother! He did! This was not possible!

"Enough, Papa. I do not want to hear this."

"Sit down, child. This is as hard on me as it is on you."

She raised a fist to her mouth. "Mother is dead. Let me have my memory of her without you disgracing it."

"Her name was Philomena."

No, her heart cried. It wasn't true.

"Philomena? What kind of name is that?" she replied in a mocking tone.

"Philomena was your mother, Lizzie."

Elizabeth felt as if the earth had shaken violently beneath her feet and she was falling where there was no bottom.

"Wh-what are you saying?"

"Your real mother died giving birth to you. I brought the babe to Sarah after you were born. Sarah loved you like her very own. Sarah's name is even on the papers as your mother."

But Sarah was her mother! That was the only mother she had ever known. Not Philomena! No! Eyes blurry with tears, Elizabeth backed up, tripping over her feet.

"Lizzie, please."

She gave a haunting laugh. "And you want me to marry some stranger? How do I know *you* are my real father?"

William Shelby seemed stricken and it was a moment before he could speak. "I will not answer that, Lizzie. But you will marry Lord Stephen Clearbrook. I promised your mother I would take care of you. I am doing this for you. Your best interest is what I am concerned with here. I ain't going to see you marry some wastrel."

Elizabeth clasped her hands tightly together. "Oh, this is grand. You would marry me off to some man who wants nothing but my money, and in return, your soul is saved. How wonderful for you. Your good deed is done."

"Lizzie, that ain't how it is at all. You don't understand."

"Don't I? I believe I do, *Father*. You never loved me. You loved only a dream of a woman that died years ago."

He took a step toward her. "None of what you say is true. I wanted you to marry a lord because Philomena begged me to marry you well. I chose Lord Stephen Clearbrook because he is one of the very best men in England, and I wanted the best for you, poppet. Don't you see?"

She put up her hand to ward him off. "Milli?"

"Milli is Sarah's daughter."

Elizabeth's heart felt ripped from her chest. "I see." No wonder Milli looked so different.

Silent tears streamed down Elizabeth's cheeks, and before William Shelby could say another word, she bolted from the room and ran down the hall, slamming directly into a solid chest of muscle.

"Elizabeth." Stephen's voice startled her as much as her collision. "What's happened?" He grabbed hold of her shoulder, his face softening with concern.

"Nothing." She gazed over his shoulder. He didn't love her either. Why should she care? "I forgot to tell you, I'm leaving as soon as it is feasible to find other accommodations."

His hands dropped to his sides, his stance rigid. "Fennington has left and should not be seen again. So douse those flames of desire, my dear. You won't be going anywhere with him. We are still engaged."

Fury filled her. Fury at her father. Fury at Mr. Fennington. And fury at this man for not trusting her. She lifted her gaze, her eyes smoldering with contempt. "You are not my husband, my lord."

"No, but you still have obligations," he said stiffly. "You don't have much time. Get dressed. We are to attend Wellington's soiree tonight."

"*We* are not going anywhere, my lord."

"Yes, we are. You have exactly one hour."

"How dare you give me orders." She turned from him, heading toward the stairs to her room.

"Elizabeth?"

She didn't stop her progress.

"You will be ready."

His command vexed her to no end. If she packed fast enough and had Milli's help, she could be away from this place before her hour was up. But then again, maybe she could show him that she was immune to him and those spellbinding charms.

They had just left Wellington's soiree. Stephen watched the odd play of emotions on his fiancée's face as she turned her head toward the carriage window. She was not speaking to him now. In fact, she had spoken but ten words to him all night.

He had to admit he was amazed she was going to follow through with her plan to leave the duke's home because she felt she had overstayed her welcome. Ha! As if he believed that.

He was not about to declare himself and bare his soul, but he would die before he let her run away with Fennington, even if she thought she loved the idiotic man. Besides, he thought smugly, Fennington was probably at sea by now.

"Your father did not love your mother, did he?" she asked.

Elizabeth's words took Stephen by surprise. Something flashed in her eyes. Dread? Pain? Regret?

"No. Why do you ask?"

She shrugged and glanced back out the window. "My mother died when I was born."

The information startled him. He could smell the touch of sweet perfume she had dabbed along her neckline, and he tried to rein in his senses, controlling the urge to sweep her in his arms and kiss her. "I did not realize your father married twice."

Her back seemed to tense. "My father did not marry twice. He married only once and that was to Milli's mother, not mine."

The implication of her words hit Stephen like a splash of ice water.

She turned, as if daring him to comment: "Does that surprise you? I thought it would. It did surprise me this morning when my father finally decided to tell me. He told me that Sarah, the lady who raised me and is the mother on my papers . . ."—she gave a cold laugh—"well, it seems her father was a baronet. I am from some kind of peerage after all. But in truth, I am not. Imagine that."

Stephen said nothing as he watched her try to hide the pain. Dash it all. William Shelby was a fool twice over. To withhold the information from his daughter and then to trade her to any man without her consent was intolerable.

"You probably will think twice about the offer you made my father," she said softly, staring down at her hands. "The gossip would be unforgivable if anyone discovered the truth."

Stephen cared nothing about the gossip. What he did care for was the woman beside him. Was she telling him the truth or did she want him to call off the engagement? "You believe this information would sever our wedding plans?"

She let out a deep, shuddering sigh. "You must not wish this marriage now. Perhaps my father will settle upon you a prodigious sum for your troubles and we can part amicably."

He detected the noted strain in her voice as the clatter of horses' hooves pounded along the street. Did she love Fennington so much to play this hand with him?

A lonely teardrop slid down her face, and he raised a finger, wiping it from her cheek. "I would never hurt you."

She pressed her forehead against the glass, stifling a sob.

He drew her hand to his lips and lifted his gaze to meet hers.

She bit her bottom lip, and he thought it enchanting. She was so innocent, he wanted to be the one to teach her about love.

He ran a thumb over her velvety cheek, then buried his nose in her hair. He felt drugged by her nearness. She smelled of sweetness and everything wholesome.

He tipped her head back and kissed her.

"Stephen," she whispered as she wound her arms around his neck.

He saw the question in her eyes and his gaze bore into hers. "I don't care about your mother." He crushed her to him, flames of passion exploding between them.

When the carriage stopped, he realized they were at the townhouse, and he dragged himself from her arms. He laughed at the sight. Her hair was tousled, and his cravat was askew.

She pressed a hand to her mouth. "Oh, forgive me. I never meant . . . I only wanted . . . oh, how I must look."

He raised her hand to his lips. "You look beautiful, and I fail to see why you need to apologize."

Her eyes filled with tears and she looked away.

He frowned. "Perhaps it is I who should beg your pardon?"

She shook her head. "A marriage of convenience would break my heart. I want to marry for love. Please, I beg you. Don't do this to me. Ask my father to dissolve this engagement. It would be best for both of us. Your family would never approve once they discover my mother's secret."

Stephen's hope sank. So, she did not love him after all.

He said nothing as they entered the townhouse. The entire fiasco would be coming to an abrupt end, he thought grimly. This had gone far enough. Elizabeth deserved better than to marry a man she didn't love. He would seek out William Shelby, intending to settle the debts once and for all.

* * *

"You must woo the lady. What kind of man are you?"

Stephen glared at Roderick, sitting like some pompous king behind his library desk, lifting a snifter of brandy to his lips.

"Woo her? You must be mad. I am already engaged to her. Wooing her is past tense here."

Besides, he had already wooed the lady, had he not?

The snifter hit the desk with a splash. "Heaven protect me from addlepated idiots. If every man thought like you, the human race would have died out years ago. Have you no decency? The woman wants to be wooed. All ladies do. How do you think I talked Jane into marrying me?"

Stephen's face flashed with contempt. "Ah, yes, I see your point. Flowers and soothing words of love might have worked for you because Jane adored you, even though you were a conceited oaf."

"Let's not delve into my personal life, if you please. You are the one with the problem at the moment. I have already jumped my fences to secure my bride. Now it's your turn."

Stephen slapped his palms on the desk. "She hates me, Roderick. How can I woo a woman who hates me because she believes I want her father's money? This entire situation has put me in a bad light, and the truth of it is, I can see no way out of it without dishonoring her."

"Miss Shelby is a debt paid," Roderick said, the condescension in his voice clear, "not well done of you."

"Hell, Roderick! It was not my plan. Shelby threw his daughter at me, as if she were nothing but a piece of land to be bartered. I could not pay my debts at the table. Thank heaven it was me and not some nefarious scoundrel that received her."

Roderick paused. "She loves you, you know."

"I believed in that kind of love for about a minute, before she met up with Fennington again."

"You must be blind or stupid. Perhaps both. That girl is in love with you. However, even if she were not, if I were in your place, I would get on my knees and beg her to marry me. A man doesn't run into a lady like that more than once in a lifetime. And if he does, she is someone else's wife."

A faint smile touched Stephen's lips. "Like Jane?"

"Quite so."

"You can say that easily enough, but it is I who will enter into a marriage of convenience, not you."

"I already told you, she loves you."

"Then why would she ask to dissolve the engagement if she loves me?" He knew the situation with her mother had nothing to do with it.

Roderick threw up his hands in disgust. "She wants your devotion, love, all that silly stuff women like."

"How the deuce am I to do that?"

Roderick's gaze narrowed perceptively. "I have heard you are a charming fellow when you want to be."

"For the love of King George, I am no monk, Roderick. I have kissed her more than once. She is not immune to me, but that is not the same as love."

He took Roderick's drink and lifted it to his lips, downing the brandy, then slapping the glass back onto the desk. "She loves that idiot Fennington."

Roderick shot from his seat. "Fennington is over and done with! Take my word, it was Fennington who was chasing her, not the other way around. Just like the weasel did with Emily. Well, no matter. He should be flying the English flag on the Atlantic by now."

Stephen blinked. So, Roderick had followed through after all. Good riddance.

"Perhaps I am mistaken, Roderick, but she still does not want this marriage, and neither do I if she does not love me."

"Confound it, you must have a brain the size of a pea."

"I think you mean peabrain," Stephen said mockingly.

There was a knock on the door, and Roderick bade the butler to enter.

"Your Grace, I am here to inform you that Mr. Shelby and his daughters are leaving the premises."

"And when was this decision made?" Stephen's glacial tone sent the butler's brows shooting upward.

"I believe after Miss Shelby returned with you last evening, my lord. Is there anything else, Your Grace?"

"No, Crosby, that is all for now."

After the servant left, Stephen shifted a knowing gaze back to his brother. "And you believed her in love with me? You must think me a complete fool."

"You are one if you don't go after her."

Stephen recognized the commanding tilt of his brother's brow and would have smiled if the comment did not demand an action on his part.

"After her? You must be joking? If the lady cannot tell me her good-byes, then I will bid her farewell from here."

"Hell's teeth, your pride will be your downfall. You are a greater fool than Fennington."

"A greater fool, no. A fool, yes."

"I cannot see why we should have to leave today, Lizzie."

Barely acknowledging her father's words, Elizabeth stood on the walk outside the Elbourne townhouse and frowned as the footmen loaded her trunks. She had said her farewells to everyone but Stephen. He seemed to be deliberately avoiding her.

But it was better this way, she thought, letting out a trembling sigh. The note she left him was to be delivered after they departed.

"Aunt Polly is ill, Papa, and I need to tend to her."

Elizabeth lied. She would never admit that she had used her godmother as a last resort. The older lady was like a general, and once Aunt Polly had received word of the forced engagement, she demanded that Elizabeth come to her if she were ever in need of a safe haven.

Elizabeth blinked back tears as she watched the horses' breath swirl in the cold spring air. Safe haven from her heart would be all but impossible, but she would do anything to escape a marriage where her husband did not love her. Seeing Stephen and knowing he did not love her was too much to bear.

No doubt he was probably glad to rid himself of her, no matter what he had said. Her mother had never married her father. That was scandalous in the eyes of the *ton*.

William Shelby shook his head. "Polly and I never got

along, Lizzie. I don't suppose you would care to send along your medical bag, and we could stay here until you marry."

Elizabeth dared a glance at her father.

She was amazed she could get him to leave the duke's home so easily, when he would not release her from her engagement. Though she could never be completely forced into the marriage, the situation had already gone too far to back out unless the parties involved were agreeable to the terms, and she did not see that happening any time soon.

"We have outstayed our welcome, Papa. I have asked that the wedding be postponed." She had said more than that in the letter. "Besides, I cannot justify staying at the duke's home any longer than need be. Aunt Polly needs me."

Liar, she thought again. *She* needed her Aunt Polly.

"But I can rent a townhouse, poppet, if that's what's worrying you. Your Aunt Polly is not going to die. Probably a silly cold. I can send the best doctor to her side before the day is out and then we can stay at the best hotel in London."

Her father had been wounded by her coolness after he had disclosed the information about her mother, but she could not offer him any sympathy. He had hurt her deeply. With the forced engagement and now the disclosure of her sordid background, she was too hurt and embarrassed to face Stephen again, let alone let him kiss her. She had to distance herself and form some kind of plan. A plan that would involve her heart as little as possible.

"I have no qualms about his lordship coming to our home and wooing you before your wedding," her father went on. "I know you have not been comfortable here, but I thought it would be for the best. Seems I was wrong."

He spoke with such an ache in his voice she almost let him have his way. Yet she could not give in to his every whim. She needed time to think. And if she had to work on his sympathy, then so be it. It could very well lead to her freedom.

Milli grabbed her black kitten and looked up. "I would not have Cleopatra if we had not come here, Papa."

"I think one cat is enough, Milli. You will not bring that to Tavton Hall. Crabby old thing won't allow it."

Milli held her kitten tighter to her bosom. "Aunt Polly's going to allow Lizzie's cat that she picked up in the alley the other day; why not mine?"

"Lizzie's cat is staying in the stables. It was a stray that needed help, and it was never meant to be part of the family."

The cat they were speaking of had been found half-dead in an alley beside the lending library. Elizabeth had mended its cuts and bruises while keeping it in the Elbourne stables. It was doing fine now. She wished her heart were as easy to fix.

"Well, then, I will hide Cleo from Aunt Polly," Millie said. "I will keep her under my bed. Lady Bringston would be horrified if I returned the gift." The tiny kitten wiggled in her hand, and she smiled. "See, the poor thing thinks I'm its mother. Did you know that Lord Stephen named one of the kittens King Tutankhamen? Is that not the silliest thing?"

Elizabeth ignored Milli's comment as they stepped toward the carriage. A fierce wind swept down the walk. Elizabeth slapped a hand to her hat, trying to keep her turbulent emotions at bay. She didn't want to think about Stephen or his charms.

His tenderness with the kittens touched her. His patience with Milli's theatrics impressed her. But his love for his family captivated her. When she had seen him hold Lady Emily's baby in the crook of his arm, she could not deny her attraction to him.

The more time she spent with him, the more she loved him.

But if she stayed in this home any longer, seeing him at every meal, she would end up married to a man who did not love her and she could not have that. Oh, he would be kind to her. He would use that undeniable charm, but it would be all one gigantic lie because he did not love her. And to add to that, her father's money would always be between them.

"Elizabeth, I would like a word with you, please."

Stephen's voice hit Elizabeth's ears the exact moment she entered the carriage behind Milli and her father. She tightened her grip on her reticule and sank back onto the velvety seats across from her family, ignoring the harsh beating of her heart.

Stephen bent his head toward the door, his dark brown hair gleaming in the sunlight. He was too handsome for his own good.

For a second she thought she saw a flash of pain cross his chiseled features, but she realized she must have been mistaken. She was seeing a reflection of what was in her own heart.

"You are leaving to visit your sick aunt?" he asked dryly.

She nodded, her lips pinched. Was it his fault she had fallen in love with him? She clenched her jaw. Yes, yes it was.

It was as if the door were slamming on her heart as she met his challenging gaze and managed a brilliant smile. "Good-bye, my lord. I do hope you thought about what I said earlier."

His eyes darkened and his hand shot out, gripping her arm. "I have need to speak to you in private."

The heat of his touch scorched a path straight to her toes. "Whatever you have to say, you may say it here."

To her shock, he sent her father a knowing look.

William Shelby grabbed his youngest daughter's hand. "Do believe I forgot a few things in the library. Milli, come along."

Milli's mouth dropped in shock. "But Elizabeth has no wish to be with *him*. He—he might kiss her again."

Elizabeth could not be more embarrassed than she was now.

"Millicent." William Shelby had already departed the carriage, tugging at his youngest daughter's hand.

Wide-eyed, Milli descended the carriage, clutching a mewing Cleopatra to her chest and dragging her feet every step of the way, barely moving aside as Lord Stephen Clearbrook hopped up the steps, closing the door behind him.

Chapter Thirteen

*E*lizabeth's senses were buzzing. The carriage instantly smelled of bayberry and leather, a dangerous combination of cleanliness and ruggedness that made her heart tumble at the mere sight of this man. "What? What is it you want of me?"

Stephen smiled, folding his hands across his chest, deliberately invading her space. "You are not indifferent to me, Elizabeth."

Her cheeks grew warm, but she remained silent.

"I believe Roderick was correct." He leaned forward and took her hands in his. "Tell me you do not love me."

"Love you? What a silly thing to say."

He shot her a devastating smile. "You do love me."

Elizabeth fidgeted in her seat, feeling his fingers running circles on her wrists beneath her gloved hands, a practice he was becoming very good at. She could not let him do this to her. She could withstand his charms. Her life depended upon it.

"You must be insane."

"Am I?" He slid closer to her, his breath a sweet caress.

There was not a moment to lose. "Open that door at once."

"Tell me you do not love me, and I will open it."

She refused to look at him because she knew, without a doubt, those warm dark eyes would instantly devour her. And then where would she be? In his arms with a broken heart.

"No."

"No, what?"

"No, I won't answer. Now if you refuse to open the door, I will take my leave of you and *you* can go to Aunt Polly's."

"Very well. But let me tell you one thing, your mother, whoever she was, has nothing to do with this."

He slipped his fingers beneath her chin and gently turned her to face him. Challenging brown eyes glittered back at her.

It seemed that minutes passed before he spoke to her again. "Venture to your Aunt Polly's then. I understand her direction is near St. James. I'll be visiting you tomorrow for a morning call and every day until we are married *next week*."

Next week? "I do not want you to visit, my lord."

His lips thinned. "Nevertheless, I will."

"But you must not."

"Why?"

"Because I asked you to postpone the wedding. And . . . because I do not want this marriage at all." *Because you do not love me.*

She thought she heard him growl. "You love Fennington?"

"I believed I was in love with the man. But I realize he was only after my father's coin." To her astonishment, her formidable glare did nothing but draw a smile from the man.

"Well, then, I have saved you from a life with a man you did not love. And now you are in my debt, are you not?"

There was a wicked gleam in his gaze that pushed her back against the seat. "Yes. I mean, no, I mean—"

"You mean you love me, then?"

"Yes . . . er, no," she replied with an obvious stutter, her cheeks turning pink with confusion. "You tricked me!"

A set of bright white teeth flashed her way. "You love me, Elizabeth." It wasn't a question, it was a fact.

She said nothing. She did love him and hated herself for that. He would only break her heart. She remembered Fennington's words. *He never told you he loved you.*

The door burst open and Milli poked her head inside.

"Did he kiss you, Lizzie? Did he? Papa still thinks I'm

playing chess in the drawing room with Lord Marcus, but I
let Cleopatra loose, and little though she is, she clawed his
lordship's favorite jacket to shreds. He is not very agreeable
at the moment, and I daresay he did not like it a bit when I
told him he deserved it."

"Good heavens, Millicent!"

Stephen let out a husky laugh. "No, Milli. I have not
kissed her . . . yet."

Milli waited patiently by the door, gawking, her innocent
black kitten peering over her cupped hands. "Well, go
ahead. Papa will be here any minute, looking for me, and
I'm afraid that brother of yours might find me out soon
enough. I do not have nine lives, you know."

Elizabeth scooted back against the corner of the carriage.
"Get in, Milli."

"Stay out and close the door, Milli."

Milli frowned.

Elizabeth tightened her grip on her reticule. "Don't you
dare listen to him. He is not your father. Get in, Millicent."

Milli opened her mouth, but Stephen pointed her toward
the walk. "One minute and then you may come in."

"But I would like to see what happens," she said, peeking further into the carriage. "I can use some practice for my
love scenes when I am on stage."

Stephen coughed, smothering a laugh, but Elizabeth
heard it, and she was furious. "Milli, get in here. Now!"

"If she stays," Stephen said, "then that is your choice."

Elizabeth gasped. "You would not dare to do anything to
me in front of a child," she hissed.

Stephen did not give her a chance to answer before he stifled her words with a kiss.

As the carriage rolled to Aunt Polly's, Milli sat as mute
as her kitten, her mouth tight and curled upward, staring at
Elizabeth as if her sister were the goddess of love.

"What are you staring at?" Elizabeth snapped, the memory of that kiss still making her bones weak.

Milli looked at her papa, then Elizabeth again. "I was
wondering if he loves you, too."

"'Course he does," William Shelby said.

"Oh, Papa," Elizabeth sighed, finally giving way to the grief that had taken hold of her since she had met Lord Stephen. He only wanted her money. And his charms would get him everything he wanted. "How could you say such a thing?"

She barely held onto a sob before she broke forth in a river of tears.

Milli glared at her father. "That was terrible."

William Shelby blushed. "What? What did I say?"

Polly Crimmons was a slender, fifty-year-old, no-nonsense type of lady who did not take lightly to the engagement of her goddaughter to a man who did not love her. "You do not want to marry this lord, Elizabeth. That point is obvious."

"He does not love me." Elizabeth sipped her tea, the lump in her throat growing larger every minute she stayed away from that pair of charming brown eyes. But it had to be done.

Polly tilted her head to study her godchild.

The lady's flamboyant gown of pink fitted her personality as much as the salon they were sitting in. The walls were painted gold with black stripes. Red velvet curtains framed the window. Plush settees of deep brown and purple filled the room in a style more suitable for an Arabian princess than an English spinster.

Elizabeth stared into her cup. "He gambles, Aunt Polly."

"Ah, a gamester, is he? How many men do not gamble today? Even your father gambles. The lout."

Elizabeth chewed her bottom lip, wishing things were different. As soon as they had arrived at Tavton Hall, William Shelby had taken Milli to Leicester Square for an ice—anything not to be within ten feet of Elizabeth's godmother, who had been a friend to his wife Sarah. The lady was not truly their aunt by blood, but that was all Elizabeth had ever known her as.

Elizabeth's pained gaze shifted back to her aunt. "Papa is adamant about this engagement. You have seen the announcement in the papers. Lord Stephen has the special license. He told me he will be visiting me every day until we are married. There is naught I can do."

Polly rang for the maid. "My dear, there is always a choice to be made. Always something you can do."

A squeezing pain claimed Elizabeth's heart when she thought of jilting Stephen. But if anyone could help her out of this precarious predicament, it was her godmother. She should have gone to her sooner instead of thinking she could foil her father's plans by herself.

"Then you will help me disappear," she said softly. "Your cottage in the country would be perfect. Once I am there, I will send word to Papa that I refuse to marry his lordship and the engagement will be dissolved." And she would never see Stephen again. She had tried to make that clear to him.

The maid appeared in the doorway. Polly asked for her carriage to be sent around, then set her gaze back on Elizabeth. "You wish to run, then? You are afraid of this mighty lord?" Her godmother's eyes narrowed. "He is a ruffian?"

Elizabeth stiffened. "No!"

A twinkling light appeared in her aunt's eyes. "An ugly scoundrel? So ugly you had to claim I was sick to visit me?"

"Certainly not. He is most handsome."

"Ah, a bounder and a rake?"

"No," Elizabeth said defensively. "Too charming at times, but certainly not a rake."

Her godmother sighed. "Ah, you love him then?"

Elizabeth fell silent, her gaze dropping to the floor. Tears filled her throat. "I love him so much it hurts."

"Then you must leave him. You cannot marry a man who does not love you. It is an intolerable situation."

The bitterness in the lady's voice surprised Elizabeth. "He will have a string of mistresses. A pile of debts. Night upon night of drunken routs. By all the king's men, it is too much, Elizabeth! I fear the knave will pick apart your life like a vulture, stealing away the very soul of your being until your heart cannot stand it anymore."

Elizabeth curled her hands into a fist. "You don't know him! He would never treat me as you say! Never!"

Before Elizabeth could vindicate Stephen, the butler came into the room. "The carriage is waiting, madam."

"Very well." Polly took one last sip of her tea.

Elizabeth's hand trembled as she placed her teacup back onto the table. The determined expression on her aunt's face did not bode well. Suddenly she did not think it such a grand idea that she had come running to her aunt. "Where are you going?"

"I am going to find that father of yours and make him withdraw your engagement. See if I don't."

"But Papa will be here tonight."

Polly narrowed her eyes. "I know your father. He is planning his departure as we speak. He will drop Millicent off and take his leave to who knows where. Then where will you be?"

Elizabeth paled, remembering how her father had left her at the duke's home. "He will not leave me." But she knew her aunt was telling the truth.

"Did he stay with you at the Elbourne townhouse?"

Elizabeth reddened and shook her head. "Not all the time."

Polly's face became a cloud of anger. "That man." The lady marched toward the hall. "Never fear, my dear. I will see that he does right by you. You will not marry that despicable lord if I have to ship you off to America to save you!"

Elizabeth followed on her heels. "Wait!"

Polly spun around.

A sob escaped Elizabeth's throat and she clutched a hand to her mouth. "Please do not call on Papa. He means well. You know he does. And I do not want to go to America. Oh, this is such a mess, Aunt Polly. I do not know what to do."

Polly gave the maid her cloak. "My dear, you know I would never do anything to hurt you. I won't go after your father if you don't want me to. At least, not yet. Now let's get you back into the drawing room and you can tell your Aunt Polly everything—including the entire story about that hideous Mr. Fennington. I declare if that man dares come sniffing around here, I will have him shot on sight."

Elizabeth looked up, shocked.

Polly smiled as she closed the doors to the drawing room and led Elizabeth to the sofa. "My dear, you must know by now, Millicent cannot keep a secret. In fact, I believe she gained some of those theatrical notions from me."

"That little gabster."

Polly poured another cup of tea and chuckled. "Yes. Well . . . . Sometimes I wonder what other information that little imp has up her sleeve."

"Papa, may I have another ice?"

"No." William Shelby wiped the sweat from his brow and heaved a tired sigh. He was too old to be running around hiding from his eldest daughter.

"But Papa, I would like another one."

"No means no, Millicent."

Milli frowned. "You never pay attention to me. You only want Elizabeth to have the best things. Why, you even won her a husband. When I am old like her, I want you to buy me a prince. Of course," she huffed, "we have only a few more years and I daresay I might be dead by then."

Shelby blinked. "What did you say?"

"I said I might be dead by then. Apoplexy, typhoid, influenza. Good gracious, Papa, it's disheartening to think about. Death and destruction! It's abominably cruel!"

The shop grew quiet and heads snapped up to stare.

William's face reddened at his daughter's outburst. "Millicent, please hold your tongue."

"But Papa, everybody dies sometime."

William pulled at his cravat and stood, taking his daughter by the arm and escorting her out the door.

"Papa, my ice!"

"We will come back another time. Now come along, Millicent."

Milli dug in her heels as he dragged her toward the coach. "You love Elizabeth more! You would never make her leave half of her ice on the table!"

A nearby couple turned to gawk at the father and daughter.

William narrowed his eyes at Milli. "Get in that carriage

and don't say another word. One would think you were eight years old. See here, my girl, I should have sent you back to Bath the minute you showed up at the door unannounced."

Milli looked furious. "I didn't like it there," she hissed, climbing into the carriage. "And the governesses you hire are all horrid too."

The creases about William Shelby's face deepened as he took his seat beside his daughter. "Now what is this about me winning a husband for Elizabeth?"

Milli folded her arms across her chest and pinched her lips into a mutinous line, refusing to speak.

"Millicent, I refuse to play these games."

Milli shrugged.

"All desserts will be put away when it comes to your dinner if you do not answer me. By Jove, I will forbid you to attend any plays or lectures for the next three years."

Milli dropped her hands to her sides and glared at him. "You made his lordship marry Elizabeth. There!"

William's brow furrowed as the sound of carriage wheels clattered along the cobblestone streets. "Poppycock! Where did you hear such a notion?"

"I have very good ears, Papa. And when I put them to a door, I can hear *everything*. Well, almost everything."

"What door?"

"Why, the duke's door. Of course I thought I would hear nothing, for you would think a duke would have better doors in his townhouse. I could not hear everything before we left, but I heard enough to know that you made Lord Stephen pay his debt by marrying Elizabeth. You wanted a titled son-in-law and in effect obtained a handsome lord for Elizabeth." Her eyes glittered romantically. "It would make a grand play, Papa."

William's face lost all color.

"You see, Papa, I would never have thought of such a dastardly plot. Not that I condone it, but if the story included a secret agent of some sort, it would—"

"Millicent!"

She closed her mouth and stared at him.

"Are you telling me you were eavesdropping on the duke?"

She nodded.

William pulled out his handkerchief to wipe his face. "Did you say anything about this to your sister?"

"No."

"Good."

"Then, will you trick a prince into marrying me, Papa?"

"Not another word about this. Do you hear me?"

Milli sat back against the seat with a pout. "I hear you."

"Very good. Your sister will be married as soon as it can be arranged and she need not know anything about this conversation. Understand me, girl."

Milli's lips thinned.

"Yes, well," William Shelby said, glancing out the window. "The only problem will be your Aunt Polly. Listen here, Milli, I'm dropping you off at Tavton Hall. I am hoping to see his lordship at the club and this entire mess about Elizabeth postponing the wedding will be ironed out in no time."

"But she does not want to marry him, Papa. She thinks he does not love her. Maybe you should not have done what you did."

"Don't matter."

"Yes, it does. The more I think of it, the more I see that Lizzie should have a choice!"

"Sometimes it is better to listen to your parents, my girl, and not make such a fuss over the little things."

"Oh, forgive me. I should not have questioned you."

William closed his eyes and sighed. "A father knows best about these things, Milli. You will see."

Milli glared out the window. "Yes, I see everything now."

Late the following morning, Stephen made his way to the kitchen, hatbox in hand. "I would like to have one of Egypt's kittens, Mother. That one there, off to the side."

Lady Bringston looked up from her kneeling position. "I'll not have you getting into mischief with my babies."

Stephen rolled his eyes. "What do you take me for?"

The lady lifted a haughty brow. "You let that wonderful girl leave here. I doubt her aunt is ill. Something happened and I have no idea what you might do next."

He stiffened. "I *am* going to marry Miss Shelby."

His mother stood, holding the requested kitten in her hand. "If you do not woo that precious girl, all is lost for you. I am hoping she will still come to our soiree this week."

"Why is it that everyone believes I should *woo* my fiancée?" Stephen was definitely going to have a word with Roderick. "I am going to give the kitten to Elizabeth, Mother. Are you willing to part with it?"

The lady smiled, handing him the kitten. "Now that is wooing, my boy. Remember, Pharaoh will need a lot of attention."

"Pharaoh, is it?"

"Yes. Then there is Cleopatra, who has been given to Milli, and you know King Tutankhamen. I have yet to name the other two."

Tutankhamen had been given to Stephen's nephew, Richard, for a christening present, though the babe could not play with the tiny kitten until both of them were bigger. Emily had been touched.

His mother returned to the kittens. "At least I know that with Elizabeth, Pharaoh will be in fine hands."

Stephen let out a twisted smile. Oh, to be a kitten . . . .

Chapter Fourteen

*H*e had come.

Lifting her chin, Elizabeth dragged her hand along the banister, slowly making her way down the stairs with her aunt by her side. The strains of a concerto rose to her ears and she stopped short just outside the drawing room. Stephen was seated at the pianoforte, his slender fingers running up and down the keys as if he were Mozart himself.

He was so beautiful her heart ached. His dark head was bowed and his eyes were closed. He did not seem to notice her or Aunt Polly as they entered the room.

"My lord." Aunt Polly interrupted the musical dream and Elizabeth felt her bubble burst.

Stephen stood immediately. The light in his eyes dwindled. "Forgive me. I found myself drawn to the keys."

Elizabeth regarded him with a thoughtful gaze. How many other things had he hidden about himself? "You play wonderfully."

Deep brown eyes met hers. "Thank you. A compliment from you is a compliment indeed."

The intimacy of his glance caused her to look away.

"Tea?" Aunt Polly broke the spell, showing him to a seat on the sofa. Elizabeth moved to a wing chair opposite him.

As the refreshments were served, Stephen peered up at her, his gaze flickering with amusement. It was as if he had known he had been kept waiting.

"You are well?" he asked Elizabeth.

"Very well, thank you."

"Mother says the kittens are growing bigger every day."

Elizabeth peered over the rim of her cup. "And the baby? How is little Richard?"

"The babe has changed Stonebridge into an unequivocal ninny. His high-pitched voice is still ringing in my ears."

Elizabeth laughed. Lord Stonebridge could never be called a ninny in her book. "And your sister?"

"Ah, Emily is the only one in that house that has a pinch of sense. They are moving back to their townhouse today."

Elizabeth dropped her gaze. "Oh, I believe the duke has more than a pinch of sense, and the young duchess outshines all those brothers of yours." Her eyes tilted to meet his.

"You think so?" he asked, a smile working its way to the corners of his mouth.

She nodded. The silence was palpable as she sipped her tea.

Moreover, Aunt Polly appeared to be watching with such indifference it was unnerving, for Elizabeth knew the lady was mentally listing everything being said.

"The duke is quite fond of you."

Elizabeth's cup stilled in midair. Her cheeks grew warm. "Well, yes, in the end we did get along quite nicely. In fact, all your brothers were extremely kind."

Stephen's hand tightened around his teacup. Was he jealous?

"Madam, your solicitor has arrived."

Aunt Polly looked up at her butler's announcement. "Good heavens, Wallace, I completely forgot about my appointment." She rose and exchanged wary glances between Elizabeth and Stephen. "You will forgive me, but I have a most pressing problem that my solicitor and I must go over. You do understand?"

Stephen stood. "Of course. Do not feel you have to chaperone us, madam. We are, after all, engaged."

Elizabeth rose unsteadily, her thoughts running wild when she saw the devilish twinkle in Stephen's eyes. She could not stay alone in this room with him and remain neutral. One touch from him turned her to mush.

She turned a pleading glance toward her aunt. "Perhaps his lordship could return tomorrow?"

Polly gave Lord Stephen Clearbrook a curt glance and patted Elizabeth's hand affectionately. "Nonsense, my dear. He is correct on all accounts of propriety, you know. You are engaged."

The lady leaned down and whispered in her ear. "But by no means let him kiss you. Once you do, he will lose all respect."

Lose all respect? Well, that was a lost cause already.

Elizabeth swallowed past the lump in her throat and watched her aunt depart. How would she keep her distance from this man?

She would inform him that on no account would she come back to him. She turned around to tell him just that and found herself face to face with his broad chest.

He gripped her shoulders to keep her from stumbling backwards. "Elizabeth, you have nothing to fear."

Her chin shot up. "I am not afraid of you, my lord." She was afraid of herself. Afraid she had fallen in love with this man who would surely break her heart.

One side of his mouth quirked upward. "Then what are you afraid of . . . my kisses?"

She pulled away. "No . . . *my lord.*"

He scowled, pushing a hand through his hair. "My lord this, my lord that. We are to be husband and wife. Can you not call me Stephen?"

He had always been Stephen to her, but he would have too much power over her if he knew the extent of her love. "I have told you that I do not wish to marry you."

He pursed his lips and then, suddenly, he turned toward the pianoforte, his strong fingers playing a simple country song she remembered from childhood. "But you have not told me why."

She glanced at the door. This was not working well at all.

"Running away does not solve this." His voice was hard, almost angry.

Elizabeth turned back to him, her brows narrowing in outrage. Why should he be the one who felt angry, when it was she who was being forced into this marriage?

"I cannot run away, my lord. You and my father have cornered me like some fox in a hunt. However, I still don't wish to marry you. Even your kisses could not sway me."

A mischievous light appeared in his eyes. "My kisses do not move you, then?"

"I did not say that, my lord."

"Then what are you saying, Elizabeth? That you do not want to be my wife?"

With a pantherlike grace he rose from his seat and strode toward her. Her stomach clenched.

"That you do not wish me to touch you?" His hand reached for hers. "Or that you do not wish me to kiss you?"

His gaze traveled to her lips. "I want you, Elizabeth."

She blinked hard. "Y-you want me?"

The smile he sent her made her heart leap. He kissed her then, brushing his lips against hers with such tenderness tears filled her eyes. "Say you love me, Elizabeth. Say you will marry me, sweetheart."

He wrapped a strong hand around her waist and drew her against him. The sweet familiar scent of bayberry seeped into her senses as she flattened her hands against his chest.

"I think I loved you from the first time I saw you," she whispered.

He groaned into her ear, kissing the soft skin beneath it. "I have waited forever for you, my darling."

He tugged her toward the pianoforte. "See here, I have brought you a present." He reached beside the bench and pulled out a hatbox. He lifted the top, and a small kitten peeped out, its ears twitching curiously. "My mother named him Pharaoh."

Elizabeth's heart swelled as he cupped the tiny kitten in his hands and gently placed it into hers.

"He's the most beautiful one of them all," she whispered, stroking the cat's fur.

Stephen's hand covered hers. "He reminds me of your heart, Elizabeth. So soft and full of life . . ."

A lump formed in her throat, and she blinked back tears. "I don't know what to say, except thank you."

"Say you will marry me. I want you. It has nothing to do with your father's money."

Her defenses immediately fell away. She believed him. "Yes, I will marry you."

He tipped her chin. "Don't cry, sweetheart."

"I'm . . . crying because I'm happy. I love you."

She pressed a hand to his cheek. "I would trust you with my life just like this kitten trusts me. You would never hurt me."

She waited for him to answer, for him to tell her he loved her, too. Instead, his mouth grew taut and he stepped away.

"Stephen?"

A frown settled in his eyes and a cold numbing silence blanketed the room.

Her heart slipped a notch. *He . . . he didn't love her.*

"Elizabeth, there is something I must tell you."

No, please, no!

Before he could speak, the door opened and Milli bounced in.

Elizabeth swallowed, trying to stem her anxiety. "You should knock before you enter a room, young lady."

Milli shrugged, plopping herself onto the sofa. "Oh! The kitten with the black and white paw. May I hold it?"

Elizabeth handed the small ball of fur to Milli. "Get it some milk. I think Pharaoh's hungry."

"Pharaoh, is it? How utterly wonderful!"

Milli frowned, taking in the sight of Lord Stephen's motionless form in the middle of the room. "What's wrong with you? You look as though you sold your soul to the devil."

Stephen's eyes snapped as if Milli had stuck him with a pin. Milli looked back at Elizabeth's flushed face and let out a heavy theatrical sigh.

"Ah," the girl said, petting Pharaoh. "He has told you about Papa, then. I promised not to tell, but since he has told you, well, you can see it is best to have everything out in the open. Secrets should not begin a marriage, you know. I was reading a play once where the lady—"

"Millicent," Stephen interrupted with a deadly calm. He was beside the girl in two seconds. "How would you like to visit Drury Lane later this week?"

Elizabeth's blue eyes narrowed with suspicion. "Told me what about Papa?"

The girl's face lit up with delight. "Drury Lane? You have a box?"

Stephen nodded, taking the girl by the elbow and escorting her toward the door. "I do. You and your sister will be my guests."

"Milli?" Elizabeth's sharp voice cut across the room.

Milli stopped and turned, the kitten riding high on her shoulder. "Hmmm?"

"What is this about Papa?"

The girl's face fell. She regarded the grim expression on the lord's face beside her and backed up toward the door.

"Oh, did I not tell you? He is staying with Lord Baxby for the next few days. You know Papa and Aunt Polly. They fight like cats and dogs." She gave a forced laugh, pulling the kitten to her cheek.

Elizabeth knew her sister was keeping something from her. "What is it, Milli? What are you hiding?"

Milli's eyes grew wide with guilt. "Uh, nothing."

"Run along, Milli." Stephen tapped her shoulder in the direction of the door.

"Milli, stay here."

"Will you two stop throwing me around like some ball? I feel as though Papa were trading me instead of Lizzie here."

Elizabeth froze. "What do you mean, trading?"

Stephen quickly turned toward Elizabeth. "No one traded anyone. It was nothing like that."

Elizabeth felt her breath quicken. "Then why are you two acting like this is some deadly secret? It is not as if I hadn't known about the monetary transaction between Stephen and Papa." But in fact for a few glorious minutes she had almost forgotten all about the arranged marriage and her father's money.

"Monetary transaction?" Milli asked. "Is that what you call it? I had no idea you would take it so well, Lizzie. I would have told you myself. I mean, when I heard that Papa made Lord Stephen pay his debt at the card table by marrying you—"

"Millicent, that is quite enough." At the sound of
Stephen's curt command, Milli dashed out of the room.

Pay his debt?

Elizabeth wrapped her hands around her stomach. She
could not breathe or remember how. Short gasps of air fell
from her mouth. Her legs were unsteady and she fought to
stand.

Her father had made this man marry her over a debt? The
sudden knowledge pierced her like a spike to the heart.

Stephen had never wanted her at all. She was nothing to
him but a wager. And honor demanded he not back down.

A fiery heat spread through her veins. What a fool she
had been! An utter fool! She could see it all now. A man like
Lord Stephen Clearbrook would never marry for money at
all. He had too much integrity to do that.

But he should have told her. It was her life, too.

"Elizabeth, I can explain." His voice was strained.

She shook her head. "Don't come near me."

"Elizabeth, please. You don't understand."

Tears clogged her throat. "Oh, I understand. You owed
my father money, and he made you pay your debt by marrying me. Is that not correct, my lord?"

"I lost, Elizabeth. I knew it. He knew it. He would not accept a debt of honor. I had no choice but to accept his
terms."

She hurt so deep inside, she felt like crumbling into
pieces on the floor and burying herself in grief. Instead, she
held her head high, concealing her tears and her heart.

"You never wanted me, then. You did not seek my father
out. He sought you. What a silly widgeon you must think I
am."

"No, Elizabeth. I think you everything beautiful."

She could no longer look at him, her heart hurt so. It felt
as if someone was squeezing it, twisting it inside and out,
until there was no life at all.

"You are free now, my lord." She gave a sad laugh. "I ab-
solve you of this debt."

"But you must marry me."

Grief and anger tossed like a storm in the very core of her

being. "I must? Marry a man who is forced to marry me over a debt? How very unconventional for you, the son of a duke, to marry such a low person as I. Ha, a wagered bride for the lofty Lord Stephen Clearbrook. How very droll. You must have had a good laugh with your brothers."

"It was not like that at all. I wanted to tell you."

"Then why didn't you?"

"It does not matter."

"It matters little to you, but if I marry you I will have to live with the truth the rest of my life. Every morning when I wake up, I will remember why you married me, what my father did. Every time I touch you, I will remember. Do not think me a fool. Though I may not be of titled blood, I still have a heart that can break, and you may consider it broken."

He grabbed her shoulders. "Elizabeth—"

She didn't give him time to finish. She slapped him hard across the cheek and was instantly horrified at what she had done. What had come over her?

A circle of white formed about his lips.

"You should have told me," she stammered, the tears flowing easily now. "I will never forgive you for this. Never."

She rushed past him and stopped abruptly, seeing her father standing like a statue in the hall.

"How could you do this to me, Papa?" she cried, her tears running in rivulets down her face. "Trade me like some pawn in a chess game? I will never forgive you, either."

Stephen swallowed hard as he watched his beloved race up the stairs, her sobs burning like a white-hot knife into his heart.

His eyes flashed as he turned to William Shelby. "I should have borrowed or stolen the money that night. We have *both* broken your daughter's heart, and I am not proud of it."

William Shelby pulled at his cravat. "The girl is strong-willed, but in time she will see I did it because I loved her."

Stephen took a step toward the man. "Infernal drivel,

Shelby! You did it because you wanted a drop of blue blood in your family. Hell's teeth! Do not speak to me of love."

Shelby's pale lips trembled. "Perhaps I was wrong. I only wanted the best for her."

"Best for her? You forced me upon her. What if I had not been a gentleman, Shelby? Heaven help her. What, then?"

If Shelby could turn any whiter, he did.

Stephen grabbed the man by his neckcloth. "If you were not an old man I would break you in two." Shelby winced.

Stephen dropped his hand, disgusted at the way he himself had hurt Elizabeth. "You don't deserve her. She is everything kind and beautiful. She deserves better than this."

"The engagement? We had a deal. Or are you not a man of your word? I am still holding you to it. Your word of honor."

"There is no engagement," Stephen snapped, knowing it was not as easy as that. "Your daughter is the one who does not wish this marriage. And the devil take it, if you wish to speak of honor, sir, you had best take a fine look at yourself."

Stephen departed in a cloud of fury, sidestepping his carriage and walking back to his brother's home. He wanted to drink himself under the table, but those days were over. He realized that now.

And heaven help him, if he wanted to woo Elizabeth back into his life, he would have to go about it a different way—and swiftly, or he would lose her forever.

Chapter Fifteen

At the sound of the knock, Elizabeth pulled her head from her pillow. "Who is it?"

"It's me. Milli. Can I come in?"

"You are already in." Elizabeth turned her head away from her sister and wiped away the rest of her tears with the back of her hand. She could hardly breathe she had cried so much.

"Will you ever forgive me, Lizzie?" Milli's voice cracked with guilt as she walked across the floor. The soft purr of kittens filled the room.

Elizabeth spun around, her sobs barely checked. "Get them out of here, Milli. I never want to see those kittens again." They reminded her too much of *him.*

"Lizzie! How could you be so monstrous to two innocent kittens? They did nothing wrong."

Elizabeth's lips trembled as she buried her face in her pillow. "I'm sorry. It's just that they bring back memories." She gave a stiff laugh. "How silly the Clearbrooks must have thought me. Oh, Milli, how could you not have told me?"

Milli rushed toward the bed. "Forgive me, Lizzie. I would do anything to make it all better."

Elizabeth stared blankly at the wall beside her. "No one is ever going to choose my husband. Do you understand, Milli? Don't let Papa or anyone decide for you, either."

"I will choose my prince, Lizzie. I certainly shan't let Papa do it!" She hugged the kittens to her breast in such a tight grip they squeaked in protest.

Elizabeth rolled onto her back and sighed. "Oh, Milli. What am I to do? I love him."

"Well, if he loves you back, would you wed him?"

"He doesn't love me, Milli. And if by some miracle he did, I would never know the truth. He would marry me because of Papa. I cannot win either way."

Milli sank into the bed and let the kittens curl up against the pillows. "I can see how it is. You might have to marry Mr. Fennington after all."

"Mr. Fennington is no gentleman, Milli. I would never marry that weasel."

"I should say not," a female voice declared. "However, marrying a wagered bride was not well done of Lord Stephen either."

Both girls looked up as Aunt Polly swooshed into the room.

Elizabeth glanced at Milli. "You told!"

Milli's brows raised about an inch. "Did not. She wiggled it out of me."

Elizabeth threw her hands to her face. "I was such a fool."

Aunt Polly put a comforting palm on Elizabeth's shoulder. "If you marry your lord, all will be forgotten, my dear."

Elizabeth blew her nose. "I . . . am not . . . marrying him."

Her godmother pursed her lips. "Well you cannot dismiss the soiree held at the duke's home tomorrow night. It would be scandalous for you not to appear. Think of Milli's future."

Frowning, Elizabeth looked up. "I forgot about that."

"You must go, my dear. Even if you mean to dissolve the engagement. You must hold your head high and show everyone that you are Miss Elizabeth Shelby, and you are made of the same flesh and blood as the rest of them."

"I will go, but after it is all over, I want you to promise me I can stay at your cottage in the country."

Milli looked horrified. "But you cannot run away!"

"I am not running away. I just need some time to think everything out. No one is going to run my life anymore. Not Papa, and certainly not Lord Stephen Clearbrook."

"The cottage will be available, my dear. And I will care for Milli while you are gone."

Glumly, Elizabeth nodded. She would not let her father or Stephen determine her life. Perhaps she would make her way to France and set up shop. She would administer her remedies to pets, and if asked, to people, too. She would live her own life and never ever fall in love again.

"I believe you have gone out of your mind! I will certainly not give you that amount of money!"

Stephen slapped his hands on the duke's desk. "I need the money now, Your Grace! I can pay you back, even if I lose. My business ventures have become quite lucrative. It's just that I don't have that amount on me now, and there are no debts in the game tonight. For the love of King George, I know I said I would never come to you again, but I'm . . . I'm begging you."

"You are begging me? I never thought I'd see the day."

Stephen had no pride left. If he lost the woman he loved, he would have nothing at all.

"I promise you, Roderick, I will return every penny. But I must play in that game tonight. You cannot be worried about theft. We will be gaming in this very house."

"Thunderation, Stephen. This is maddening."

"Maddening or not, I must have it."

"And what if you lose? What then?"

Stephen made a fist. "I have already lost what is most precious to me. I *will* pay you back."

Roderick shook his head, throwing his brother the key to his safe. "My money is yours. But I want you to know, I do not condone this action."

Stephen grinned. "Yes, but you have Jane and you are so very agreeable now that you are married to such a woman." Roderick's lips curled into a wicked grin. "Quite agreeable, indeed. But I daresay if she gets wind of this escapade I am funding she will have my head."

Stephen's brown eyes glittered. "An interesting prospect, but alas, one that will never come to pass."

"You know, I do believe Mother picked you up off the

street like that cat Elizabeth scooped out of the gutter last week. You never were like the rest of us with your carefree spirit."

Stephen stuffed the money into a sack and strode toward the door, leaving the key to the safe on Roderick's desk. "Thanks. I know I've done some stupid things the past few years, but I've changed. I see things differently now."

"Father didn't die because of you."

Stephen's boots halted. A brittle silence ensued as the two brothers stared at one another.

"You knew?" Stephen finally asked.

"I eventually put two and two together. You argued with Father before he was killed and you took the blame. I thought time would be your friend, but it became your enemy instead. I was the oldest, Stephen. I knew Father loved another. Oh, not a mistress, but a lady whom he cherished from afar. I just didn't know who it was until Emily married. I also saw our mother's pain. I tried to ignore it because there was nothing I could do."

Stephen rubbed a hand across his face as painful memories clouded his vision. "It was more than that, Roderick. I killed a man in the war. He—dash it all . . . he had children."

"It was war, Stephen. We are all mortal beings with faults." The duke poured his brother a glass of sherry. "Take this. And know that many men have had to kill in war. It's something I have done myself. However, carrying the guilt for two men's deaths is not right. Forgive yourself for being human and move on."

"Yes, move on," Stephen muttered, realizing Roderick was right. Why had he not seen it before? The past seemed behind him now, but what of his future? What of Elizabeth?

"I never knew for certain your role against Napoleon," he said to Roderick, "but now I believe you were a secret agent of sorts. You seem to have answers for everything."

Roderick's right brow rose. "You always had a vivid imagination, even as a child. But I have heard some things about you and Wellington, so I believe we are even. Except it seems we have a hero in our midst who for some humble reason is keeping it a secret."

Stephen pushed his drink aside and smiled. So Roderick knew. "Thanks for everything. And wish me luck."

"Now, poppet, you must see I did what I thought was right."

As the Shelby carriage rolled toward the Duke of Elbourne's townhouse, Elizabeth avoided her father's worried gaze and stared at the lampposts gracing the cobblestone streets.

"I am not speaking to you, Papa."

"Lord Stephen Clearbrook is a good man, Lizzie. I never would have wed you to anyone who was not worthy of your love."

"Love?" She let out a pitiful laugh. "I fell in love with a handsome lord. Is that what you planned? To have your daughter's heart broken? To have the man love someone else?"

Her father bristled. "Someone else?" She refused to answer. "You tell me now, Elizabeth. I thought you were jesting before. No daughter of mine will marry a man who loves another."

"Like you did." She regretted the words as soon as she said them. Her father sat in silence. "Papa, I did not mean that."

"Fair is fair, Lizzie. I ain't saying I was perfect. I was not fair to your mother. She deserved better."

Elizabeth fought the lump in her throat. "Did you love Mama?"

He looked out the window and sighed. "I loved her, Lizzie. But not enough. Ah, here we are." He turned and patted her knee. "Everything will be fine, my dear, just trust me. By the way, did I tell you I like your hair that way? Does something for your eyes, you know."

Stephen eyed his mother warily as she closed the library doors and told him to take a seat on the sofa.

"Pray tell me, my dear mother, why do I have the grand pleasure of your company tonight instead of Bringston? I thought your new husband had returned to London today."

The lady blushed. His new stepfather had made his mother feel young again, and if she was happy that was all that counted.

"You oaf!"

Stephen's head snapped to attention. "Beg your pardon?"

The lady stabbed her finger in the air and Stephen would have laughed if she weren't pointing it at him. "You take that girl into your arms and declare yourself or else."

His lips fell into a crooked grin. "You love her, too."

His mother's face instantly softened. "Of course I do."

"Well, then. At least I have you on my side."

His mother looked up expectantly. "What can I do?"

"Can you make certain I have Elizabeth alone?"

Two violet blue eyes lit up with delight. "My dear, you may think me a delicate woman, but when it comes time to enter into battle, I am always ready." She raised a right brow as Roderick did when he was planning something entirely wicked.

Had he underestimated his very own mother all these years?

"You knew about your father, did you not?"

He blinked. "Beg your pardon?"

"Your father always loved another and you knew that."

Stephen could not speak.

Her gaze softened. "I loved your father and he was fond of me. But he loved someone who could never return that love."

"You had a marriage of convenience, Mother. I have no wish for that. I have to make things right with Elizabeth."

She smiled. "You know I loved your father. I had five beautiful children with him. Do I regret it? Certainly not. But now I am married to a wonderful man, and my life is complete. If you love Elizabeth, marry her, her father's edict or not."

"You knew?"

"There is not much I do not know that goes on with you."

He stared at her thoughtfully. "I have a plan."

"Plans sometimes go astray. Tell her the truth."

"It's too late for that. This is a chance I have to take."

"Very well, then. Include me in your plans. I will have Elizabeth at my side at half past ten. Is that satisfactory?"

"Yes, and thank you."

Her eyes danced. "What are mothers for if not to help their sons trap innocent young maids in the garden?"

"Mother!"

"Goodness, Stephen. Do not be such a prude. I have had five children and two husbands, you know." Turning on her heel, she left the room, leaving him openmouthed and speechless.

Chapter Sixteen

*T*he soiree was more a ball than an evening party, with at least a hundred people crowding the floor. An army of candelabra lit the perimeter of the room, giving the appearance of a thousand twinkling stars. Elizabeth stood between the duchess and Stephen's mother. It was amazing that the Elbourne household could host another party so soon after her engagement ball, but Stephen's brother was a duke after all.

Elizabeth took in the sight of the couples gathering for the country dance that was about to begin. A pinprick of tears lined her lids. It was all she could do to keep her embarrassment over what her father had done to a minimum. To be a wagered bride was unforgivable. She wondered how many people knew the truth.

The duchess? Stephen's mother? How many people were laughing at her behind her back?

The thought of running into Stephen made her all the more determined to follow through with her plans. She had regretted slapping him the second she had done it. And her guilt had magnified a thousandfold when she had seen him walking lazily into the room an hour ago.

He had been dressed in black evening attire, making him appear even more devilishly handsome than she remembered. His stride was confident and graceful. Many of the ladies, young and old alike, fluttered their fans and batted their eyes as he gave them his most irresistible Clearbrook smile. His easygoing self-confidence exuded such masculine charm it was unnerving.

Her heart plummeted as she regarded the dancers.

But Stephen would never truly love her. He was just too honorable to refuse the terms of her father's wager.

After years of marriage he would eventually begin to pity her, and she would begin to hate him. It was all too much to bear. She had to make up her mind what she was going to do about her life before it was too late.

"You look lovely tonight."

The low whisper broke into her reverie. She glanced over her shoulder. Stephen's cheek was an inch from her ear, setting the hairs on the back of her neck tingling with warmth.

"Good evening, my lord."

His hand pressed possessively on the small of her back. "Would you honor me with the next dance?"

The heat of his words flowed like warm honey through her veins, and before she could think of a way to excuse herself, he had pulled her onto the floor for a waltz.

"What? Not happy to see me?"

She lifted her eyes, finally coming to her senses. "You should have told me."

The tenderness in his gaze compelled her to look away. She would not fall for his charms. She would not.

He smiled and pressed her closer, turning her around the dance floor as if nothing were amiss. "You are as light as a fairy with wings, my love."

Her steps faltered. "Don't," she said, holding back a sob.

The lines around his mouth hardened as he twirled her toward the ballroom doors that led to the garden. An ache tightened about her chest when he took her arm, taking their conversation outside.

"What your father did matters not to me. I want to marry you, Elizabeth."

She avoided his dark gaze as the cool night air caressed her cheeks. Her heart struggled with her conscience. But he had lied by keeping the truth from her. How could they ever be happy?

"Don't you understand?" she said in a hurt tone. "I would always believe you married me because of my father. I was beginning to believe a marriage of convenience between us was something I could live with. But I cannot do it."

She gathered her courage and tried to hold her heart together as her eyes locked onto his. "The fact that my father pushed me upon you will always come between us. Our fate together has been doomed from the very start, my lord."

He gripped her arm more tightly and pulled her down the path toward the darkness of the trees. "But none of that signifies."

"Yes, it does."

No, not down that path again! She dug her heels into the pebbled walkway, knowing that if she wanted to keep her heart from shattering forever, she had to stay in sight of the couples standing outside the ballroom.

"We would never be happy," she added. "*You* could never be happy."

He stopped and turned. "You do not trust my love?"

Love? No, he was only doing the honorable thing. It was only a word to him.

"No," she finally said, wondering if he did love her just a little. But a little would never do. Her father's interference would always be between them. She would never be able to tell fact from fiction.

He raised his arm and clasped her waist, dragging her body tightly against his. "Tell me you do not love me, Elizabeth. Tell me. By heaven, the truth this time. I need to know."

She felt the beat of his heart against hers and drank in the sweetness of the bayberry scent she loved so much.

"The truth, Elizabeth," he whispered.

Tears spilled down her cheeks. She had to pick up the broken pieces of her life before there was nothing left to mend. She had to lie. "I never loved you. I don't want this marriage. You are a gamester like my father. I could never marry you."

For a few seconds he stood there, his muscles slowly stiffening beneath his clothes. The air between them grew thick with silence. He stepped away.

"I would never force you, madam, despite what you think

of me. I am not an ogre. If you do not love me, then it is done."

She bit her lip, wanting to bury her head against his chest and tell him she loved him. But the coolness of those brown eyes told her it was over.

A deep aching pain sliced across her chest as he escorted her back to the ballroom, his determined stride making her hurry. "Smile, my dear. People will think we have argued."

Her pain quickly shifted to anger. He had given in all too easily. He should have fought for her love if he truly loved her. "I am not married to you. Do not tell me what to do."

"And that is the crux of the matter, is it not?" His lips thinned as he made a curt bow, kissing her hand. "You leave me no choice," he murmured more to himself than to her, then handed her off to the duke for the next dance.

Stephen sank back in his chair as he took in William Shelby's flushed face. The blue room in the Elbourne townhouse was theirs to command. A small fire crackled in the hearth, giving the impression of a cozy ambience. But icy tension enveloped the room like a wicked winter storm, making the stakes undeniably real.

The card game had gone on for at least two hours. Shelby had lost a great sum. Grumwell and Hewitt had taken their leave a while ago.

Stephen laid his cards on the table, his eyes never leaving Shelby's face.

The older man looked up. "I fear you have me again, my lord."

Stephen pursed his lips. "Another hand, perhaps?" He knew men like Shelby. Winning was everything to them.

Shelby pulled at his cravat and took a mouthful of brandy. Stephen eyed the liquid, wanting just a drop to touch his tongue. Just a taste. Shelby must have realized his suffering.

"Soothes the throat, my lord. Sure you ain't wanting just a pinch? A bit thirsty?"

Smiling, Stephen shook his head. "I need to stay awake." He reached out to pour a cup of tea from the small tray table beside them.

Shelby frowned. "The engagement is still on, my lord. No matter what my Lizzie says. Or you. It would be a breech of contract, it would."

Stephen curled his lips deliberately. "Don't want that, do we? Would not look good for the Clearbrook name, now would it?"

As if a cool wind blew into the room, Shelby stirred in his seat. "Now, see here, my lord. We are to be family soon and I see no reason for any hard feelings. This is a business arrangement after all."

"A business arrangement, of course. What else?"

Shelby looked up, frowning, but he said nothing as he dealt the cards for another hand of vingt-et-un.

Stephen studied the man before him. The notion that he could have lost Elizabeth forever because of Shelby's machinations numbed his conscience.

"No hard feelings, Shelby. Shall we continue?"

Shelby's eyes gleamed at the amount Stephen threw in. "You seem to have more than enough money tonight, my lord."

Stephen shrugged. "Believe it or not, a man in my situation has a few business dealings on the side."

Shelby looked him over with a critical eye and laughed. "You won't be thinking to have all this back in Elizabeth's dowry now, would you?"

Stephen calmly took a sip of tea. His business dealings the past few weeks had given him a lively income with most of the money still tied up in investments. Nevertheless, he would like to have thrown Shelby's money in his face, but he needed to win. He needed to follow through with his plan. "Looks as though I will have to win enough for the honeymoon, eh?"

Shelby laughed. "Always knew you had a sense of humor."

Stephen picked up his cards. Sense of humor, indeed.

"If you are looking for my brother, Elizabeth, he can be found in the blue salon playing cards with your father."

Elizabeth glanced up to find Stephen's brother Marcus

standing in her path. The hall had been deserted only a minute ago. She lifted her chin, pulling together her pride as she tried to walk past him. "I am not searching for your brother. You can be rest assured of that."

"My dear girl, you are not as good an actress as your little sister."

Elizabeth bit back a retort and tried to move past the man blocking her advance.

He touched her arm, stopping her. "You love him."

"I do not."

"You lie, Miss Elizabeth Shelby."

She shot him a haughty scowl. "Are all you Clearbrook men so arrogant?"

Marcus chuckled and gently pulled her further down the hall. "I fear you have found us out. We are an arrogant lot, to be sure. But we fight for what we believe in, and whether you want to believe it or not, Stephen wants to marry you."

She halted and folded her arms across her chest. "It matters not. The situation as it stands now is not one I choose to stay in. He obviously does not love me."

Marcus frowned. "But I believe the engagement papers are signed. You will be ruined if you pull out of the agreement now. You cannot jilt him. Millicent would be touched by scandal as well. Do you want that? Besides, you love him. Give him another chance. I know my brother. He is an honorable man. He will do right by you. Mark my word."

Give him another chance. She had been thinking that exact thing when Stephen had left her to dance with the duke.

"But what if he never loves me? What kind of life will I have then?"

"You mean, what kind of life will you have because you have been tossed about in a game of cards?"

She stared back in shock. Humiliation overwhelmed her. So he knew.

Marcus took her hand in his. "It has naught to do with your worth, my dear. This is between your father and Stephen."

He tilted his head toward the stairs. "I believe Roderick mentioned to me that your father and Stephen are in the blue salon, second door on the left. If you wish to have a conversation with both of them in the same room, I would think this is as good a time as any. But it's up to you."

Elizabeth realized he was right. She still loved Stephen. She had to have this out with the two of them, no matter what happened. She turned toward the stairs. But a hand on her elbow stopped her.

"And if by chance you do not marry my brother," he gave her a devilish wink, "I will be here."

She felt herself color. "You would thwart your own flesh and blood?"

He smiled. "If what you say is true, and Stephen does not love you, then it should not matter at all."

"But I can never believe him." Could she? Yet a little seed began to grow, making her think that anything was possible.

Marcus sent her an irresistible smile. "As I said before, you are not a very good liar. You have already answered your own heart. You love Stephen, and somewhere inside you believe he loves you, too. No matter what your father has done or what Stephen agreed to, you were meant to be together. Believe me, if it is true love, nothing will stand in your way."

Her throat spasmed as she bent to kiss his cheek. "Thank you."

To her surprise, his face bloomed with color. "What for?"

Her lips split into a meaningful grin. "For understanding what the heart sometimes does not want to hear. After the wedding, I will find you a lady worthy of your love."

Elizabeth planned to tell her father and Stephen that she had had enough of their foolishness. This would be settled once and for all, and she would ask Stephen point blank if he loved her or not.

"See here, now. Let's not go as far as that. This was just a brotherly talk. It certainly did not pertain to me."

She glanced over her shoulder as she climbed the stairs toward the gaming salon, her blue eyes gleaming with promise. "I will not forget. You will have a lady worthy of your love and there will be no substitute."

Marcus stood at the bottom of the stairs, staring at the vacant hallway.

"Problem, Marcus?" He turned at the sound of Roderick's amused voice. "Misplace something?" the duke asked.

Marcus scowled. "You could say that."

"And what, pray tell, have you misplaced on this grand night of diversion?" The duke raised a right brow in mock inquiry.

"My mind, Roderick. My blasted mind."

The door to the blue room eased open just as a servant departed, carrying a silver tea set. Elizabeth stood in the hall, not intending to eavesdrop, but the sudden sound of her father's voice kept her frozen in place.

"You must be mad. I cannot hold you to that amount. The duke would call me out, my dear boy."

"Shelby, if you continue to call me dear boy, I will call you out myself." The crisp sardonic response belonged to Stephen.

"Very well, then. If you insist, my lord. But Lizzie ain't going to be happy about this."

There was a slight scrape of a chair, the clearing of her father's throat, the cracking of knuckles.

Elizabeth was about to step inside and put a stop to the game when she thought better of it. She rested her forehead against the wall outside the salon.

How could her father treat Stephen so, knowing his weakness at cards? And how could she humiliate Stephen by breaking into the game? She realized with a start that he needed her. Needed her to take care of him, save him from himself.

She picked her head up and straightened. She could do it for the man she loved. She could.

Stephen stared at his cards, knowing that unless Shelby produced a miracle, the man was going to lose.

"Vingt et un, Shelby. Knave and an ace."

Shelby's face turned crimson. "But how?"

Stephen did not rejoice in seeing the man sweat. But it was something that had to be done.

The older man flipped out his hand. "You surprised me.

my lord. You find me a bit indisposed." He threw out his purse. "I can pay the remainder of my reckoning tomorrow."

Stephen leaned back in his chair. "Sorry, old boy. But the rules of the game, you know. I will have to call you on it."

Shelby swallowed. "A note perhaps. Tomorrow, the bank—"

Stephen leaned forward, a gleam of determination in his gaze. "No tomorrow, sir. You owe me the sum. Now."

Shelby's Adam's apple gave a pronounced bob. "I find myself at a loss."

Stephen finally poured himself a glass of port and sipped, peering over the rim of the glass. "Of course, there is something else that may be used instead of your purse. I could call the matter even if you wish."

Shelby knitted his bushy white brows in confusion. "Exactly what are you saying, my lord?"

Stephen shot the man a cool deliberate smile. "Do you not remember, one daughter for one debt?"

Shelby rose unsteadily from his chair. "I fail to see how that applies here."

Silence thickened the air between them.

Stephen's chair scraped back as he stood. "You may have her back."

"I beg your pardon?" the older man asked, his face beet red.

"Elizabeth. Your eldest. You may have her back. I don't want her. We are even now."

Shelby looked shocked. "This is maddening! I won't do it!"

"Oh, won't you?" Stephen said, throwing the man's purse back at him. "But it is done. I believe I will still keep Creighton Hall, though. However, fair is fair, my good man. In fact, I believe I have been more than fair in handling your debts."

"I won't have it. You hear me. She will be the laughing-stock of all London."

Stephen's lips thinned as he took his seat. "Then you should have thought of that when you made the deal with me, sir. You have made Elizabeth a pawn and now you have been checked."

"Checkmated, my lord," Shelby said between gritted teeth. "You have me cornered. Always knew you were a smart one."

"We are even, then. You owe me nothing and I owe you nothing."

"And I owe neither of you." The voice was a bare whisper beyond the door, but when Stephen heard it, it was like a blast of cold air to his soul. She took a step inside.

"Elizabeth," Stephen said, shocked.

"I am not a pawn," she said calmly. "I am a person."

Stephen rose slowly, his face white. "I—"

"No. No more. I don't know how I ever thought I loved you. And, Papa, I am ashamed. I am ashamed of both of you." Blue eyes peered at Stephen with such disgust he felt ill.

"You don't understand," he said, starting toward her.

She put up her hand. "I understand everything now. I am a female with no rights except the ones you two deem necessary to bestow upon me. I cannot stand the sight of either of you. I am leaving now and don't you dare follow me."

A sob broke out and she turned from the room, her head held high, her chin wobbling, her footsteps echoing the hall in small little thwacks of pain until they could no longer be heard at all. Stephen's lungs ached from holding his breath.

Shelby threw his hands to his face. "Goodness knows I tried. Tried to give her everything. And somehow I failed."

"We were both wrong," Stephen replied, as he stalked across the floor and threw open the door. Instantly he felt a sinking in the pit of his stomach, worse than he had felt when his father died, worse than he had felt at Waterloo. She was gone.

Elizabeth ran down the hall and staggered into the first room she came to around the corner. Hot tears pooled in her eyes. She hurried to the window seat, hiding behind the curtains, pressing a hand to her mouth.

How could they play her like a fool? How could Stephen

throw her back to her father as if she were a piece of property?

She had been ready to confront the two most important men in her life and forgive them, but they had betrayed her again.

Footsteps stopped near the door and she stilled. Her heart pounded as if the hounds of hell were after her.

"Elizabeth?"

She held her breath.

"Lose something, little brother?"

Elizabeth's stomach knotted as Clayton's voice sounded only a few feet from her hiding place.

"No, I did not lose something," Stephen snapped. "I am merely looking for my fiancée."

"Ah, a lover's rendezvous?"

"I don't have time to entertain your sick mind. If you see Elizabeth, tell her I am looking for her. Can you do that?"

"I believe I can follow those instructions."

"I won't even ask why you are lying prone on that sofa."

"Three words, Stephen. Miss Briana Garland."

"The one with the mother that looks like a penguin?"

"The very one. Now, if you would be so kind as to shut that door, I can retire to the book that I was reading."

With a groan, Stephen shut the door and Elizabeth crumpled to her knees, too ashamed to face anyone.

The next moment Clayton was at her side. "Are you ill?"

"No."

He helped her to the sofa and locked the door.

Walking back, he stood over her and frowned. "Then it is my duty to my brother to tell you that he is looking for you."

Her response was a strangled laugh. "Well done of you, my lord."

He cleared his throat. "Being a gentleman I won't ask why you are weeping. But if you have any need of my services . . ."

She looked up. "Could you obtain a carriage for me?"

His dark brows rose about an inch. "Zeus, Miss Shelby, Stephen would have my head."

A lonely tear dropped to the carpet. "I understand."

Clayton winced. "Oh, very well. The carriage will be waiting around back. But I must know where you are going."

"My Aunt Polly's. That is where I have been residing since I left here."

Though Elizabeth liked Clayton, she certainly was not going to divulge her plans to him, either. He was a Clearbrook after all. Moreover, he wanted to help her, but she knew that as soon as she left, he would tell his brother of her departure.

"Ah, a lovers' spat?" he said dryly.

"Your brother and I are not lovers," she blurted out and immediately realized her faux pas.

He gave a little chuckle. "Hmmm. My brother must be losing his touch with the women, then."

"I truly do not wish to discuss your brother. I would merely like accommodations for travel back to my aunt's home. If you would be so kind as to help me, I would forever be in your debt."

"Oh, not that, my dear. If you are in my debt, Stephen would call for pistols at dawn. But I will help you. And being the gentleman I am, I will accompany you to your destination."

She narrowed her eyes. "You think I have cause to lie to you?"

The older brother smiled, the rakish expression reminding her too much of Stephen.

"Oh, no, my dear Miss Shelby. But Stephen would never forgive me for letting you travel without an escort."

She gave him a wary look. "Very well."

He walked back toward the door, glancing over his shoulder. "Do not open this door for anyone. I will return with your wrap in five minutes. And if perchance a certain Miss Briana Garland or a dowager penguin breaks down this mighty oak barrier to see me, tell them I have died and gone to gaming hell." His eyes twinkled. "Understand?

Elizabeth smiled faintly as he closed the door. He thought he was helping her. But a wrap would do nothing to avert the icy grief that had seeped into every pore of her soul.

Chapter Seventeen

"What do you mean she took the carriage?"

Stephen stared in disbelief as Clayton sat in the library, his shoes on the desk, sipping his wine as if nothing were amiss.

"I took her home," his brother said calmly. "And you will be pleased to know I did mention you were looking for her."

With one quick move, Stephen swiped his brother's feet off the desk. "You are more stupid than I remembered."

Clayton lowered his gaze to the spot of red wine sprinkled on his shirt. "No, I believe you are the stupid one here. You threw her back to her father like some cursed toy."

"It wasn't like that at all. Blast it! I love her!"

"Fine way of showing it, little brother."

Stephen's hands fisted at his side. "I only meant to give her back to her father so I could marry her free and clear."

"You should have told her."

"Hell and thunderation, you stupid idiot! I wanted to, but it seems you went about hiding her from me."

"I have had about enough of you."

"And I have had about enough of you. Reading Byron while escaping Miss Garland. Or is it her mother that terrifies you? Never knew I had a coward for a brother."

Clayton's eyes shot daggers. "If you weren't so mad over Miss Shelby, I would box your ears. I won't try to talk to you in this state, but I daresay your fiancée has had enough of you as well. Sleep it off, and tomorrow morning, fetch her back."

Clayton had barely a second before he was spun around

and thrown to the floor with Stephen's fists pummeling his face.

Fifteen minutes later, the duke found Stephen slouched against an overturned chair, breathing hard. Across the room, Clayton held his handkerchief to his bleeding nose.

"Do you want to tell me what the hell is going on here?" Stephen glared at the duke.

"We were fighting over who is the biggest idiot," Stephen said sarcastically, "and as you can see, Clayton won."

Aunt Polly sat primly on her sofa, sipping her tea and eyeing Stephen over the rim of the cup as she contemplated answering his question. "She is gone."

Exasperated, Stephen tried to control his anger. "Well, I know that, but where has she gone to?"

"That is not for your ears, my lord."

Stephen gripped the side of the chair, his knuckles turning white. "Madam, I am fully aware of Elizabeth's feelings toward me, but yesterday was not what it seemed."

Polly set her cup down and let her gaze linger over him as if he were last night's supper, spoiling in the pantry. "You and William have bounced my girl's heart around as if it were nothing at all. I fail to see what good it will do for her to meet with you again. She wants her privacy and I will give it to her."

"Enough of this piddling talk!" William Shelby strode into the room, his cravat askew, his jacket rumpled.

Clenching his jaw, Stephen regarded the man. It looked as if Shelby had not slept a wink either. The notion was little consolation compared to the loss of Elizabeth.

A flash of pained recognition glittered in Shelby's eye as he acknowledged Stephen before he shifted his gaze back to the lady. "Now, madam, you will tell me where my daughter is. This is not the time to trifle with me."

Polly Crimmons laughed. "La, William. Surely you cannot think me such a fool. Your daughter has no wish to let anyone know where she is. But since you are her father, I can assure you she is quite fine. Not that you have anything to do with that, you half-witted idiot. She needs time to heal from what you two have done to her."

Red-faced, the older man pulled at his cravat. "Listen here, Polly, you will tell me her direction."

"I will, will I?" the lady said haughtily. "How dare you tell me what I should do when it was you who shoved that poor girl off on this roguish gamester."

Stephen swallowed a curse. "If you would do me the honor of giving me your niece's direction, I would be forever in your debt."

"An interesting prospect, but why should I divulge such confidential information to you, my lord?"

Stephen's brows snapped. "Why? Is this the Spanish Inquisition? Because I love her, that's why!"

"I believe you do," Polly said. "But I gave Elizabeth my word that I would not disclose her destination. She needs time to think, time you two have obviously not given her."

"Now see here," William blurted out, "This ain't seemly."

Stephen's piercing gaze settled on the lady. "Are you going to tell me where she has gone or must I follow her trail myself?"

"I fear my lips are sealed, my lord."

Stephen gave her a stiff bow and retreated from the room. William followed in his shadow. "By Jove, you do love her. Been thinking about last night. You deliberately gave her back to me, did you not, my lord? An interesting maneuver."

Stephen grabbed his hat from the hall table. "Yes, well, Napoleon had interesting maneuvers and look where that led him."

William looked penitent, but Stephen's blood was pounding so hard he thought he might plant Shelby a facer right there.

Shelby colored. "Yes, I know you would like to box my ears. And rightly so." Tears glittered in the man's eyes. "But you find her. She needs you. I only did what I thought best. I chose you because I thought you would make her the best of husbands, not some wastrel wanting to spend my money."

With a sniff, Shelby pulled out a starched white handkerchief and started down the hall.

Stephen felt a twinge of pity for the man, but before he could think of something to say, he was distracted.

"Pssst."

Raising his gaze, Stephen found Milli hanging over the banister with Cleopatra and Pharaoh tucked inside the folds of her gown. "Come down from there, you imp. You might fall."

Milli's eyes flashed as she pulled away from the banister and started down the stairs. "You cannot tell me what to do."

"May I remind you, you called me, not the other way around."

Instantly, she threw a hand to her head and sighed. "La, I fear all is lost in love if one does not follow one's heart."

Stephen rolled his eyes. "What is it, Milli?"

"I know where she is."

"Elizabeth?"

"She will not like it if I tell."

"I love her, Milli. I will make her happy if it takes me a hundred years. You have my solemn word."

Tears pooled in Milli's eyes. "If you take her, I will have no one. Papa is always leaving and I don't like it at that stupid Seminary for *Females*. And governesses are horrid creatures."

"You will have someone, Milli. You will have a brother-in-law. And I would never take your sister from you."

Her delicate lips folded together as she absorbed his words. "May I come live with you and Lizzie then?"

"Your father will have to approve. But you must tell me where your sister is. You must trust me."

The girl walked down the last of the steps. "Elizabeth is staying at my aunt's cottage in the country. I have the direction since I told Lizzie I wanted to write to her, but all the time I knew you would want it." Her eyes sparkled with a devilish gleam as she handed him a paper with the information.

"You little minx."

"I am that, am I not?" she answered wickedly. "Here, take Pharaoh. Tell Elizabeth he has not been eating or sleeping."

Stephen frowned, examining the black-and-white ball of fur in his hands. "Is that true? He looks healthy enough."

"'Course it's not true. But if your kisses do not work, you will need another plan. You cannot be that stupid."

Stephen laughed, tucking the kitten gently into his coat. "I hope I do not have to resort to plan B, but just in case, I'll be fully armed."

And armed he would be. One special license, one kitten, and a few passionate kisses of undying love should do it. But he would rather face Napoleon than face Elizabeth's rejection.

"Oh, and my lord." The girl threw a hand to her heart. "Best tell her you would die for her." She sighed dramatically. "Tell her your heart aches for her. Tell her you would cross the ocean for her. Tell her no woman could ever take her place."

Though he was eager to find Elizabeth, Stephen could barely hold back his laughter. "Milli, I am not an actor."

"Well, if you do not want her running off with someone like Fennington, you had best do something spectacular."

A muscle twitched in his jaw at the sound of Fennington's name. And what the blazes did that girl have in her hand? Hell's bells! It was Fennington's quizzing glass!

"A knight on a white horse might do it," she said, the quizzing glass swinging at her hip. "All girls dream of such things."

Stephen had no idea what she was blabbering about. "Go bother Marcus with that thing. Vexes him to no end, you know."

Her gray eyes sparkled with delight. "No, I didn't know. Thank you for the information, white knight."

Scowling, Stephen turned on his heels. White knight, indeed.

Elizabeth threw on her cloak and strolled down the stone walkway leading from the cottage. A biting wind touched her cheeks, sending the red tulips at the edge of the fence dancing against each other, reminding her all too well she was no longer in London.

"Looks like rain, Miss Shelby," the housekeeper called as she bent to pull a weed from the flower garden. "Would you care for a ride to the village? Mr. Baskers can have the hack ready in a few minutes."

Elizabeth smiled at the plump, older lady. Poor Mrs. Baskers had been keeping a keen eye on Elizabeth ever since she had showed up at the door. Aunt Polly's doing, no doubt.

"I do not believe a little rain will hurt me, Mrs. Baskers. And I do need the exercise."

The plump housekeeper frowned. "Mayhap you should take Mr. Baskers along with you, my dear? A young thing like you should always take an escort into town."

Elizabeth laughed. The town included a quaint little inn, a church, a few shops, and a blacksmith. "I won't be but a few hours. I am in need of some writing materials. A good walk will help me gather my thoughts."

The housekeeper shook her head. "A man, it is, then. I knew it the minute you showed up at the door, all pale and unhappy looking."

Elizabeth clutched her reticule, refusing to let her misfortunes show in her face. "It was the ride on those bumpy roads, Mrs. Baskers. Nothing more."

The elder lady tugged on another weed. "And 'tis a rose I just pulled."

"You are too smart for your own good, Mrs. Baskers."

"I be that and more, at least Mr. Baskers says so. As a matter of fact, good husband that he is, he is cleaning that old shed right now. He's a pack rat, did you know? Saves things from thirty years ago. Now, if it rains, you stay in town. I'll be sending Mr. Baskers to fetch you."

Chuckling, Elizabeth waved as she made her way down the graveled road. The lady's protective streak was like a breath of fresh air. She frowned suddenly, looking toward the village. Too bad everyone in life was not as good as Mrs. Baskers.

When Stephen passed the soaked figure stumbling down the lane, his heart stilled. He called to the driver to stop the carriage. Pulling the door open, he jumped down from the vehicle. "Elizabeth!"

She turned to him, her surprised face a small oval inside the hood of her wet cloak. Rain splattered against her pink cheeks. Blue eyes impaled him with such pain he winced.

She silently turned and kept walking.

Stephen hurried alongside her, clutching her elbow. "Elizabeth. Talk to me."

She avoided his gaze. "Please unhand me, my lord."

He set his teeth and let her go. "Oh, for the love of King George, at least get inside the carriage. I can give you a lift."

She pulled back her shoulders and ignored him.

Stubborn was the only word that came to Stephen's mind. He kept pace alongside her. "Very well, then. If this is what you wish."

"Do not let me keep you from staying warm and dry, my lord."

"Would you stop calling me 'my lord'? Use my Christian name."

Surprisingly, she stopped and tilted her face to stare at him. She looked so delicate, so vulnerable, he drew on all his strength not to haul her over his shoulder, throw her into the carriage, and kiss her senseless.

"Very well, *Stephen*. Let me inform you, since you have not deemed it necessary to ask. Your visit is a waste of time."

"Is it, Elizabeth?"

Thunder sounded in the distance.

She shifted her gaze toward the fields. Wind rushed past his ears, almost drowning out her words. "You never wanted me. Why come all this way to tell me so?"

He stepped in front of her, sheltering her from the battering rain. "I want you, Elizabeth, or I would not be here."

She glared at him, tears now flooding her sky blue eyes. "Yet you handed me back to my father as if I were nothing."

"I had my reasons."

She brushed past him. "Reasons? That is no excuse for breaking my heart."

Hope lifted inside him. "I broke your heart?"

She faltered and took a right turn down another lane.

Stephen followed, the carriage clattering behind them. "You have every right to think badly of me. But why do you think I reversed your father's debt?"

He heard her sniff and his own heart stumbled as if it had been given a push. "Do not judge what you did not see." He raised his hands for the coach to stop and the jingle of harnesses ceased.

"Elizabeth, wait. I have something for you." He opened the carriage door and pulled out a small covered basket, handing it to her. "I thought you might need this."

"I have no need of your gifts, my lord." She shoved the basket into his stomach.

He kept his hands like leaden balls at his sides, refusing to take back his gift. "Take it anyway."

Without another word, she turned and approached the cottage, basket in hand. He stood rooted in the graveled path, the rain streaming down his face, watching her, wanting her.

"I love you, Elizabeth. Does that not matter?"

He saw her hesitate and then run toward the cottage.

"I love you," he shouted. "I love you! Blast it!"

But it seemed Elizabeth wanted nothing from him. She opened the cottage door, disappearing from sight.

Stephen brushed a hand through his wet hair. He would not give in to her silence. He would not. She loved him, and by heaven, he would prove it to her.

Elizabeth whipped off her cloak, but not before she peeked inside the basket to see the small black kitten curled up asleep.

"Oh, Stephen," she said, stifling a sob.

Mrs. Baskers came up behind her, shaking the water off the cloak. "Goodness, child. I knew you should have taken Mr. Baskers with you. He would have made you stay in town until this nasty weather settled. I just told him to go fetch you."

"You were right, Mrs. Baskers." Elizabeth wiped her face, trying to conceal her tears. "What a ninny I was to go out in that."

Mrs. Baskers regarded her, then gazed perceptively at the small kitten in the basket and took the burden from her.

"Love is not always what we want it to be, my dear. Now you get out of those wet things. I'll make you a nice warm drink and you can sit by the fire. I can take care of this wee little thing too."

"Its name . . . is Pharaoh," Elizabeth said with a sob and fell into the woman's soft arms.

"There, there, dear. Is it that bad?"

Elizabeth nodded, her throat tightening with grief. The soft aroma of lavender lingered in the air. Milli's scent from the basket. Her sister had trusted Stephen enough to give him her direction. Could Elizabeth trust him too?

With a few words of encouragement, the lady helped Elizabeth upstairs and into some dry clothes. The entire history of Stephen and William Shelby came out in one long rush. All the while Mrs. Baskers listened without judgment.

A few minutes later, they made their way into the kitchen where the housekeeper brewed some tea.

Elizabeth sat on a scarred oak chair and warmed her hands around the cup before her. "I must look a sight after all that crying."

Mrs. Baskers' lips curved into a sympathetic smile. "You still love him?"

Elizabeth blinked back the tears. "Yes. But how can I live with him after what he did?"

"He did what he thought best, dear. Everyone makes mistakes, even sons of nobility."

Elizabeth raised her blurry gaze toward the window Mrs. Baskers was opening. The rain had stopped and the air smelled of freshly cut flowers.

"He said he loves me," she admitted, knowing she didn't care a whit if Stephen was the fourth son of a duke or not.

Mrs. Baskers took a seat beside her. "Love is never a simple thing. 'Tis work sometimes."

"At first I thought he gambled with my father to trade back the debt so he would be free of me."

"And now you believe differently?"

She heaved a trembling sigh. "Since I've had some time to think, I realized he freed us both from an obligation that hindered our relationship. But he should have told me the truth from the very beginning."

"I see, and he finally came to claim you, and you, with your pride, told him to leave you alone."

She nodded again, stifling another sob of regret. Afraid she would be hurt again, she had pushed him away.

The older woman patted Elizabeth's shoulders. "If he does not come back, he is not worthy of your love. But I believe that if he came this far with that adorable kitten in tow, he will come again and again until he has you for himself."

A few hours later Elizabeth was reading a book by the fire when Mrs. Baskers came rushing into the parlor, her face flushed with excitement. "My dear. Come quick."

Startled, Elizabeth rose from her seat, setting her book aside. "What is it?"

"Saints preserve us! A sight I have not seen in at least twenty years!"

Elizabeth was a bit worried at the way the lady's hands were wringing her apron as she ran out the door and down the path. She was moving far too fast for a woman her age.

Elizabeth followed. "Mrs. Baskers, please slow down."

"Mr. Baskers just informed me," the housekeeper said breathlessly, gazing over the hill, "and I cannot believe it."

"Informed you of what?"

"He will be coming soon."

"Mr. Baskers? Is he hurt?"

Mrs. Baskers spun around. "Goodness, child! Not Mr. Baskers!"

A heartbeat passed and the elderly woman turned toward the lane, her finger shaking in the air. "There, dear. Look there!"

Elizabeth squinted in the noted direction where the sun began to peek through the clouds. Water glistened like diamonds, both on the road and on the limp branches of the trees. "A rainbow?"

"No, no. Can you not hear it?"

Elizabeth paused. There, in the distance she could hear the clopping of hooves and the jangle of metal.

"He's here!" Mrs. Baskers grabbed Elizabeth in a death grip. "Did I not say he would come?"

Elizabeth blinked at the rider coming into view. The horse was as white as snow, and the man . . . what on earth—

"Oh, my dear, how romantic," the older lady sighed, tears settling on her short lashes.

Elizabeth's heart came to a sudden halt as the magnificent knight in full mesh galloped toward her, his metal suit clanging like that of a medieval warrior's.

The large ominous figure stopped before the gate and turned his helmeted head toward Elizabeth.

Mrs. Baskers clapped her hands together, pushing Elizabeth forward. "Go on, my dear."

"Miss Elizabeth Shelby." The velvety timbre of Stephen's voice sent Elizabeth's knees knocking. *He had come back.*

"W-what are you doing?" she asked faintly.

With some effort he slipped from the horse and walked toward her, his suit of armor rattling like ten buckets of nails. "I have come to sweep you off your feet, my lady."

He knelt down in the mud, tugging his helmet off his head, and grasped her hand in his metal-gloved one. "I came to ask for your hand in marriage, my sweet, adorable Elizabeth. I am a poor dumb knight begging your forgiveness. Begging, mind you."

The clank of metal turned her heart as he shifted his balance. "I will love you and honor you all the days of my life. I never meant to hurt you. You are everything that is precious to me. I gave you back to your father so that I might love you without any obstacles between us."

Deep brown eyes peered up at her, pleading. "What say you, my beautiful princess? Will you marry a dumb knight such as I?"

Mrs. Baskers let out an audible sigh.

Elizabeth's heart soared as she fought back a giggle. His charms were as devastating as ever. Not only that, his hair was mussed in a devil-may-care style, making him look like a dashing rogue of old. He was beautiful. And he loved her.

She drew in a shaky sigh, knowing he would not have

come if he did not want her. She brought his hand to her heart. "I say yes. I love you, my dear knight."

A bright white smile flashed across his face as he struggled to a standing position. "Give me a moment here, sweetheart." He was just about upright when he fell flat on his face in the mud. A muffled curse flew from his mouth.

She bent down to help him, trying not to laugh. "Stephen?"

He sat up, a wicked sparkle in his gaze. "And I love you, dear Elizabeth." It took a few amusing seconds before he stumbled to a standing position.

He grunted and groaned as he pulled Elizabeth toward him and cursed as his armor snagged against her gown. "Devil take it!"

Mrs. Baskers came to his rescue. "Come into the house, my lord. We can fix that as right as rain."

Grinning from ear to ear, Stephen grabbed hold of Elizabeth's hand and clanked into the cottage. Within minutes his suit was off, and he had cleaned the mud from his face.

He stood arm in arm with Elizabeth in the parlor while the housekeeper went to fetch some tea. "Now, my sweet," he said with a kiss, brushing his warm lips against hers.

Elizabeth could not help but laugh. "Where did you obtain your proposal suit?"

He lifted a brow in amusement. "Mr. Baskers had the suit back in his shed. It seems he used it years ago. The white horse, you ask? It's owned by the blacksmith in town."

Elizabeth laughed. "No!"

Stephen snaked a hand around her waist and hauled her against him. "Yes. And if you dare say one word of this to my brothers, I will have to take drastic measures."

She gazed up at him, teasingly. "Oh, my, drastic measures?"

He gave her a delicious smile that told her he meant every word he said. Before he could speak again, he glanced over his shoulder as Mrs. Baskers entered with the tea tray. The older woman smiled and took a seat across from the couple.

Stephen frowned when Elizabeth stepped away from him to sit near the fireplace. "Do you have some cakes to go with this, Mrs. Baskers?" he asked hopefully, looking down at the lady.

The lady smiled up at him. "'Course I do."

Yet to Stephen's displeasure, the lady sat there, not willing to move. He cleared his throat, taking a look out the window, then back at her. "Well, do you mind fetching some?"

She lifted her head and smiled back. "'Course I do."

Elizabeth's eyes twinkled when she noted Stephen's hand curl at his side.

"I wish to be alone with Elizabeth," he said stiffly.

"'Course you do."

Elizabeth bit back her laughter.

Stephen heaved a frustrated sigh and scratched his head. "Have you something against me, Mrs. Baskers?"

Rather intrigued, Elizabeth regarded the scene between the steadfast housekeeper and the handsome lord. This was better than Milli on stage.

"'Course not, my lord." Mrs. Baskers gave a knowing look toward Elizabeth. "But drastic measures will not be taken here. They are reserved for *after the marriage vows*. Beggin' your pardon, your lordship."

Elizabeth could not believe the crimson color that blotted Stephen's cheeks.

"Mrs. Baskers!" The woman jumped as Mr. Baskers appeared in the doorway, his bulky figure shadowing his wife.

The lady smiled at her husband. "Yes, dear."

"I have need of your assistance."

The lady shifted her gaze between Stephen and Elizabeth, and sank back comfortably into her chair. "It can wait, Mr. Baskers."

The older man heaved a sigh and strode into the room. "Forgive me, my lord." He shot Stephen a wink. "But I believe this calls for drastic measures." Before his wife knew what was happening, the man scooped her into his beefy hands, sweeping her over his shoulder.

She yelped in protest. "Mr. Baskers, please!"

Eyes gleaming, Stephen rolled back on his heels. "Ah, drastic measures, Mr. Baskers? May I invite you to the wedding?"

Mr. Baskers brandished a gap-toothed smile. "'Course, my lord," he said in a mocking tone, then disappeared around the corner, Mrs. Baskers yapping in his ears.

Elizabeth rose. "Should we go after them?"

Stephen laughed, swinging her into his arms. "Certainly not. It seems Baskers takes drastic measures quite seriously."

"And you, my lord? What say you to drastic measures?"

Stephen let out a deep growl as he kissed her with a hunger that sent her senses spinning. "I love you, Elizabeth. Do not ever run from me again. I could not live without you."

Tears pricked her eyelids as his lips slowly descended to meet hers once again. But Mrs. Baskers's giggling screech pierced the air, separating the two. "Mr. Baskers . . . please!"

Stephen's chest rumbled with laughter. "What say *you* to drastic measures, dearest Elizabeth?"

Elizabeth backed up, pressing a hand against his chest. "Drastic measures may be taken after the wedding, my lord."

Stephen's eyes devoured her as he slipped out the special license from his pocket. "Is tomorrow soon enough?"

She ran from him, laughing. Stephen was hard on her heels and caught her in the hall, pulling her against him. "Is it?"

"What?" she asked, her heart singing with happiness.

"Soon enough?" His words were a whispered caress and a hot ache of love grew in her breast.

She sank against him. "I would like my family to be there."

"Very well. We can travel today and marry tomorrow. But you may inform Milli I won't be galloping in on a white horse or wearing a suit of armor. Speaking of that imp, I think she dropped an entire bottle of lavender in Pharaoh's basket."

Elizabeth muffled a laugh against his shoulder. He smelled distinctly of lavender. "Tomorrow will be soon enough."

He fitted himself along her body and buried his face in her hair. "Perhaps we should call in Mrs. Baskers after all."

"She won't be coming now," she said, smiling wickedly and lifting her head. "Drastic measures, you know."

He laughed, then his gaze turned serious. "I love you."

She touched a hand to his face. "And I you, Stephen."

A half hour later they rode from the cottage as the last of the sinking sun hit the horizon in wide ribbons of pink and orange. Elizabeth smiled, petting the wide-eyed feline in the basket beside her. "Stephen?"

He took her hand in his. "Yes, my love?"

"How old was that suit of armor?"

He looked puzzled. "Not certain. Why?"

She gazed out the window of the carriage and put on her spectacles, staring back at him. "Oh, I just wanted to know all the answers when your brothers asked."

Within a heartbeat, she was on his lap, laughing.

Stephen whipped off the spectacles and held her hands against his chest, a slow grin spreading across his face.

"Should I tell you now what drastic measures I will take if you dare say a single word to them? Or if you ever try to scare me with those spectacles or another inkwell?"

She nodded, her eyes lit with tenderness. "Tell me."

All playfulness fled from his face. "You are everything I ever hoped for in a wife, my dear, sweet Elizabeth."

"And I don't care if you are the fourth son of a duke."

A small rumble of amusement broke from his lips. "I gather drastic measures will be accepted from the fourth son of a duke?"

She wrapped her hands around his neck, wondering how God could be so good to her. "Very drastic measures, *my lord.*"

"Hoyden," he said huskily and closed the lid to the basket holding the wide-eyed kitten. "Drastic measures, indeed."

He kissed her fiercely, wondering how God could be so good to him.

As time passed, one lavender-scented coach hastened along the road to London, its clattering wheels and jingling harnesses drowning out the mews of one curious kitten and a couple very much in love.

Drastically in love.